Butterfly

A NOVEL

Butterfly

A NOVEL

SYLVESTER STEPHENS

SBI

STREBOR BOOKS

NEW YORK LONDON TORONTO SYDNEY

Strebor Books
P.O. Box 6505
Largo, MD 20792
http://www.streborbooks.com

© 2013 by Sylvester Stephens

ISBN 978-1-59309-447-8
ISBN 978-1-4516-8647-0 (ebook)
LCCN 2012933945

First Strebor Books trade paperback edition January 2013

Cover design: www.mariondesigns.com
Cover photograph: © Keith Saunders/Marion Designs

10 9 8 7 6 5 4 3 2 1

Manufactured in the United States of America

For information regarding special discounts for bulk purchases, please contact Simon & Schuster Special Sales at 1-866-506-1949 or business@simonandschuster.com

The Simon & Schuster Speakers Bureau can bring authors to your live event. For more information or to book an event, contact the Simon & Schuster Speakers Bureau at 1-866-248-3049 or visit our website at www.simonspeakers.com.

To my mother, Orabell,
and my daughters, Bria and Simone Stephens

Acknowledgments

I would like to acknowledge the educators who graciously contributed to the book, Kim Clark-Freeman, Cassandra (San) Horton, Kimberly Phillips and Nic Starr.

Chapter One

My name is Shante Clemmons. I was fifteen years old when my life started to unravel. I was skinny; about six feet tall. I had a medium tone, or caramel skin color. I had light brown eyes, with naturally long eyelashes. I had a cute face, or at least that was what people told me. Because of my height, I looked very mature for my age. I was a foster care child but looking the way I did, foster care wives were not really feeling me being around their husbands.

"Get outta my house!"

"Where am I gonna go?"

"I don't care where you go! Just get outta my house!"

"I ain't got nowhere to go, Mrs. Redmond!"

"You shoulda thought about that before you climbed into bed with my husband!"

"I swear to God! It was him! He climbed into bed with me!"

Mrs. Redmond opened the door and threw my duffle bag with all of my possessions outside on the ground. I did not move, hoping she would have some compassion for me, but she didn't. Mr. Redmond stood at the bottom of the stairs in a robe, still wearing nothing underneath, and watched.

"It's two o'clock in the morning. Can I at least stay until daylight?"

"Shante, please," Mrs. Redmond said softly. "Just get out my house!"

I walked past Mrs. Redmond and when I got to the door, I stopped in front of her.

"I didn't do nothing with your husband. And you know that!"

Mrs. Redmond looked away, too embarrassed to even try to pretend that she could hide the truth. But as I was closing the door behind me, she grabbed my arm so that Mr. Redmond could not see, and without saying a word, she placed one hundred dollars in my hand. I realized that Mrs. Redmond did not make me leave to hurt me, but to protect me.

As she closed the door, I could see the tears coming from her eyes. I did not know whether to feel sorry for myself for having to leave in the middle of the night, or for her, for having to stay behind with that bastard. I picked up my duffle bag and walked down the dark empty street.

It was two a.m. and I had to find a place to sleep. I didn't want to spend the hundred dollars on a hotel because I would have had only a few hours before check-out. I decided to sleep in back of a nightclub where there was a lot of foot traffic until morning, and then I'd get a cheap room. I put my duffle bag against the building and slept sitting up. It seemed like I had just fallen asleep when some gigantic man kicked my feet.

"Hey!" the man said.

I looked up and saw this big, black humongous man standing over me. He had big red pop-eyes with a bald head and rolls of fat on the back of his neck. I was so sleepy I dozed back off.

"Hey, get up! You can't be sleeping out here like this."

"Oh, I'm sorry," I said. "Can I just sleep here until in the morning? I promise I won't ever come back."

"Naw, I can't do that."

I stood up and picked up my duffle bag.

"Damn! You slim, but you fine as hell," he said. "I'm Anthony, but they call me Big Ant. How old are you, babygirl?"

"Fif…" I knew that if I said I was fifteen, Big Ant would have chased me away, so I lied, "Um, I'm eighteen."

"Eighteen?"

"Yeah, I just turned eighteen."

"What you doing sleeping out here on the street?"

"I had to get out of my situation at home, man. I can't go back there."

"Turn around."

"For what?"

"You wanna ask questions or do you want a place to sleep?"

I turned around with my arms held out for Big Ant to see my body. "See?"

"Damn, you slim. But I think you might work."

"Work for what?"

"You wanna make some money?"

"Look, Mr. Big Ant, I just need a place to sleep. I'm not trying to make no money like that."

"You don't even know what I'm talking about, babygirl."

"Well, what you talking 'bout then?"

"Dancing."

"Dancing? What kind of dancing?"

"The kind of dancing that will keep money in your pocket. You interested?"

"I'm interested, but…"

"Ain't no buts. Get your shit and come on."

I grabbed my duffle bag and followed Big Ant into the night-club, which happened to be a strip club. As we entered I saw the big neon sign with the name of the club shining brightly: Emerald City.

Big Ant led me to a small office in the back of the club. Nobody paid any attention to me as I walked by, but I paid close attention to the beautiful women grinding their naked bodies against the men. When we passed the stage, I nearly tripped watching a lady slide up and down on the pole. Her body was doing things I could not imagine my fifteen-year-old body even attempting to do.

"Mr. Harry, I think I got some new talent for you."

"Oh yeah," Mr. Harry said.

Mr. Harry was a round man. I could see his stomach overlapping onto the desk as he counted money. He had rings on every finger. He had very fair skin, balding on top with dark rings around his eyes.

"Check it out," Big Ant said. "Show him the goods."

"What you mean 'show him the goods'?"

"Show that ass, girl!"

"Oh," I said and turned in a circle.

"Naw, take off your clothes so he can see all of that ass."

"Wait a minute! You ain't said nothing about taking off my clothes."

"Get this girl out of my office!"

"Hold on, Mr. Harry, let me talk to her."

Big Ant whispered in my ear, "Look, you can make us a lot of money, and you can make yourself a lot of money, too, so stop acting so damn scary and show the man the goods!"

Although I was scared as hell, I was also tired and sleepy. I pulled my shirt above my head and dropped it to the floor. I placed my hand behind my back, unsnapped my bra and let it drop to the floor.

"She got some ripe-ass little titties. How old are you, darling?"

"Fif...eighteen."

"Damn, you got some pretty titties to be eighteen!" Mr. Harry stopped counting his money and sat back. "Let me see what else you got."

I looked at Big Ant and then I unzipped my pants and slowly

pulled them down my leg and stepped out of them. I had on short-cut boxer-briefs that only revealed the bottom part of my ass.

"Drop them draws, girl," Mr. Harry said.

"I ain't never did nothing like this before, so can I practice before I take everything off?"

"What you think, Big Ant?"

"Hell, we can see what she workin' with right now. She straight!" Big Ant took the back side of his hand and rubbed up and down my thigh. "Look a-here."

"Yes, Lawd, Big Ant! Look at them damn long legs! Mmm! Mmm! Mmm! We got a star in this one. Can she dance?"

"Dance for the man," Big Ant paused momentarily to try to think of my name, "uh, what do you call yourself?"

"Uh, I call myself, uh..." I did not know what to say so I said the only name I felt described me at the time. "Butterfly."

"Butterfly? That's too soft, baby," Mr. Harry said.

"But I like Butterfly."

"Naw, that ain't gon' work. How about Climax?" Mr. Harry yelled.

"Hell yeah!" Big Ant smiled and looked at me. "Climax!"

I could not believe they wanted to call me Climax. What the hell did I look like to them? A damn walking orgasm?

"No disrespect, Mr. Harry, but I kinda like Butterfly."

"It really don't matter to me as long you make me some money. If you want to call yourself Butterfly, Butterfly it is."

"Thank you," I said humbly. "Can I go to sleep now?"

"You don't have to worry about nothing from here on out, Butterfly. Mr. Harry gon' take care of you," Mr. Harry said. "Take care of her, Ant."

Big Ant took me to a hotel and paid a week's rent. I slept until noon and I would have slept longer than that if Big Ant had

not pounded on my door. I stumbled to the door and opened it.
"Yeah?"

"Time to get up! You got dancing classes to attend."

"Huh?"

Big Ant walked past me with a bag in his hand and sat in a chair
that was way too small for his huge frame.

"Try some of these clothes on," Big Ant said as he threw the
bag of clothes to me.

I opened the bag and pulled the clothes out. "Whose clothes
are these?"

"Yours now! Get dressed and let's go. Mr. Harry wants you to
start working tonight. He wants you to come dance for him, so
he can see what you working with."

"Dance?"

"Yeah, dance."

"Why are you and Mr. Harry being so nice to me?"

"Nice? This ain't nice, Babygirl. This business!"

I did not ask what he meant by "business," but did I have to?
When we arrived, the club was not open and there were only a
few people in the building. I was nervous and did not know what
to expect. It was not a difficult formula to figure out, though.
The DJ started playing loud music and Mr. Harry made me go
on stage and I began to dance. Mr. Harry was not happy with my
dancing when I first started.

"Come on now, Butterfly, pick it up," Mr. Harry said. "I need
more sexy; and less *Soul Train*."

I moved more seductively and Mr. Harry responded more agree-
ably. "Yeah, baby, like that. Move them hips. Make me want to
give you my money!"

As I watched myself dance in the mirror, I began to turn myself
on. I looked like a beautiful, full-grown woman. There were other

strippers in the club who stopped and watched me dance. The more eyes that watched me, the sexier I felt.

"How was that?" I tried to catch my breath.

"That was fantastic!" Mr. Harry said. "I'm giving you a spot tonight."

"Thank you." I was enthusiastic about having a "spot," but to be honest, I didn't really know what the hell having a "spot" meant.

Mr. Harry scheduled me to start at ten o'clock that night and it was a packed house. I sat in the dressing room contemplating if I should go out or not. Not should, but could I go out or not. I put my head in my hands and closed my eyes. When I opened them, there was a lady standing behind me. I could tell that she was much older than me but she was very beautiful. Her skin was dark and smooth, almost without a blemish. Her hair was cut short, but neat. Her eyes were symmetrically oval and light brown. Her body was thin, but toned, even her arms. I think I was most mesmerized by her straight and even teeth.

"Hi, I'm Sparkle."

"Hi, I'm Butterfly," I said.

"Butterfly? That's original." Sparkle laughed.

"Is Sparkle your real name?"

"What do you think?"

"Well, what's your real name then? My name is Shante."

"Never tell anybody in here your real name, even those you think you're making friends with."

"Oh."

"Okay, so what are you? Runaway? Escort? Single mom? What?"

"What do you mean?"

"What brought you here? No little girl has aspirations of being a lifelong dancer. Not this type of dancing anyway. So what brought you here?"

"Different circumstances, but only one really matters...I need money."

"You seem like a nice girl, Butterfly, so let me give you some advice."

"Okay." I spun my chair around and faced her.

"Do what you have to do and get the hell away from here."

"I'm just doing this to pay back Mr. Harry and make a few more..."

"You don't owe Mr. Harry shit! You do what you have to do as quickly as possible and get the hell away from here! You hear me?"

"Yeah."

"Good," Sparkle said while taking off her clothes.

"I'm scared, Sparkle. I'm scared and I'm nervous."

"Don't be. Remember, you're in control out there. Those men are here to worship you."

"Nobody has ever worshipped me before. Other than my daddy, I ain't even had nobody to really love me before."

"Trust me, Butterfly, you're about to get more love than you can handle."

"Well, I guess I better get out there."

"Here," Sparkle handed me a glass, "this will make it a lot easier."

"What is that?"

"Something that will make you feel really good."

I took a swallow and spat it out.

"What is that?" I shouted.

"Gin and Coke," Sparkle said. "Do you drink?"

"Nope."

"How old are you?"

"I'm eighteen."

"Stop lying!" Sparkle snatched the glass out of my hand. "Now how old are you?"

"Seventeen."

"You better not be lying to me."

"I'm not lying. I'll be eighteen on my next birthday."

"Does Harry know you're only seventeen?"

"No, and please don't tell him. I don't have nowhere to go, and this about the only job I can do without a diploma that's going to keep me off the streets."

"I won't tell him, but you better be telling the truth. You can get Harry in a lot of trouble and get us girls on the unemployment line. And I'm not ready to quit the business just yet. I have a few more bills to pay."

"Okay."

"Come on and get out there and show 'em your goods."

Sparkle smiled and walked out of the dressing room. I took a deep breath and followed her. I walked around too nervous to ask those men if they wanted me to dance for them. But once I felt that first ten-dollar bill in my hand, I was hooked. After that, taking money from the patrons of Emerald City, men and women, was like taking candy from a baby. Sparkle said I was a natural.

Over the next six months, I turned sixteen and with a little fake I.D. assistance from some anonymous friends, I got me an apartment, I got my driver's license, and bought me a car.

Sparkle and I became close friends. I turned to her whenever I had a problem and we shared all of our current secrets to each other, but nothing about our past.

Keeping my past a secret, I had fooled Mr. Harry, Big Ant, the clients, and the rest of the girls at Emerald City. It had gotten to the point where I was beginning to believe my lies, myself. However, Sparkle was at the point where enough was enough!

"Okay, so what are you going to do?"

"Do about what?"

"Workin' at the club."

"I gotta work, Spark."

"You can't keep workin up in that club underage. I'm tellin' you it ain't worth it."

"What else I'm gon' do? I ain't got nobody to take care of me, but me."

"I tell you what. You can come stay with me until you turn eighteen and we'll go from there."

"You sure?"

"What did I say?"

"I don't want to get over there and then you kick me out on the street."

"If you mind your business, you won't have to worry about that."

"Okay, but I got to work these next few nights to put me a little money up, though. You cool with that?"

"That's cool, but after that, you gots to go."

"All right."

Getting out was easier said than done. A few nights later, I went to Mr. Harry's office at the end of the night when I knew he would be tired and not feel like doing a lot of talking. Mr. Harry had money tied into me, and he was not going to let me out of the business just because I wanted out.

"Mr. Harry?" I knocked, and then opened his door. "You got a minute?"

"Of course, I got a minute for my superstar; what's up?"

"I appreciate everything you've done for me here at Emerald City, but I think I'm ready to do something a little different."

"What do you mean, do 'something a little different'?"

"I don't want to dance no more."

"Then what you gon' do?"

"I don't know, go to college."

"You? In college?" Mr. Harry laughed. "Butterfly, baby, you were born to do this. From the very first time you stepped on that stage, you were a superstar. You can be the best. Why you want to give up on your dream?"

"This ain't my dream, Mr. Harry. This is how I pay bills."

"Have you seen yourself out there? It's been women who have been at this business for years that ain't half as good as you. There's a lot of money to make in this business and you got what it takes to make as much as you want."

"Thanks, Mr. Harry, but this ain't what I wanna do."

"Okay, well," Mr. Harry paused and gave me a mean look, "what about the money you owe me?"

"I have the money. I can pay you. It's no problem at all."

"How much you got?"

"I got enough to pay you back for my hotel and my clothes, and my..."

Mr. Harry interrupted me while I was speaking, "Fifty-thousand dollars! You got that? Because that's how much you owe me, fifty-thousand dollars."

"Mr. Harry you know I ain't got no fifty-thousand dollars. And I don't owe you no fifty-thousand dollars, either."

"But I said you do!"

"How do I owe you that much money, Mr. Harry, for a hotel room and some clothes?"

"Interest."

"Please, Mr. Harry, don't do this to me. I don't have that much money."

"There is another way."

"What other way?"

Mr. Harry turned his chair to the side and rolled from behind his desk. He unzipped his pants and pulled out his stick.

"Here you go, baby."

He grabbed his stick in his hand and started to pump it up. I could see it harden right before my eyes. Mr. Harry, himself, was disgusting to look at, but his shriveled-up, nasty, little prick was even more disgusting than his nasty fat body.

"What you want me to do with that, Mr. Harry?"

"Just come touch it."

"I can't do that."

"You wanna pay your debt, don't you?"

"Not like this, I don't."

"Well, you gotta choice. Either you give me some ass, or I'm going to have Big Ant take my fifty-thousand dollars out on your ass! What's it gon' be?"

I slowly walked over to Mr. Harry and he made me kneel down. "Please, Mr. Harry, I'll give you all the money I got, but please don't make me do this!"

"Shut up!" Mr. Harry grabbed my head and started to lower it toward his stick. I closed my eyes as I got closer to it. I opened my mouth and then he screamed at the top of his lungs, "*Oooooo shit!*"

Mr. Harry pushed me away from him and fell to the floor with his stick in his hand. Sparkle burst through the door and shouted, "What's going on in here?"

"She bit my shit!" Mr. Harry screamed.

"She did what?" Sparkle was standing in the doorway when I ran past her. "Butterfly? What happened?"

I kept running out of the club and into my car. Sparkle ran out of the club and knocked on my window. I backed up and zoomed off. By the time I got to the first traffic light, Sparkle was in my rearview mirror flashing her lights. I saw her, but I was not going to stop for her or anyone else. She pulled beside me and honked her horn.

"Stop runnin' from me, fool!"

I was running scared like the sixteen-year-old child that I was. At that moment I did not want to be an adult! I did not want to be grown!

"Butterfly? Shit! Shante? Will you pull your car over before somebody gets hurt?"

That was the first time Sparkle had ever called me by my real name, and it had a calming effect on me. I pulled into a gas station and parked. I did not know what to do so I cried like a lost child. Sparkle parked her car and ran toward mine.

"Baby, you okay?" Sparkle pulled me out of the car and hugged me. "I told you this business is not for you!"

"That man tried to make me suck his...oh my goodness!" I became so overcome with emotion, I began to hyperventilate. Sparkle did her best to try to calm me but I was hysterical.

"It's okay! You're okay! Calm down and breathe, Shante!"

"I...I...I can't!"

"You're safe now! You're safe! Just calm down and breathe!"

"That man...that man..."

"Shante! Shante! You're with me! I'm not going to let him hurt you, okay?"

I put my head on Sparkle's shoulder and cried. She held me until I stopped crying and then we went to her high-rise apartment in Buckhead. That apartment was so high I could almost see over the entire city.

"Wow! This is nice."

"You like, huh?"

"I thought I was making money at Emerald City, but you must really be making a lot of money to afford all of this."

"I do, okay."

"Wow! Thank you for letting me stay here."

"If you want to thank me, tell me your real age."

"Okay. But if I tell you, you have to promise you won't be mad at me."

"I'm not promising shit! Now tell me."

"Okay, I'm sixteen."

"You've had a birthday since you've been working at the club, so that means you were only fifteen when you started working at Emerald City?"

"Yeah."

"Girl, I need to take my belt off and whoop your tall, grown ass!"

"I had to make some money, Sparkle."

"But you're just a child, Shante."

"I'm not all the way grown but I'm not a child, either."

"Whatever! Being tall don't make you grown," Sparkle snapped. "I need to contact your relatives. I know they're worried sick."

"The only relative I know of is my father. He's locked up and I don't even know how to get in contact with him. Oh yeah, I have a little sister and a little brother but I don't know where they are, either."

"Where's your mother?"

"She's dead."

"I'm sorry to hear that."

"That's okay."

"We have to find somebody in your family because my lifestyle is not role-model material for a sixteen-year-old."

"Why not? You're one of the nicest people I've ever met."

"I never said I wasn't nice. I said I don't live a role-model life-style."

"I don't need a role model. I just need somebody to help take care of me."

"That's what I'm saying, dear; I can't take care of you like that."

"You look like you're doing pretty damn good for yourself to me."

"I don't mean financially, Shante. You need guidance. You need someone to put you on the right track so that you can have a successful life. I'm too screwed up for that."

"Can we try? Just for a little while?"

"Don't worry, dear. I would never put you out, or turn my back on you. And you're welcome to stay as long as it takes for me to find you suitable living arrangements."

"Thank you, Sparkle."

"Call me Ida."

"Ida?"

"Yes, that's my real name."

"That's an old person's name."

"Well, not that it's any of your business, but I was named after an old person that I loved very much, my grandmother. Is that okay with you, Shante?"

"Hmm, I guess," I said sarcastically.

Chapter Two

The very next morning Big Ant paid us a little visit on behalf of Mr. Harry. Sparkle was coming in from a night shift at a new strip club. She was going to bed to end her night as I was getting up to begin my day.

"How was the club last night?"

"It wasn't that packed but a few of my regulars from Emerald City stopped through, so I made a little money."

Knock! Knock! Knock!

Sparkle stopped talking when someone banged on the door. She pulled her pistol from her purse and then gestured for me to go to the bedroom. I stood behind the bedroom door as Sparkle yelled to the person outside of her door.

"Who is it?"

"It's Big Ant from the club!"

"What do you want?"

"We need to talk."

"We don't need to talk about shit!"

"Come on, Spark," Big Ant yelled, "I know that girl is in there and Mr. Harry wants to talk to her."

"I don't know what you're talking about."

"We can do this the easy way, or we can do this the hard way; it don't make no difference to me."

"Okay, wait a minute."

Sparkle came into the bedroom to try to figure out what to do with me before Big Ant forced his way in.

"Look, we have to get you out of here!"

"How? You're on the sixteenth floor!"

"Damn!" Sparkle looked around the room over and over again. "Come here."

I followed Sparkle into her living room and hid in a closet. Sparkle took off all of her clothes and stripped down to her underwear. She put on a robe and then opened the door for Big Ant.

"Damn, what you doing in here?" Big Ant cased the apartment as he walked in. "Where she at, Spark?"

"She's not here."

"Uh-huhn. What took you so long to open the door?"

"I was about to get in the shower. How the hell I know you were going to be pounding on my door like a fool."

The door to the closet was opened barely enough where I could see parts of their bodies as they spoke. My heart was beating so fast I could hear it pounding.

"Yeah, right."

Big Ant went into the bedroom and Sparkle gestured for me to run out of the closet. I tiptoed toward the front door as she went into the bedroom with Big Ant. On my way out of the door, I heard the sound of a loud crash so I ran back in. I rushed into the bedroom and Big Ant had his knee in Sparkle's chest with both of his hands around her throat.

"Get off of her!" I screamed.

"Ru...!" Sparkle tried to speak but Big Ant's grip was too tight around her neck.

"You the one I'm looking for anyway!"

Big Ant jumped off of Sparkle and started chasing me. I turned to run out of the door but he grabbed me and threw me on the couch. But by the time he reached me, Sparkle had reached her gun and she pointed it directly at the side of his head.

"Get off her!"

"Hey! Hey! Hey! You better think about what you doing!"

"Naw, you better think about what *you* doing, niggah!" Sparkle yelled. "Get your ass up before I put a slug in your big-ass head!"

"Sparkle?" Big Ant said nervously.

"Sparkle, my ass! You think I'm playing with you, niggah?" Sparkle cocked the barrel of the gun and shoved it into Big Ant's head. "Huh, niggah?"

In the year that I had known Sparkle, I had never seen her that angry. Shoot, I had never seen her angry, period. I guess if you back anybody into a corner, they will either fight or flee. Sparkle did not feel like running that day.

"Back up, Sparkle, and I'll let her up!"

"Naw, niggah! You let her up and then I'll back up!"

Big Ant slowly raised his hands in the air and climbed his big ass off of me. Sparkle kept the pistol pointed at him as he backed his way out of the apartment. She followed him into the hallway until he got on the elevator and went down. She ran back into the apartment and screamed at me to move quickly.

"Let's go! *Now!*"

Sparkle snatched a bag that was already packed and ready to go. It was as if she knew someday she would have to make an emergency exit. I ran to the elevator and pushed the button, but Sparkle grabbed my hand and pulled me toward the stairs.

"No! The stairs! Come on!"

"That's sixteen flights!"

"COME ON!" Sparkle screamed.

Sparkle was in great shape because she ran down all sixteen flights without stopping once. I had to take a couple of breathers around the eleventh and third floors. Sparkle cursed me every time I stopped. "*Come on!*" Sparkle yelled at me while she was standing at the bottom of the stair. "*Get your ass down these stairs!*"

"I'm trying!" I yelled back as I leaned on the rail for support.

"If you get us killed, I swear I'm gon' kick your ass, girl! "

When we reached the first floor, Sparkle pulled out her gun and slowly opened the door to the lobby area. We could see Big Ant and Mr. Harry standing near the elevator. Sparkle tapped me on the shoulder and I followed her through a rear door, which led to the parking lot. We slipped into her car quietly and unseen, but once she started the car, she put the pedal to the metal! She burned rubber speeding out of that driveway.

"I got to find you a place to stay."

"I have money, Ida. We can go stay at a hotel."

"That's not safe, baby. Mr. Harry and his goons will finds us in no time."

"Well, what we are we going to do?"

"I don't know, but we have to do something quick."

Sparkle pulled into the parking lot of a Waffle House restaurant and cut the car off. "I have to take you to DFACS!"

"No! I'm not going back there. I'll only end up in a foster home."

"I'm sorry, Shante, but what else can I do? I have to get out of town for a while, and I can't leave you behind living on the streets."

"I'll be okay."

"Like you're okay now?" Sparkle looked at me sarcastically. "You're sixteen years old trying to survive in a world where most adults can't even make it."

"I have to do what I have to do."

"*Stop saying that!*" Sparkle screamed. "Living on the street is not what you have to do! There are people who can help you, but you have to want them to help you."

"Those people don't care nothing about me!"

"Well, you have no choice, baby."

"I'm sixteen now and I can make my own decisions on where I want to live."

"Okay, you're sixteen. You think you're grown, so where are you going to live?"

I tried my best to think of an adult answer to Sparkle's question before she hit me with her follow-up response, but I couldn't.

"That's what I thought! So, this is what we're going to do. I'm going to take you to some close friends of mine and they'll take good care of you."

"Please, Ida, I know you're trying to help me, but I don't want to live with anybody else. I'm too big. They're only going to kick me out."

"Not these people. They're good people."

"That's what they always say."

"I know these people and they will take good care of you. I promise."

"How do you know they will let me live with them?"

"Because I just know, that's how."

"Shoot," I sighed, "I'm going to have to go through foster care all over again. I can't stand that shit!"

"Watch your mouth, girl!" Sparkle snapped. "You're tough. You can handle it."

"I don't mean to whine, but you just don't know what it's like to be in and out of foster care."

"I don't know about foster care? Let me tell you something, Missy..."

SPARKLE'S STORY:

I was born in Saginaw, Michigan, the eighth child of a young mother of twenty-eight. She had my oldest sister, Tiffanie, her first child, when she was fifteen years old. She dated an older man who made her addicted to drugs and him. She pretty much stopped taking care of us. My sister Tiffanie fed me; cleaned me and dressed me so many times I had started to call her mama.

Eventually the state took us away from my mother and split us up. In the state of Michigan, they had three different forms of custody for the children of the state, Relative Care, Child Receiving Home, and Foster Care.

Relative Care was when a relative or close family friend assumed responsibility or guardianship of a child. I never had anyone close enough who wanted to take in my siblings, or myself. But I frequented the other two processes.

Child Receiving Home was a place they took children when they had nowhere else to go. I was there often and it was rough. But it still beat living on them damn streets. They gave us three meals a day and even though they bathed us two children at a time, we still got the chance to wash our asses. We slept two to a twin bed, which was quite uncomfortable, but again, it beat sleeping on the ground with a box as a blanket.

When we were in foster care, they would drop us off and pick us up early so that the other kids would not know that we were living at the Child Receiving Home. You know how children are; they were trying to prevent us from public humiliation.

They would closely monitor us during school hours to make sure we did not run away. They would also privately interview us about our mother's past situation and our current foster care situation.

On those rare occasions when my mother was allowed to see us, we would have to go to the Department of Human Services, or DHS for short. Those were the only times I saw my mother and my siblings. We would gather in this small room where the DHS staff would watch us through a glass window and they recorded our every move. I was happy to see my mother but it felt strange meeting in such a peculiar manner. At the age of eight, the visits stopped and I have not seen or heard from my mother or my siblings since.

At nine, they gave me the responsibility of caring for three of the younger children in the home. I had to dress them, feed them and make sure they did not get into any danger as if they were my own children. If I did not handle my responsibility of taking care of the babies properly, I was severely disciplined. It is odd because as much as I hated taking care of those kids, I think I craved the attention and love they were giving me.

I was twelve when I had my first menstrual cycle. I did not feel comfortable telling my foster mom, so I told a friend who had just started her first cycle as well. She took me to one of our teachers, Mrs. Glenn, who showed me how to use a pad. Mrs. Glenn was concerned and called my foster mom and told her about the situation. My foster mom was mad as hell because she felt I was telling our family business. When I got home, she whooped my ass. I ran away, and never went back. I ended up staying with a nice family for a while, but then they moved out West, and I ended up back in the Child Receiving Home.

Around fourteen, I went to a foster home with a family who had three daughters and a boy. The girls were my age and younger, but the son was three years older than me. He was cute and I had a little crush on him. We would wrestle when there was no one else around and always end up with him grinding between my legs. One day, I came home early from school and he was the only one there. He was lying on the floor when I walked into the living room.

"Hey, Ida."

"Hey, Andre."

I sat on the couch and started watching television. I eventually fell asleep and when I woke up, Andre was on top of me grinding. I was startled and wanted him to get the hell up. We had done this numerous times before, but I was always awake. Finding him on top of me made me feel as if I was being ambushed.

"Get up, Andre."

"Shhh!"

Although I had a big crush on Andre, I did not want to lose my virginity like that. "Get up!"

"Come on, Ida."

I pushed his chest with both of my hands but he did not budge. "Get off of me!"

Andre did not respond to me; instead, he held my hands above my head and pulled my shirt up. He sucked my breasts into his mouth and squeezed extremely hard on my nipples. It was anything but pleasurable. I screamed for him to stop but he was like a crazed dog.

He ripped my shirt from my body and then pulled my pants down. I tried to resist him but Andre was a big guy and after a while, I was too exhausted to fight. All that I could do was try and keep my legs closed. He pulled out his penis and tried to force it inside of me. I screamed, cried, fought, but nothing I did was going to stop him from doing what he wanted to do that day.

I squirmed at the point of penetration, and then I felt the total impact of his thrust and I was paralyzed. It was tremendously painful. He was rough and rammed me as hard as he could.

"Please, Andre, stop it! I don't want to!" I cried.

"You like it? Huh? It feels good, don't it?"

"No! No, it hurts! Stop it!"

His body was moving so hard on top of me that it caused me bruises. He moaned loudly and then his body relaxed. He rolled off of me and onto the floor. He breathed heavily with his pants around his ankles and private parts still exposed. I balled in the fetal position and cried hysterically.

"What's wrong with you, Ida?"

Hearing Andre's voice made me go from the mindset of a victim to an angry-as-hell vigilante, and I ran to the kitchen and picked up a knife. I ran back into the living room, put the knife to Andre's neck and screamed as loud as I could, "If you ever put your hands on me again, niggah, I will kill you!"

I grabbed my clothes and took a long shower. I packed my suitcase and got the hell out of that house...

END SPARKLE'S STORY

"I never stayed another night in a foster care home. It was me against the world. I won a few times, but the world won an awful lot. But over the years I have met others who have had different experiences with foster care homes. Some were adopted and some just felt, great gratitude for the people who took the time to care for them. I just came to terms that some bad people are going to abuse good situations."

"Damn, so you were raped?"

"Is that all you got out of my story?"

"That's enough, don't you think?"

"No. My point is that everybody has been through something. But if you continue to blame the world, or somebody in particular, it's not hurting them; it's hurting you. They're going to move on and you're going to be stuck in the same miserable place."

"But ain't you mad at that Andre boy for what he did to you?"

"I was. I was mad for a very long time, but not anymore."

"How can you not be mad when that boy took your virginity from you like that?"

"Time heals all wounds. And for those who cannot forget their painful past, they will forever live in pain. It was more painful for me to dwell on what happened, than it was to finally let it go and start living my life."

"So you're not angry anymore?"

"Nope."

"So what would you do if you saw that boy right now?"

"Get out this car and cut his shit off!" Sparkle and I laughed.

"That's what I thought."

"All kidding aside, I want you to do good with these people. Don't disrespect them and give them a chance to help you."

"Okay."

"I'm serious, they're good people and they can help you."

"A'ight."

"No, don't a'ight me; speak correctly."

"All right."

"I want you to promise me you won't pull any tricks in school and get thrown out."

"I promise."

"I'm serious, the only way you're going to be anything in life is to get an education. I know what I'm talking about."

"I will, I promise. Now can I ask you a question?"

"Go ahead."

"Where are you going?"

"It's best that you don't know where I am, Shante. I know Harry and he's going to come after the both of us. He knows all of my spots. That's why I have to get out of town."

"Why can't you come stay with us?"

"I can't bring my problem to that family."

"He's looking for me, too."

"That's true. But he doesn't know anywhere you could be, but with me. That's why he came to my apartment the last time. He'll think you're with me and that's why I have to get far away from this city."

"Will I ever see you again?"

"One day."

"Okay. Can you tell me about these Powell people?"

Sparkle told me when she left Michigan and caught the bus to Atlanta, she had no money, nothing to eat and nowhere to stay. She ended up going to the Powells' church for help and they took her in. They let her stay with them for a few years until they caught her and their son in the bed together. They were madly in love and wanted to get married but they were too young. Sparkle was embarrassed and moved out on her own. The Powells advised her not to do it, but she did and they were disconnected until she talked to them on my behalf.

I felt better and Sparkle drove me to her friends' house. She explained my situation to them and they were happy to let me stay. We went to the Division of Family and Children Services, and in no time at all, the Powells officially became my foster parents. Sparkle hung around long enough to make sure I was safe and secure with them, and then she disappeared from my life like everyone else. She did not leave any forwarding information.

Speaking of the Powells, they were a longtime married couple in their mid-sixties. Mr. Powell was a pastor and Mrs. Powell was a retired schoolteacher. Mr. Powell lived comfortably off of his church salary, and he was very devoted. Mrs. Powell went to church almost every night of the week with Mr. Powell and made sure we had three square meals a day. She also set me on the path to speaking and writing grammatically.

The Powells were the exact same age, sixty-six. But Mr. Powell was a mature sixty-six whereas Mrs. Powell was a youthful sixty-six. I appreciated, and learned from them both, for being who they were. They had one grown son, Stanley, who lived in California and rarely visited so I was like a prodigal child returning. They were very nice people and I became close to them, very quickly.

I affectionately called Mrs. Powell, Ma, and Mr. Powell, Reb, short for Reverend.

Initially, I suspected two things: one, they were as happy to get the foster check as they were to get me. Two, I was going to have my way in that household with those old-ass people. I was wrong on both counts. A week after I was there, I tried my first stunt.

"Good night, Reb."

"Good night, Shante," Reb said as he locked the front door.

I pretended I was going to bed and waited for Reb to cut off all of the lights in the house and go to bed, too. I tiptoed out of my bedroom and down the stairs. I was not going to try to go out of the front door because it squeaked and made a lot of noise when it was opened and closed. Instead, I had left a window unlocked in the kitchen and climbed out.

I went out feet first and by the time my toes touched the ground, my head was also coming out where I could see the outside. I looked both ways; the coast was clear. I closed the window and tiptoed toward the front of the house. As I passed the porch, I heard Reb say, "So where we going tonight?"

He scared the living hell out of me! I stopped in my tracks and I did not move.

"What's the matter?" Reb laughed. "You look like I done scared the living hell outta ya."

"I...I...I was just, um..."

"What? You thought the old man was just a pushover, didn't you?"

"No."

"Excuse me?"

"I mean, no, sir."

"So, where you going?"

"I was just going down the street to hang with some of my friends. We weren't going to do anything, but just hang out."

"Hang out where, child? Ain't nothin' good happenin' this time of night."

"It's only eight o'clock, Reb."

"Right! God go to bed at eight! So if you ain't did what you need to do by eight o'clock at night, it ain't got nothin' to do with the good Lord!"

"Uh, okay."

"So what you think we should do about this?"

"About what?"

"About you tryin' to escape?"

"I mean, I didn't go anywhere so I don't think we should do anything."

"Think again!" Reb stood up and gestured for me to follow him.

"Damn!" I whispered under my breath.

Reb made me sit down while he practiced his next week's sermon on me. Every time I looked as if I was falling asleep, he would elevate his voice and wake me up.

"*And Jesus said, 'Judge not that ye shall be judged, for with what judgment ye judge, ye shall be judged!'*" Reb screamed.

I almost jumped out of that damn chair! All of the screaming woke Ma, and she came downstairs to find out what the hell was going on.

"What is all this screaming and yelling going on down here?"

"We havin' church, old lady."

"We who?"

"Me and the girl."

"What did you do, Shante?"

"I, uh, I tried to sneak out."

Ma looked at me and I gave her a look like, *please, please help me!* But instead of helping me, she went the other way.

"Hmm," Ma looked at Reb, "preach on, Preacher!"

Ma turned around and went back upstairs. Her approval seemed to inspire the Reb because he turned it up a notch or two.

I tried a few more escapes and Reb caught me every single time. I think he looked forward to catching me as much as I looked forward to getting out of that house. It had gotten to the point where we did not have to speak when he caught me. I would follow him into the living room and just sit in my chair. He would open his Bible and start preaching. In all honesty, after a while, I kind of looked forward to hearing my own personal sermons.

As far as my education was concerned, I became a student of the DeKalb County School System. I went to a rough school. I was tough and from the streets, but these kids were an entirely different animal.

The first person I met was a girl named Keisha Warren. Keisha was short, I mean really short, like four feet eleven or five feet tops. She had a strange hairstyle, like a peacock. At the top, and toward the back of the head, her hair stood straight in the air and it was blue. Yeah, I said blue! She had a brown complexion, not light, or dark, kind of like my complexion. We met my first day when I was trying to figure out how to catch the Metro Atlanta Rapid Transit Authority, or what we Atlantans call MARTA, from the school to downtown. I grew up in southwest Atlanta, also known as the *SWATS*, and I was not quite familiar with DeKalb County or MARTA.

"Excuse me?" I asked.

"What's up?" Keisha said.

"How do I get to Lenox mall from here?"

"Get on the MARTA train and go west to the Five Points station. You're going to have to get off at the Five Points station and then catch the North train to the Lenox station. When you get off there, the mall is only like a few blocks away."

"Can I see the mall from the train station?"

"Yeah, you should."

"Okay, thanks."

"I'm about to go to Perimeter Mall so I can show you where to get off."

"That's cool."

"What's your name?"

"Shante, but they call me Butterfly."

"Butterfly? That's a strange nickname. Why they call you that?"

"It's a name my father gave me when I was a baby."

"It's cool, though. My name is Keisha, and they call me Keisha." Keisha chuckled.

"All right, Keisha."

We got on the train and Keisha was like a pro. She was not afraid of the weirdos at all. I sat by the window and she sat on the aisle. Keisha decided to get off at the Lenox station with me instead of going all the way to Perimeter Mall. From that day on, she was my official best friend.

For the remainder of my junior year, I was a normal teenager with normal responsibilities and expectations. Reb made sure I legally obtained my driver's license, but when I did, I became the official gopher for the family. It was a long, black 2005 Cadillac. But I drove that joint like it was a Mustang!

Ma knew how to drive but refused to drive herself with me in the house. So, I either drove for her, or drove her, to all the places she wanted to go. I didn't mind, though, they truly felt like my grandparents. They disciplined me with love and followed with an explanation for their discipline. They embraced and loved me and never made me feel like an outsider. Oh, and did I mention that they showed me plenty of love? And I loved them just as much.

My friend Keisha introduced me to a few of her friends: Jacqua Dortch, Toya Laury and Janae Johnson. One day after school we were listening to music over Keisha's house and it got way out of control.

Toya and Janae were cousins. Toya was about five feet three, small waist, big butt, small breasts, flat stomach, long straight hair, and dark skin with Asian-looking eyes. People said she looked like a baby doll.

Jacqua was an inch or two taller than Toya. She was dark-skinned, too. She was not as flamboyant as Toya with her looks, but in my opinion, she was even prettier. She was thicker, and when she said hers was "in all the right places," it was. Jacqua also had long hair, but she kept her hair styled every week.

Janae, now Janae was a different story. She was like five-ten, or five-eleven, close to my height. She towered over the rest of them. She was thick, but she was thick-thick, and not toned-thick like Jacqua. Her hair was very short, but it was styled. She was light-skinned with a skinny nose and full lips. The boys liked her lips because they were always making obscene comments about them, comments that Janae seemed to enjoy.

Jacqua and Janae had boyfriends, but Toya had a girlfriend and a boyfriend. All of them were sexually active, but I was still a virgin. I had more life experiences than them, but they had way more sexual experiences than me.

As she normally did, Keisha snuck her stepdad's car out of the garage and went to the store for snacks. While she was gone, my other friends decided to show me how to kiss and prepare me for my first sexual experience.

"I can show you how to kiss, Butterfly," Toya offered.

"How are you going to show me?"

"Open your mouth and close your eyes." Toya moved closer to me and I could feel her breath on my lips. "You ready?"

"Ready for what?"

She moved closer and smacked me on the lips. "This."

Toya rotated her head from side to side and kissed me over and over again. It felt good! It felt warm and I had like this tingling sensation. She slowly slipped her tongue into my mouth and I could feel the moisture of her kiss. "And this!"

Eventually, I started to kiss back and we kissed more passionately, twirling our tongues around in each other's mouths.

"*Da-yum!*" Janae shouted as she covered her mouth and jumped up and down. "She all up in your mouth, Butterfly!"

"Shut up, Janae, and just watch 'em," Jacqua said.

"Mmm," Toya moaned as she pulled me closer to her. I could feel her breasts pressed against mine. It was an awkward, but pleasant feeling.

We kissed for a long time while Janae and Jacqua quietly watched us. Toya lay back and opened her legs. She pulled me on top of her and we started to grind. Toya reached between my legs and I moved her hand away. "We better quit before Keisha get back."

"Damn, that looked sexy!" Janae patted between her legs. "I'm wet as hell."

"Me, too," Jacqua added.

"I thought y'all didn't like girls, Jacqua."

"I don't, Toya, but after watching y'all, I might have to rethink the whole girl-on-girl situation."

"I ain't never said I didn't like girls; I just got a boyfriend right now," Janae said.

"Here y'all go." Keisha walked in with a bag full of fast-food and passed it around. "What y'all doing in here?"

"Man, ain't nobody doing nothing!" Janae said. "Hey, who paid for the food?"

"Me," I said.

"I'm gon' pay you back tomorrow, Butterfly, when I make my money." Janae unwrapped her sandwich and took a bite.

"Where you work at?"

"Well," Janae looked at Toya and smiled, "I keep it on the low-low."

"She runs an escort service!" Jacqua shouted.

I looked at Jacqua and then Janae waiting for one of them to tell me that Jacqua was joking, but they gave each other a high-five and took a bite from their sandwiches.

"You're kidding, right?"

"Yeah, they're kidding," Keisha snapped. "Stop telling all your business, Janae."

"Keisha just want to make you think we're good girls, Butterfly. Ain't none of us good girls."

"I am!" Keisha sat on the bed next to me. "You crazy if you believe all these stories these fools telling you."

"You wanna make some money, Butterfly?" Janae asked.

"Hell naw! I'm not going to be no escort!"

"You don't have to be no escort. All you have to do is be a lookout."

"That's okay. Butterfly's not interested."

"You can't speak for her, Keisha! You don't know what she wanna do."

"Not that I would, but just out of curiosity, if I'm not an escort, what would I be doing and how much would I be getting paid?"

"You'll be the lookout and you'll get twenty-five percent of everything I make."

"Where do you escort?"

"At school."

"*At school?*" I shouted. "How do you escort at school?"

"I have men come through the custodian's room between two and three o'clock every day when the janitor is cleaning the gym. They give me my three-hundred dollars and I give them whatever they want for fifteen minutes."

"Are you for real?"

"Hell yeah, I'm for real."

"So all I have to do is watch out and I get seventy-five dollars for every man that come through?"

"Damn, you figured out that twenty-five percent out fast as hell, Butterfly."

"I don't play with money, Janae."

Chapter Three

*T*he next day at school Janae and I met in front of the gym at two o'clock on the dot. When Mr. Moore, the custodian, went into the gym, Janae gestured for me to follow her in front of the custodian's room. She looked both ways and then opened the door.

"Stay here. If you see Mr. Moore comin' down the hall, don't call my name; call my phone! I just put a new ringtone on especially for you."

"Okay."

Janae walked in, and then closed the door behind her. I opened a book like I was reading it so that if anybody passed by, I would not look suspicious. Ten minutes later, Janae peeked through the door.

"You cool?"

"Yeah, I'm good," I answered.

"I got this other dude pulling up outside now. I'll be back in a minute."

"Okay, I got this out here."

"A'ight."

Janae closed the door and went back inside. Whoever the next guy was must have been putting it down right because I could hear Janae moaning loud and clear. I pulled out my cell phone and called her on speed dial.

"Somebody comin'?" Janae was breathing hard and I could hear the man in the background still doing his thing.

"No, but I can hear you out here making all that noise."

"For real?"

"Yeah, lower the volume, man."

"Oh, okay," Janae moaned. "Oh shit!"

"Janae! Be quiet!" I whispered sternly.

"Okay! Okay! But this niggah feel good!"

"Bye!" I hung up the phone.

I looked left and right down both hallways and the coast was still clear. Janae peeked through the door again. This time she was breathing hard and her pants were not pulled up all the way to her waist.

"That's a quick six hundred dollars." Janae was completely out of breath.

"Just like that?"

"Yup! Just like that!" Janae's cell phone rang and she looked down at it. "And it's about to be nine hundred!"

Janae closed the door and went back to her business. Two more men came before she left out for good. She slipped me three-hundred and seventy-five dollars and we walked away as if nothing had happened. As we were leaving Mr. Moore was coming toward us. Janae played it so smoothly I could tell she was used to the game.

Keisha walked up from behind and playfully pushed Janae. "So did you make that money?"

"Hell yeah! Fifteen hundred dollars!" Janae said. "I had to give Butterfly her cut, though. That could have been you, niggah!"

"Naw, I'm cool."

"I ain't no joke!"

"Let's go to the mall, y'all," I suggested.

"How we gon' get there?" Janae asked.

"I can get my grandparents' Caddy," I said.

"I got about twelve hundid dollars in my pocket so let's ride!" Janae shouted.

We picked up Toya and Jacqua and went to Greenbriar Mall. We spent almost all of the money we had made in a matter of a few hours. And as much as Keisha did not want us to do what we did, she had no problem helping us spend the money.

I ended up being Janae's lookout for the next two months until the police pulled a sting operation and busted some of her clients. I thank God that Keisha was looking out for me on that day. She had a strong feeling that something bad was going to happen, and she kept nagging me until I said I agreed not to be the lookout. Toya took my spot, but she did not get caught. Once she saw what was going down, she did not warn Janae or anything; she just ran.

The scandal was on television, but because they were minors, Toya's and Janae's names were not released through the media. However, the men's faces, names, occupations, everything, was on the news, and in the newspaper. Those guys ended up doing some serious time, but Janae was only expelled and given probation. You can believe I left that shit alone after that. If the Powells would have found out, they would have been crushed! They had so much faith in me and I was betraying them.

Janae had to come up with another hustle to make money, so she let some boys talk her into being their *"fight girl."* A fight girl was a female bully the high school boys betted on to fight other girls who had a reputation for being bullies. I watched Janae kick so many girls' asses I felt sorry for them. She would pulverize them to the point where the boys would have to pull her off of them. They would record the fights and put them on the Internet. That hustle was cut short when one of the girls filed assault charges against her. Janae ended up spending some time in the juvenile home but only like a month or two.

One afternoon, I skipped school with Keisha, Toya and Jacqua to go to a Braves afternoon game. We went just to be going. We didn't know anything about the Braves or who played for them. I know I didn't, anyway. The game started at one o'clock, so I thought that if we left early, I would have plenty of time to drop everybody off and get home without being late. I got stuck in the afternoon traffic and it went downhill from there.

There was an accident and we had to sit still for an hour. When we finally started moving, I started speeding. Once I dropped everybody off, I really started flying then. I ran through red lights, ignored stop signs, and I think I hit a couple of mailboxes on the way home, but I made it safely. I went to the living room for my sermon, but instead of Reb, Ma was there waiting on me. I didn't know what to expect from Ma because she was not the disciplinarian of the family.

She was sitting with the telephone in her hand and a blank look on her face. I assumed she had been calling me, but I had purposely cut my phone off so that they would not have to ask questions until I got home. I sat impatiently and waited for my sentence.

"Ma, I'm sorry for coming in late, uh, I got lost. I did not have any bars on my phone, so I could not receive any phone calls and…"

"Shante?" Ma interrupted me and closed her eyes. "Reb just went into cardiac arrest at the church and they had to call an ambulance."

"Come on, let's go! Let's go to the hospital! Where he at?"

I stood up and held Ma by the hand. She pulled her hand from mine and then dropped it on her lap. "It's too late, baby. He's gone."

"Gone where, Ma?"

"He didn't make it, baby."

I collapsed to my knees and put my head in Ma's lap and I cried like a newborn baby. She patted my back and tried to console me. "Shh! Shh!"

I wiped my eyes and said, "I need to see him, Ma. I need to tell him good-bye."

"All right, sweetheart, all right." Ma sighed.

I think Ma was in shock. She was totally emotionless. We drove to the hospital but when we got to Reb's room, I was afraid to enter. I stopped at the door and began to back up. Ma held my hand and tried to guide me in.

"You okay, baby?" Ma asked.

"I...I...I...I can't go in there."

"What's the matter?"

"I'm sorry. I don't want to see him like that, Ma."

"It's okay, baby."

I gripped Ma's hand as tight as I could and we walked through the door. Reb was lying peacefully on the bed. He looked younger, like some of the wrinkles on his face had disappeared.

"Ah, he looks so handsome, doesn't he?"

"Yes, ma'am." I rubbed Reb's face and then kissed him on the forehead. "I love you, old man."

I sat beside Reb as other people came to the hospital to say their good-byes. Their condolences gave me strength. So much so, I did most of the planning for Reb's funeral. Their son, Stanley, flew in and helped me with a few details, but all in all, I did everything myself. He was grateful and thanked me for taking care of his parents and looking after them. I made it perfectly clear that it was them who needed to be thanked for taking care of me.

Reb was a well-loved man because there was a huge turnout for his sendoff. There were so many ministers requesting to speak at his funeral, we had to turn some down. I thought that Sparkle would show up to offer her condolences to the family since she was so close to them, but she was a no-show.

I was so devastated by the loss of Reb, I cried from the time I found out he died until we laid him in the ground. But throughout it all, I did not see or hear Ma cry one single time. Not until the night I woke up in the middle of the night and I walked past her bedroom to get to the bathroom. Her light slipped beneath the bottom of her bedroom door, which never happened, and so I knocked.

"Ma, you okay?" Ma did not answer so I knocked on the door again. "Ma, everything all right in there?"

"Yeah, baby, I'm fine."

"Can I come in, Ma?"

"Uh-huhn."

I walked in and Ma had a box of tissue on the bed with her. Judging by the number of used tissues, she had been crying a lot.

"Aw, what's the matter, Ma? You thinking about Reb?"

"Yeah, I'm having a conversation with him now."

"Oh-kaaaay," I said as I looked around the room.

"I don't mean like that, crazy!" Ma chuckled. "I got to figure out how I'm going to take care of you."

"No, Ma, don't worry about me. I'll be fine."

"No, baby, I have to find somebody to help take care of you because I just can't do it all by myself."

My heart was broken. My dream of finally having a family was coming to a screeching halt. I loved Ma, and I did not want to leave her.

"Please don't make me leave, Ma!"

"What are you talking about, child?"

"I don't want to leave you. I love you!"

"Baby, I love you, too! I don't want you to leave, but you are my responsibility and if I can't take care of you properly, I have to find help. "

"I can take care of myself, Ma. Just don't make me leave!" I kneeled on the side of her bed and put my head in her lap.

"Get up off of that floor right now and get in this bed!" I slid into the bed with Ma and cried. "Listen to me child, I love you like you're my own flesh and blood, and I would never make you leave. Never! But I received two letters this week and I think they are God's way of telling me what we should do."

"Two letters? What letters?"

"I received a letter from my son and he asked me to come out West, so that he could take care of me."

"Oh, I understand."

"Hush it up! I told him that I would only come if I could bring you with me."

"And what did he say?"

"He said, yes."

I was so excited that I jumped out of the bed without even realizing it. "He did? I can come with you?"

"Wait a minute now; that was only the first letter."

"Oh, Lord," I said, slumping back down in the bed.

"The second letter I received was from the Georgia Department of Human Resources, and they said they have located your father in prison through a Doctor Johnson Forrester. He's a friend of your father. That's what I was in here discussing with my husband. Should I, or should I not tell you about the letter? I guess I'm being selfish by wanting to keep you all to myself. But I can't help it. I love you."

"My dad? What did he say?"

Ma took her time answering but finally she said, "The letter said that on behalf of your father's request, and a promise that he made to your father, Dr. Forrester, uh, he wants to talk to you about visiting your father."

"Oh my God! Of course I want to see my dad! I can't believe this!"

"Then we'll call them tomorrow and arrange a meeting with you and this Dr. Forrester."

"Thank you so much, Ma. I love you soooooo much!"

I kissed Ma on the cheek and gave her a big hug. Ma tried to playfully push me away, but I continued to kiss her all over her face. "Get back, girl; you gon' give me the heebie-jeebies!"

My first meeting with Dr. Forrester was just between him, Ma and me. He wanted to get a feel for me before he introduced me to his wife. He was a tall, handsome man. He had dark smooth skin, a clean-shaven face with a clean-shaven head to match. He wore a nice suit that fit him very well. Ma and I peeked through the curtain as he stepped out of his car.

"Well, he's a handsome something, isn't he?"

"Yes, ma'am!" I said with enthusiasm.

"My, oh my!"

"Ma?"

"Look at us in here salivating. I'm too old and you're too young."

"Ma, he's married," I joked.

Knock! Knock! Knock!

"Go answer the door, child."

"Oh, okay!" I looked back at Ma one last time for moral support and then I opened the door. "Hi, Dr. Forrester, I'm Shante."

"How are you, young lady?" Dr. Forrester shook my hand and then shook Ma's hand. "And how are you, ma'am?"

"I'm fine, son," Ma said. "Have a seat, please."

We sat in the living room and Dr. Forrester told me the story of being my father's cellmate. He told me how much my father loved and adored me and that he made a promise to my dad to find me when he was released from prison.

Ma was understandably concerned about Dr. Forrester's prison record, but he explained that he was unrightfully accused and was awaiting the dismissal of the charges held against him through an evidentiary hearing. He was totally open and honest with her and that made her believe him. At the end of the conversation, Dr. Forrester presented the question of visiting my father.

"Shante, your father would give anything to see you."

"I want to see him, too."

"We have arranged for me to take you to see him this Sunday, if you would like to go."

"Oh my God! Are you serious?"

"Yes, if you want to go."

"I can't wait!"

"Well, if it's okay with Mrs. Powell, I'll pick you up Sunday afternoon."

"Ma?"

"Of course, baby."

"I guess I'll be seeing you Sunday, Dr. Forrester," I said with a huge grin on my face.

"You go on and do your homework and I'll walk the doctor to the door, child."

I knew that meant that she wanted to talk privately with Dr. Forrester, so I got the hell out of there immediately.

"I thank you for stopping by, Doctor, but this child means an awful lot to me. I need to know that she's not going to be hurt in all of this. She's been through so much in her short lifetime."

"I promise you, ma'am. Her father wants nothing but the best for her."

"Then I'll take your word for it."

"Have a good day, ma'am."

"You too, son."

I was nervous when we arrived at the prison. It was the first time I had seen my dad in almost ten years. When I first laid eyes on him, he looked different from what I remembered. His hair was a lot longer. He wore his hair bald when he was on the outside, but in prison, it was long and in a thick ponytail. He was also much more muscular, with tats on his neck and hands. He had a couple of scars from what I assumed to be prison battles. All that did not matter to me. I was just so happy to see him, I wanted to cry. I wanted to reach out and hug him. But I couldn't because he was behind those bars.

When I first walked in, I thought he did not remember who I was. He spoke to Dr. Forrester but did not say a word to me.

"Hey, Doc," Dad said. "How's life out there?"

"Not much different from in here," Dr. Forrester joked and handed the telephone to me. "I brought somebody to see you, man."

"Hi," I said.

"Oh wow, man! Look at you. You're taller than me. My little caterpillar is turning into a beautiful Butterfly," Dad said. "Do you remember when I used to call you my butterfly?"

"Yes, Daddy."

"Do you remember anything else about me?"

"Of course."

"What do you remember about me?" Dad chuckled.

"I remember one time when I was little, I had a dance recital and you were out of town. I asked you if you could come. Mommy said you were too far away to make it back in time. It was raining and thundering and I just knew you weren't going to make it. But after the recital, I saw you standing there with my flowers in your hands. I was so happy I didn't know what to do! Now! Do you remember that?"

My father may have been hard to the rest of the world, but he was like a marshmallow when it came to me. "Yeah."

"And I remember that time when I was sick. I think I had the measles or something like that," I said. "You remember that?"

"Yeah," Dad said. "I remember that, too."

"I remember when you had to wear sweaters, and T-shirts, and long pants, because you didn't want to catch the measles. I was sleeping on your lap for like five days." I laughed. "Mommy kept telling you to put me down, but you wouldn't. You spoiled me!"

"How do you remember all that?" Dad said. "You were a baby!"

"'Cause you my daddy!"

"I'm sorry, Butterfly," Dad said. It looked as if he wanted to cry, but I did not see any tears. I wanted to tell him so badly that it was okay for him to cry if that is what he wanted to do. "I should be out there protecting you, but instead, I'm in here locked up."

I truly believe my father tried to be the best father he could. But he was who he was, and no matter how hard he tried, he could not separate parenthood from the street, even when I was little. He was always apologetic for his lifestyle. That got on my nerves then, and it still got on my nerves.

"Why are you talking like that?" I asked.

"Because," Dad said. "I'm letting you down."

"You're not letting me down!" I said. "You can't change what you've done, Daddy. All you can do is pay for what you did."

"I can't believe you even want to see me."

"Why wouldn't I want to see you? "

My father lowered his head and waited before he responded to my question, even though he did not answer the question I asked. "Are you going to come back and see me?"

"Yeah, why wouldn't I?" I asked. "You're my father."

"You promise?"

"Wait a minute! I promise on one condition," I said. "I'll come back if you behave yourself while you're in here and get paroled so you can be my daddy like you're supposed to."

"Oh, so you're giving orders now?" Dad turned to Dr. Forrester and cracked one of his lame jokes. "She's trying to blackmail me, man."

"Right! I sure am."

"In that case, I guess we got a deal."

"You better keep your promise, too, Daddy!"

"I always keep my promises."

"Well, we better be going, Shante," Dr. Forrester said.

"Okay."

Time had flown by and I was not ready to leave my dad just yet. I probably could have stayed a month and I still would not have been ready to leave. I stood up and waved good-bye. "Bye! I love you, Daddy."

My father stared at me but did not respond. That was the second time that had happened and it was pissing me off. "Did you hear me? I said I love you, Daddy."

"I'm sorry, baby," Dad said, "I love you, too. I love you so much."

"All right, Stone," Dr. Forrester said, "Keep your head up, bro."

"Doc," Dad said, "Can I talk to you privately?"

"What y'all talking about?" I asked jokingly. Ma had taught me that when grown-ups wanted to talk in private, they were probably going to talk about me.

"You!" Dad said while pointing at me.

"It better be good," I said. "I'll wait for you out here, Dr. Forrester."

"Okay."

I walked out to the exit room and waited for Dr. Forrester. I am not going to lie; I started to cry like a little baby. I missed my daddy! By the time Dr. Forrester came out, I had wiped my tears away and he never even knew I had been crying. However, that lasting image of my dad being locked up and behind bars stayed in my mind.

The private conversation between my dad and Dr. Forrester was a very important one. My dad asked Dr. Forrester to take me into his home until he was released from prison. Ironically, Stanley made an impromptu visit to Ma to try and convince her to come out West with him. Our decisions were quick and final. Ma was moving out West with Stanley, and I was moving to Gwinnett County with the Forresters.

My next interview, so to speak, with the Forresters, included the Missus herself, Mrs. Alicia Forrester. Dr. Forrester and I met her at an elegant restaurant in Midtown. She was beautiful. I mean absolutely gorgeous. It took her a minute to warm up to me, but when she did I knew that pending the result of Dr. Forrester's evidentiary hearing, I would be having yet another family. The hearing proved that the State did not have enough evidence to prosecute his case, so it was dismissed.

My first night in the Forresters' house was unbelievable! They were having this party in celebration of Dr. Forrester's murder charge dismissal. I stayed in my room until the party was over and then I helped Ms. Alicia clean up.

Shortly after that, two of Ms. Alicia's sisters came to town and told her some sad news. Her father had died and she had to go to Ohio for the funeral. While the Forresters were gone, I stayed with Keisha. Mr. Forrester, Dr. Forrester's dad, had just moved in with the family as well, but I guess he needed a babysitter, too, so he stayed with Dr. Forrester's brother, Michael. I called him Uncle Mike.

They were gone for only a few days, but when they returned, I could tell that things were different. It was a positive difference, but things were different all the same. The Forresters seemed to be looser and carefree, even Mr. Forrester had a friendlier disposition, and that made me feel more comfortable about the living situation.

Excluding the Powells, all of the people I lived with were unemployed and were only foster parents for the checks. As a matter of fact, foster parenting was their jobs. Ms. Alicia seemed like she genuinely cared about me, and my welfare. She was not looking for a check. She was not looking for a pat on the back. She was just trying to help me.

Chapter Four

When it was nearing the end of the summer, Ms. Alicia registered me in school. She was very thorough and wanted all of my background information. While adding me to their health insurance, she showed me my birth certificate and I noticed the name listed as my mother was not my actual mother's name. At the age of seventeen, I found out the woman I loved, and knew, as my mother was not my mother at all. And there was some woman out there who had abandoned me. In my mind, I finally had someone to blame for all of the negative shit that had happened to me in my life.

The following weekend Ms. Alicia invited some of her friends over to meet me. She called them the "office girls." I went from having no aunts whatsoever, to having a clan of aunties in a matter of minutes. She was so excited when she introduced me.

"Hey girls, I want you to meet the new addition to our family. Her name is Shante." Ms. Alicia pointed to the "office girls." "Shante, meet your new stable of aunties."

"Hi, Shante, I'm your Auntie Cynthia. You'll be seeing a lot of me."

"Good to meet you, Auntie Cynthia."

Auntie Cynthia was short, with a ponytail and she dressed very conservatively.

"Me too, I'm Auntie Pam. You look familiar, girl."

"You look familiar, too, Auntie Pam."

Auntie Pam had a youthful athletic body. She was dark-skinned with a tight-ass, short hairstyle. She dressed like she was young.

"I'm Auntie Wanda, and I don't like children! I used to be Dr. Forrester's patient, but he stopped seeing me because I'm just too damn crazy!"

That lady scared the shit out of me! She was kind of husky with big-ass eyes. She was adorable, though, in her own crazy way.

"Quit it, girl!" Ms. Alicia laughed.

"I'm Auntie Tina. I have a daughter around your age. Y'all might be able to hang out sometime."

Auntie Tina was about five feet four inches, dark, slightly over-weight, and she had long hair but it was not styled at all. She was soft-spoken and timid.

"That'll be nice."

"I'm Auntie Susan. Alicia and I used to work together."

Auntie Susan was white. She was short, cute and acted like a black woman. Her husband was a black man and that may have something to do with it.

"That's the white sheep of the family!" Auntie Wanda joked.

"Okay." I chuckled. Nobody else laughed, but I thought Auntie Wanda's joke was hilarious.

"I'm Auntie Tazzy. Good to meet you."

"Good to meet you, too, Auntie Tazzy."

Auntie Tazzy was short, petite and also soft spoken. She had a certain charisma about her that everyone seemed to respect.

"Hi, Shante, I'm Darsha. I'm too young to be your aunt, but you can call me auntie anyway."

Darsha did not look much older than me. She was young but she sounded like she had herself together.

"Y'all about the same age, Darsha!" Auntie Wanda joked.

"Don't pay no attention to her. She's just mad because her old ass ran out of Geritol this morning!"

"Damn, that's cold. I just made a little joke and you coming at me with ageism."

"Forgive these ladies, but they don't know any better. I'm your Auntie Lisa."

Auntie Lisa was prim and proper. She was kind of tall, not nearly as tall as me, but tall. Her hair was long, and her face was unblemished.

"Hi, Auntie Lisa."

"Hey, I'm your Auntie Valerie."

Auntie Valerie dressed like a dude. Her hair was cut like a dude. And she talked like a dude. She reminded so much of a man I almost called her Uncle Valerie.

"She's our version of Ellen DeGeneres!"

"Wanda, shut your big-ass mouth!" Auntie Valerie yelled.

"Stop cussing like that in front of that girl, Val!" Darsha said.

"I'm sorry, Shante."

"That's okay."

We drank tea, and then two very fine masseurs came over and gave all of us relaxing massages. By the way, I found out that day that a masseur was a male who gave massages and a masseuse was a female. Anyway, we also got our hair and nails done, too. I felt like a queen. The only time I was treated like that was when Mr. Harry groomed me for the stage.

It took me a while to feel comfortable because those women looked important and I did not want to say the wrong thing. I was not used to being around those kinds of professional people. I will always love the Powells and consider them as my real family, but they were not exactly Buckhead type of folk. Buckhead is a very upscale area of Atlanta. No, they were educated but old school. These women were hip and knew what was going on in the world.

I studied Auntie Valerie all day because she was a little peculiar from the rest of the "office girls." She was pretty but she was also very masculine-looking. That night, my curiosity got the best of me and I had to ask her.

"Are you a lesbian?"

"Don't you answer that!" Auntie Wanda covered Auntie Valerie's mouth.

"Move!" Auntie Valerie pushed Auntie Wanda's hand away. "Yes, sweetheart, I'm a lesbian."

"Oh Lord! She done corrupted our youth!" Auntie Wanda said.

"One of my best friends is a lesbian. We messed around a little but nothing major," I said.

Ms. Alicia spat out her drink and sprayed on her friends.

"Man, damn!" Auntie Wanda shouted. "You done gave me a damn shower!"

"What?" Ms. Alicia asked.

"Good for you and your friend!" Auntie Valerie laughed and then kissed me on the cheek.

"I believe the children are our future!" Auntie Wanda pulled Auntie Valerie away.

"But uh," Ms. Alicia said, "but you're not a lesbian, right?"

"No, ma'am. It was just a curiosity phase."

"Lawdy Clawdy!" Auntie Wanda shouted.

"What do you know about lesbianism, Shante?" Ms. Alicia asked.

"Nothing," I said.

"Nothing?" Ms. Alicia asked. "You just said, *'it was a curious phase.'*"

"I meant to say, um, I'm, um, I'm good." I knew that did not make sense, but I was nervous and said the first thing that came to my mind.

"Excuse me, ladies, but I think me and Ms. Shante needs to have a little talk."

"Oh-oh!" Auntie Wanda said. "Somebody's in trou-ble."

"You gon' be in trouble if you don't shut the hell up!" Auntie Valerie said.

"I'm serious, girls, the party's over! Shante and I need to be alone."

The "office girls" grabbed their jackets and purses and left. Ms. Alicia asked Auntie Valerie to stay behind to talk to me. They sat on both sides of me and talked very cautiously as if I had some kind of a disease or something.

"Do you want to talk about it, Shante?" Auntie Valerie asked.

"Talk about what?"

"Lesbianism!" Ms. Alicia said.

"Calm down, Alicia! I got this," Auntie Valerie said. "Go 'head, baby."

Ms. Alicia sat back and folded her arms.

"Well," I said, "I don't really have anything to talk about."

"How old were you when you started to have those urges?" Auntie Valerie asked.

"What urges?" I asked.

"Urges to touch another girl."

"I'm sorry, Auntie Valerie, but I never really had those urges."

"Then why do you think that you're a lesbian?"

"I never said I thought I was a lesbian. I just fooled around with a girl, that's all. We all did."

"We all who, Shante?" Ms. Alicia sat up.

"Alicia! Don't overreact!" Auntie Valerie shouted. "Okay, we all who, baby?"

"My friends from school." I looked back and forth at Ms. Alicia and Auntie Valerie.

"When you say 'fooled around,' what exactly did you do?" Auntie Valerie asked.

"I mean like, we would kiss each other. Touch each other."

"Touch each other where?" Ms. Alicia asked.

"Everywhere," I said.

"Everywhere like where, the breasts, the vagina? Where?"

"The breasts, the butt, you know."

"OH MY GOD!" Ms. Alicia shouted.

"I'm sorry!" I shouted back.

"Would you stop it, Alicia?" Auntie Valerie said. "If you want her to open up and talk, you're going to have to stop tripping every time she opens her damn mouth!"

"I'm sorry! I'm sorry! I'm sorry!" Ms. Alicia said. "I won't say another word. Y'all go on. Act like I'm not even here."

"It's hard to do that when you won't be quiet," Auntie Valerie said. "Now Shante, did you enjoy touching your friend?"

"It was okay."

"Did this happen only one time, or more than one time?"

"Way more than once."

"Lord Jesus!" Ms. Alicia screamed as she covered her mouth. "Okay, that's enough!"

"No, let her talk! Ignoring it is not going to make it go away, Alicia."

"I don't know if I want to hear any more of this, Val."

"I don't believe you, Alicia."

"What do you mean, you don't believe me?"

"You know what I went through at Shante's age and now you're doing the same thing to her!"

"I'm not doing anything to her but trying to protect her!"

"Protect her from what, Alicia?" Auntie Valerie said. "Hell?"

While Auntie Valerie and Ms. Alicia were arguing, I sat back and hoped they would forget about me.

"You said it, Val, I didn't!"

"What good are you doing this girl by making her think the Lord won't love her if she likes girls?"

"The Bible clearly states that homosexuality is a sin!"

"The Bible also says that lying is a sin! Adultery is a sin! And judging is a sin! I don't see you condemning yourself to hell."

"That's different and you know it."

"Let me tell you something, Alicia! If your God is like you claim, He loves everybody! It's not Him that's turning people away in Heaven. It's hypocrites like you who are turning people away from His churches!"

After listening to them go back and forth, I figured they would never stop so I tried to step in. If it meant answering all of their questions, so be it.

"Can I say something, please?" I asked.

"Sure, sweetheart," Ms. Alicia said.

"I don't like girls," I said. "I..."

"If you like girls, you like girls. There's nothing wrong with that," Auntie Valerie interrupted.

"And there's nothing wrong with liking boys, either, Shante." Ms. Alicia raised her voice to talk over Auntie Valerie.

"I'm afraid you can't just turn it on and off like that, sweetheart."

"I'm not turning it off and on, Auntie Valerie," I said. "I never really liked girls like I liked boys. It was just that I was always in that situation with girls, and not boys."

"Which do you prefer?" Auntie Valerie asked.

"I mean, I don't have to prefer because I just like boys."

"Did Ms. Alicia's reaction intimidate you into saying that?"

"I didn't intimidate her! This house is a free society!" Ms. Alicia snapped.

"No, she didn't intimidate me. I just like boys; that's all. Some of my friends still like girls, but I don't."

"Have you ever had sex with a boy, Shante?" Auntie Valerie asked.

"No, ma'am."

"Thank you, Jesus!" Ms. Alicia clapped her hands together.

"Then how do you know you like boys?"

"Valerie!" Ms. Alicia shouted. "She doesn't have to have sex with a boy to know that she likes boys!"

"You got to have a test drive to know if you like the car, Alicia."

"Okay, that's it!" Ms. Alicia said. "Good night, Val."

"We're not through yet."

"Oh yes we are! Good night!"

"So we're going to end the conversation all up in the air like this?"

"Yes, 'bye!" Ms. Alicia grabbed Auntie Valerie's hand and led her to the door.

"You have her batting for the wrong team, Alicia," Auntie Valerie said. "The girl is confused!"

"Okay, thank you for all of your assistance. Good night!"

Ms. Alicia pushed Auntie Valerie out of the door and closed it behind her. She came back into the dining room and asked me to sit down.

"Sit!" Ms. Alicia pointed to a chair.

I sat down and put my hands underneath my legs.

"Okay, let's discuss some of the rules of the house."

"Okay," I said.

"In this house, we are allowed to speak our minds but in a respectful and articulate manner. Is that understood?"

"Yes, ma'am."

"And I want you to know that you can talk to Dr. Forrester or me about anything that concerns you. I should not have judged you just now. I should have listened and discussed it with you. That will never happen again. In this house we keep no secrets. Now I want you to promise that if anything bothers you, or if there's anything you want to discuss, you'll let Dr. Forrester or me know, okay?"

"Yes, ma'am."

"Promise?"

"Yes, ma'am, I promise."

"Shante, if you call me 'ma'am' one more time, girl!"

"I'm sorry, ma'am," I said. "Oops! I mean, Ms. Alicia."

"Girl! Are you trying to get yourself hurt?"

"It slipped." I chuckled.

"Seriously," Ms. Alicia said. "I know I'm not your mother and I'm not trying to be, but…"

"Please! My mother was a bitch!"

"Oh my God! Why would you say such a thing?"

"Because she gave me up for adoption!"

"Shante! You're not going to use that language in this house, and I don't want to ever hear you talk that way about your mother!"

"But you don't understand, Ms. Alicia. That woman abandoned me!" I started to cry and Ms. Alicia consoled me.

"It's okay, baby." Ms. Alicia leaned over and put her arms around me. She handed me a napkin from off of the table to wipe my eyes. "Here you go."

I don't know where the words came from, but they began to spill out and I screamed. "I hate that woman! I hate her! I hate her! I hate her! I hate her! I hate her!"

"You don't mean that, sweetheart!"

"Oh yes I do!"

"Hey, what's going on in here?" Dr. Forrester peeked around the corner. "Is everything okay?"

"Yes, everything is fine, honey. We're just having an important girl conversation, that's all."

"Well, that's my cue to exit," Dr. Forrester said. "If you need me, I'll be upstairs."

"We won't need you. So go to sleep."

"Good night, ladies."

"Good night, baby."

I would have said "good night," but I had my face stuck on Ms. Alicia's shoulder and was crying my tears out.

After Dr. Forrester went upstairs, Ms. Alicia raised my head. "Baby, listen, I don't know what you've been through, but you're home now. There's no reason for you to hate anybody. Not your mother, not anybody. It's time to start forgivin' so you can start livin'."

"I can't." I lowered my head.

"Why not?"

"Because it hurts."

"I understand more than you realize, but you shouldn't hold on to that anger, Shante. It's not going to do you any good."

"But if my real mother had been there for me, my life probably would have turned out differently!" I said. "She didn't even care what happened to me."

"I'm sure she did."

"If she cared about me, she wouldn't have left me."

"It's not that simple, sweetheart."

"It's not that simple? How hard is it to love your child, Ms. Alicia?"

"Maybe she was going through a difficult period in her life."

"So?" I snapped.

"So you better watch your mouth!" Ms. Alicia snapped back.

"I'm sorry."

"When you learn how to control that mouth of yours, you'll stop having to say I'm sorry so much."

"I know."

"Now go get some sleep. We have a busy day tomorrow."

"Okay, good night."

Chapter Five

I was so excited about going shopping I could barely sleep that night. I had never gone shopping for school clothes before. You feel me? Never! Most of my school clothes came from some type of donation drive. But don't trip; sometime I got some good stuff.

I tossed and turned until the sun came up. As soon as my eyes closed for some real sleep, Ms. Alicia walked in beating on a frying pan. The noise was so loud I sat straight up, and covered my ears.

"Okay, I'm up!" I said. "Stop it, please!"

"Can you cook?" Ms. Alicia asked.

"Yes, ma'am!" Ma Powell had taught me how to cook everything from boiled water to a four-course gourmet meal.

"Good! You got five minutes to meet me in the kitchen to help cook breakfast."

"Can I shower first, Ms. Alicia?"

"You don't need to shower. All that you're going to be using is your hands. So just make sure they're clean and you're good to go."

"It's like boot camp around here." I chuckled.

"You ain't seen nothin' yet, sister! Wait 'til Mr. Forrester get ahold of you."

I washed up and went downstairs to help cook breakfast. Ms. Alicia already had pans on the island, eggs in a bowl, waffles on the counter and her hands on her hips.

"You ready for Cooking 101?" she asked.

"What's Cooking 101?"

She explained, "101 is college terminology. It means your very first level of classes in college. They're introductory classes that freshmen take. Understand?"

"I'm not a freshman yet."

"You're a freshman in this kitchen. What do you know how to cook? Eggs? Bacon? Sausage? What?"

"Waffles!" I laughed and then ran over to the toaster.

"You wish!" Ms. Alicia pulled me backward by my robe. "Get your behind over there to that stove."

"I might mess up."

"That's okay; you'll be all right."

I looked over my shoulder and I saw that Ms. Alicia had turned around to walk out of the kitchen.

"Where are you going, Ms. Alicia?"

"To take a shower."

"But I thought you said I only needed to wash my hands to cook breakfast?"

"I did."

"Then why are you leaving me to go take a shower?" I whined.

"You're right. I did say *you* only needed to wash *your* hands, not me." Ms. Alicia walked out of the kitchen. She yelled back to me as she was going upstairs, "And if that breakfast does not taste good, there will be no shopping. You feel me?"

"Please don't try to act young, Ms. Alicia."

I did not know if Ms. Alicia was joking or not about shopping, so I made sure I cooked a tasty breakfast. I fixed golden yellow eggs, with dark-brown sausages. I made biscuits from scratch to go along with crisp light-brown bacon. The orange juice was poured in everybody's glasses, including Dr. Forrester's and Brittany's.

They came to breakfast at the same time. Dr. Forrester was holding Brittany in his arms. They were inseparable. She wanted to spend every minute of the day with him. She loved her father a lot, but that little girl had enough love for everybody. She was the apple of all of our eyes. She was a very affection four-year-old who looked up to me as her big sister. I really enjoyed being a big sister.

"Can I have a hug?" Brittany said as she jumped out of Dr. Forrester's arms and ran to me.

"Of course you can!" I picked her up and spun her around.

"Mommy said we're going to the mall today!"

"Yes we are!" I walked over to the breakfast table and extended my arms across the buffet of food. "Breakfast, anyone?"

"Homemade biscuits?" Dr. Forrester shouted. "I thought you didn't know how to make homemade biscuits, baby."

"I don't," Ms. Alicia rolled her eyes at me sarcastically, "Ms. Thang over there made them."

Dr. Forrester took a big bite out of one of my biscuits. "These are delicious. Melts in your mouth."

"Okay! That's enough! If I didn't know any better, I would think that you were trying to show me up, girl."

"No! Uh-uhn! I'm not trying to show you up, Ms. Alicia!" I laughed.

"Well, just for that, you have cooking duties every morning until you start school. We'll see who's going to get the last laugh!"

Ms. Alicia threw a napkin at me and we both laughed. I never knew life could be so enjoyable. People always try to explain what a family is, or is not. I do not care if it is biological or not. A family is being around people who love and care for you.

After we ate breakfast, Ms. Alicia asked me to help out with Brittany. It really made me feel like I was one of the family.

"Okay, Rachel Ray, take your little sister upstairs and help her run her bath water."

"Okay." I grabbed Brittany's hand.

"Oh, I'm sorry. I got caught up in the family moment thing, Shante. Take Brittany upstairs and help her with her bath."

"That's okay," I said. "We already call each other sisters, anyway. We got this under control. But, um, like you told me, Ms. Alicia, when you learn how to control your mouth, you'll stop having to say 'I'm sorry' so much."

"No that heffa didn't!" Ms. Alicia laughed and chased after me.

"Come on, let's go, Brittany!"

I ran Brittany's bath water and played with her while she took her bath. After she was finished, I took a shower. I was not used to having my own bedroom and my own privacy. It was wonderful. I cut on the shower to let the water heat up. I liked taking very warm showers. Baths, on the other hand… I loved hot! Steaming hot!

I took off my clothes and I stared at myself in the mirror. My breasts were the size of a full-grown woman. I touched my left breast and then my nipple became hard. I was excited. I do not know if it was the privacy of having my own room turning me on, or the curiosity of my own body, but I was hot and horny.

I never cared too much for touching myself. It never really turned me on. Now when dudes touched me, it made me hot as hell. I never let them touch between my legs, though; that was my forbidden fruit.

I sat on the toilet and opened my legs. I could see myself in the full-length mirror that was directly across from me. When I'd first moved in with the Forresters, I'd asked myself why that mirror was there. Come on now, who wanted to see themselves crapping? But seeing myself naked gave me an entirely different perspective of that mirror.

I looked in the mirror and then I opened my legs. I used my finger next to my thumb and I began to touch myself. I touched my clitoris and it felt so good my legs began to tremble. I opened my legs wider and touched myself faster. I had one hand on my breast and one hand between my thighs. I felt the sensations getting stronger and stronger. I leaned my head back and I closed my eyes. I was about to have an orgasm, so I wiggled my finger really fast. I felt like I was about to explode. You know, like a bottle when you shake it up really hard. Just when I was right there, my worst nightmare happened.

"Girl, what are you doing in here?"

Ms. Alicia burst through the door and stood in the doorway of the bathroom with her mouth wide open. I was so embarrassed I didn't know what to say.

"Nothing!" I slammed my legs together and then slammed the door in her face.

"Shante! Open the door!"

"Uh, can I get a minute? Damn! Damn! Damn! Damn! Damn! Damn! Dammit!" I jumped in the shower and then jumped back out. I didn't know what to do.

"Put on a towel and open this door!" Ms. Alicia yelled.

"Okay, hold on." I ran around looking for my towel. "Shit!"

I wrapped a towel around me and cracked the door. I stood behind it and peeked around.

"Uh-huhn?" I asked.

"Uh-huhn, what?" Ms. Alicia asked.

"Did you want something?"

"What's going on in there?"

"Nothing much."

"Nothing much? Girl, I saw you with your legs all gapped open," Ms. Alicia said, "what you doin' in here?"

"Nothin'! For real! Nothing."

"It's nothing to be ashamed of, Shante."

"I'm not ashamed. I wasn't doing nothing."

"Okay," Ms. Alicia said, "Well, hurry up and finish doing nothing so we can go. You holding up the party."

"Okay," I said. "Can I finish my shower now?"

"Go 'head. But make it a quickie!" Ms. Alicia joked.

"Very funny, Ms. Alicia."

"Hurry up and come on. We're waiting for you downstairs."

I hurried and took a shower. I threw on some short shorts and some open-toed high-heels. I put on a wife beater with no bra and ran downstairs. I stopped dead in my tracks when I got to the last step. Ms. Alicia was waiting for me at the bottom of the staircase with her hand directly in my face.

"Errrrrr! Where you think you going dressed like that?"

"Uh, to the mall?"

"I don't think so."

"Huh?"

"Follow me." Ms. Alicia walked upstairs.

I followed her upstairs, one step at a time. Brittany followed behind me, grabbing my shorts and nearly pulling them down.

"Okay, here we go." Ms. Alicia slid her closet door to one side. "Pick out something decent so we can go. If we don't hurry up, all the good sales will be over by the time we get there."

"I can't believe you even buy clothes on sale."

"Girl, you better get real. I buy on sale! I use coupons! I'll forget my driver's license before I forget my Kroger card." Ms. Alicia sat on the bed and crossed her legs. "Hurry up, pick out something so we can go!"

"Can I wear this?" I picked out a short summer dress.

"Nope! That's my Vera Wang! Here, wear this."

Ms. Alicia handed me a short, spaghetti-strapped dress that

was very colorful. I liked it. Not as much as the Vera Wang dress, but it was cute.

"Okay, I'm ready."

"You sure are. Now go take off those stripper shoes and we're ready to go."

"What's wrong with my shoes?"

"You're going to the mall, not Magic City."

"I can tell you old. Magic City done played out. Emerald City is what's happening now!"

"Whatever! Here, put these on." Ms. Alicia handed me a pair of sandals.

"These are cute!" I held them up and looked at them before putting them on my feet.

We picked up Auntie Cynthia on our way to Discover Mills mall. Auntie Cynthia brought her three kids with her. The two oldest were not her biological children. They had different mothers from Uncle Mike's two previous wives: Ms. Tonita, Bri's mom; and 'Celia, Alexiah's mom. The youngest one was from her current marriage with Uncle Mike. It is a good thing we were in that SUV. It was a bunch of us.

The oldest girl's name was Brimone. Bri was fifteen and becoming a sophomore at Duluth Christian Academy. She was cute. Bri was about five feet two inches with real long, straight black hair. She was not dark and she was not light-skinned. She was kinda like, in between. Her body was thick but she had a nice shape. She looked a lot like her father, Uncle Mike.

The middle child, we called her Alex. She was ten. She was a skinny, little, light-skinned girl. She looked more like Uncle Mike than Bri, but Bri and Alex did not look much alike at all. Alex was; what's that word they used to call me when I was younger? Rambunctious. There were two words always associated with me when I was growing up: *rambunctious* and *Ritalin!*

Then there was the baby. His name was Michael. He was named after Uncle Mike. He was a pretty good baby. He did not cry or whine when we were in the car or in the mall. We made way more noise than him.

We went into almost every store in the mall. I guess they were used to it. I had so many clothes I felt guilty and asked Ms. Alicia not to spend so much money on me. She laughed at me and told me I had better get them while the getting was good.

Brimone and I asked if we could go to the food court. They let us go, but made us take Alex and Brittany with us. We didn't care. We grabbed their hands and got away from the grown-ups as quick as we could.

"Is Chick-fil-A cool?" I asked.

"Yeah, that's cool."

We got in line and then a group of chicks walked up behind us. They must have known Bri because they kept calling her name. I know she had to hear them because I heard them loud and clear. But for some reason she just kept ignoring them.

"Bri, those girls are calling you."

"I hear them." Bri did not turn around to look at them.

Bri held Alex's hand. They were standing in front of Brittany and me. I was between them and those girls. A girl named Asia Coleman tapped me on the shoulder and asked me to step to the side so that she could talk to Bri. She was a pretty little, light-skinned chick. She was short but had a nice little shape on her. Nice face, nice petite body. I could tell she thought she had some swagger.

"Hey, Brimone, what you wearing on the first day of school?" Asia asked.

"I don't know yet." Bri did not show the girl much attention.

"You oughta be able to wear anything with your rich-ass daddy."
The other girls started to laugh.

"Whatever!" Bri said. "Come on, Alex."

Bri moved closer to the counter and tried to block the girls out.
A girl named Valencia Williams stepped around Asia and started
to ask questions. Valencia was even prettier than Asia. She was
dark-skinned. She was about five-four or five-three-and-a-half,
something like that.

"You still going to DCA this year?" Valencia asked.

"Yeah."

"We are, too."

"I know."

"How do you know?"

"Because Asia already told me."

"Is your father going to buy you a brand-new car this year, Bri?"

"I'm too young to drive a car and you know it, Asia."

"So what?" Valencia said. "He buys you everything else."

"So what?" Bri yelled. "I can't help if your daddy can't buy you
nothing!"

"Don't be yelling at me!" Valencia yelled back.

"You better shut up. You know what happened to you last year!"
Asia said.

"I'm not scared of y'all!" Bri let go of Alex's hand and balled
her fists. She opened her nostrils and breathed hard.

I was supposed to be the bad girl from the wrong side of the
tracks. But those rich, suburban chicks were acting like Bloods
and Crips in the mall. All of their parents were rich. What the hell
did they have to be fighting for? Who had the biggest trust fund?

The third girl in the group, Jheri Rose, finally spoke up and
made her little comment. She was dark-skinned, too, but not as
pretty as Asia or Valencia.

"You know you scared, Bri!" Jheri said.

"I'm not scared of y'all!"

"Then do something!" Valencia said.

The girls surrounded Bri and all of them started yelling at her at one time. Ms. Alicia and Auntie Cynthia walked up as they were yelling and walked in the middle of them.

"Hey! Hey! Hey!" Auntie Cynthia said. "What's going on here?"

"She's about to get her ass whooped!" Valencia said.

"And who are you?" Ms. Alicia asked.

"None of your business!"

Up until that point I had been quiet. I think those girls thought I was scared. I was not scared and really didn't give a damn if they thought I was or not. I was confused about everything. They started off acting like they were friends, and then all of a sudden, they were about to throw hands.

"You need to watch your mouth, young lady!" Auntie Cynthia said.

"You're not my mother!" Valencia shouted.

"You're right! But I'm hers!" Auntie Cynthia stood in front of Bri.

"I'll go get my mother on you!" Asia shouted.

"I can't believe these grown-ass women are trying to fight us!" Jheri said.

"Nobody is trying to fight you, little girl!" Ms. Alicia said.

"We ain't scared of y'all, either!" Asia said.

I looked at that girl like she was crazy. If she thought I was going to stand by and let her disrespect Ms. Alicia like that, she had lost her damn mind.

"First of all, you need to get out of her face and just back the hell up!" I pushed Asia to the ground.

"Shante! Stop it!" Ms. Alicia said. "All of you! Just stop it!"

Ms. Alicia and Auntie Cynthia stood between the five of us and tried to get us under control. The mall security guard showed up, but it was nothing he could do, either. He was white, about sixty-five, or seventy years old. He had a big belly that hung over his belt. That old man would have had a heart attack trying to stop us from fighting.

"What's going on?" the security guard asked.

"We don't know. That's what we're trying to figure out," Ms. Alicia said.

"Those girls are trying to start stuff with us!" Valencia pointed at us.

"And those grown ladies tried to fight us!" Jheri said.

"That's ridiculous," Auntie Cynthia said. "All of them were arguing like they had no sense."

"I think everything is under control now, officer," Ms. Alicia said.

"Okay," the security guard said. "But I'm going to have to get their names, and they're not going to be able to come to the mall anymore without parental supervision."

"That's a good idea," Auntie Cynthia said. "They don't have any business in here anyway without us."

"Here are our children's names." Ms. Alicia wrote our names on the officer's notepad.

"What are your names?" The security guard pointed to the other three girls.

"None of your business!" Asia said and then ran off.

Jheri and Valencia ran behind her. The security guard didn't even move.

"Aren't you going to catch them?" Auntie Cynthia asked.

"They're probably on the bus by now," he said. "Give me their names. I'm sure you know who they are."

"I don't know them," I said. "I just met them today."

"Has either one of you seen those girls before?" the security guard asked Ms. Alicia and Ms. Cynthia.

"No," Auntie Cynthia said. "Today was the first time we've ever laid eyes on those girls. Our girls don't get into fights."

I looked at Bri and she looked at me. We both knew that the other had probably been in a fight before, but we kept quiet and pretended to be the perfect little angels they thought we were.

"What are their names?" the security guard asked again.

"I told you, I don't know," I said.

"I don't know, either," Bri said.

Bri looked at me and then I looked at her. I did not know why, but she was protecting those girls.

"Well, you two stay with your mothers until you leave the mall. You understand?"

"Yes, sir," I said.

"Yes, sir, we understand," Bri said.

"You all have a nice day."

"You, too, sir," Auntie Cynthia said.

The security guard limped away, and as soon as he walked off, Ms. Alicia and Auntie Cynthia lit into Bri and me. Bri was upset and embarrassed. I was appreciative that someone cared enough to even chastise me.

"What is wrong with y'all?" Auntie Cynthia said.

"We didn't do anything!" Bri said.

"Somebody did something. I could hear you all screaming way down there by Burlington!" Ms. Alicia said.

"They walked up and at first, they were acting nice and then they started to act all mean and crazy," I said.

"Shante don't know those girls, I do. They're girls from my school."

"Well, why didn't you tell the security officers their names, Bri?" Auntie Cynthia asked.

"Because I'm not a snitch, Ms. Cynthia."

"I'm telling your father, Bri."

"Okay," Bri said.

"Naw, that's too easy. I'm telling your mother!"

"Please, Ms. Cynthia," Bri said, "don't tell Ma."

"Yeah, I kinda thought you'd sing a different tune," Auntie Cynthia said. "You better tell me what happened then."

"Okay! Okay!" Bri said. "Those girls jumped on me last year and they were just trying to start something."

"Why would those girls want to jump on you, Bri?"

"Because my daddy is richer than theirs."

"What?" Auntie Cynthia asked. "Are you kidding me? Does your mother know this?"

"No, ma'am."

"Why haven't you told anybody, girl?"

"Because it's only going to cause more trouble for me at school."

"I'm sorry, but we're about to go see Tonita right now and tell her," Auntie Cynthia said. "Alicia, can you drop me off at my car?"

"I can take you over there, if you want."

"Are you sure?"

"Girl, please, come on."

"Y'all grab these bags and let's go," Auntie Cynthia said.

We grabbed the bags and went over to Bri's mother's house. Bri's mother looked young for her age. I do not know how old she was, but she still looked young. She had a short haircut and it was styled. She was funny, too.

"Oh-oh," Ms. Tonita said as she opened the door and stepped to the side. "Somethin' ain't right! You brought the whole crew with you."

"Yeah, we have a little problem, Tonita," Auntie Cynthia said.

"Y'all come in." Ms. Tonita walked into the living room. We followed her and everybody sat down.

"Okay," Auntie Cynthia said, "we just came from the mall. Bri and Shante were about to fight with three other wild girls."

"Who were you about to fight, Bri?" Ms. Tonita asked.

"Just some girls from school," Bri said.

"And I take it you're Shante?" Ms. Tonita asked.

"Yes, ma'am," I said.

"What did I tell you about saying 'ma'am'?" Ms. Alicia asked.

"That's okay, Alicia," Ms. Tonita said. "I'd rather have them saying 'ma'am,' than calling me some of those other names they call adults nowadays. I just take it as a token of respect. How are you, Ms. Shante?"

"I'm fine."

"Good," Ms. Tonita said. "Now who were those girls, Bri?'

"They jumped me last year because they said Daddy was rich and stuff."

"Why would they jump you because your father is 'rich and stuff'?"

"They say I think I'm spoiled and I act like I'm better than them, but I don't. They're always pickin' on people. Just because I don't cuss and smoke like they want me to, they say a bunch of stupid stuff to make people not like me."

"All of this goes on at that Christian school your daddy is paying all that money to send you to?"

"Yes, ma'am," Bri said.

"Can I say something?" I asked.

"Sure," Ms. Tonita said.

"That goes on everywhere," I said. "It doesn't matter what school you go to, public or private. Kids are going to pick on you for whatever reason. You just have to fight back."

"I understand that, but we teach Brimone not to fight. We teach her to tell a teacher, the principal, or whoever's in the authoritative position."

"But what if they're not around?" I asked. "Who do you tell then?"

"You're minors," Ms. Tonita said. "There should always be an adult around somewhere."

"There were adults around today, Ma," Bri said, "and they didn't do anything."

"They sure didn't," I said. "They just looked because they wanted us to fight! They don't care!"

"Still, fighting is not an option," Auntie Cynthia said.

"You're an adult and those girls were about to fight you, Ms. Cynthia," Bri said. "So how do you think we can stop them if they want to fight us? They jumped me last year and I didn't do anything to them. But if they put their hands on me this year, they're going to wish they hadn't."

"Bri, don't talk like that!" Ms. Tonita said. "Where did you get talking like that from?"

"She didn't get it from me!" I said quickly.

"Nobody thinks she got it from you, sweetheart." Ms. Tonita chuckled.

"I got it from me," Bri said. "I'm tired of being bullied. I'm tired of being picked on. And telling on those girls won't fix anything."

"So what do you propose we do, Bri?" Auntie Cynthia asked.

"I don't know," Bri said. "Stay out of it, I guess."

"Well, that ain't gon' happen!" Ms. Tonita said. "I'm not letting you get involved with those juvenile delinquents. You could get hurt."

"I can get hurt if I'm not involved with them, too. It doesn't matter. They're not going to stop picking on me until I stop them from picking on me."

"Brimone," Auntie Cynthia said, "We love you and we don't want to see you get hurt. Don't you understand that?"

"Yes, ma'am. But can't you understand that no matter how much you love me, that's not going to stop those girls from jumping on me?"

"When school starts, I'm going to go up there and make sure that never happens again," Ms. Tonita said.

"You don't get it, do you, Ma?" Bri shouted. "You can't fix this! Kids are not like they were when you were in school. You can't just go tell the principal and everything is going to be fine! If you tell on them, I could not just get hurt, Ma; I could get killed!"

"Don't be so dramatic, Bri," Ms. Tonita said. "You're overreacting."

"I don't mean to be disrespectful but she's not being dramatic, Ms. Tonita. That's how it is for us."

"Shante, are you trying to tell me that a fifteen-year-old girl can get killed for telling on her friends?"

"I'm saying a fifteen-year-old girl can get killed for anything."

"You seem to be very streetwise. How do you know so much about the streets?"

"I came from the streets."

"Okay, Ms. Streetwise," Auntie Cynthia said to me, "do you have any ideas on how to handle this?"

It made me feel appreciated to be around grown intelligent women who cared enough to listen to me, even though I was a teenager.

"I think that Bri has to stand up to them."

"Do you mean fight?" Auntie Cynthia asked.

"Not necessarily. But she can't keep running from them, either."

"So how do we protect her?" Ms. Tonita asked.

"You can't."

"What do you mean, I can't?"

"Bri gotta stand up to them on her own, even if it means fighting back."

"What is this?" Ms. Tonita asked. "The Wild, Wild West?"

"No, ma'am. It's life as a teenager. I'm tellin' you that's how we live."

"Oh my God." Ms. Alicia clutched her chest. "What the hell?"

"But y'all really don't have nothin' to be worried about."

"Why not?"

"Because I'm going to the same school, Ms. Tonita."

"And who are you suppose to be?" Auntie Cynthia asked. "The muscle?"

"I'm just sayin'."

"Well, I don't want you getting in trouble, either, Shante."

"As long as they don't mess with us, we won't mess with them, Ms. Alicia."

"If they mess with you, you better tell us."

"Oh, we will." I looked at Bri.

"Don't be looking at each other, either," Ms. Tonita joked. "I see that! If there's any trouble, you better tell us."

"Is that understood?" Auntie Cynthia asked.

"Yes, ma'am," Bri said.

"You, too, Shante," Ms. Alicia said.

"Yes, ma'am, I mean, yes. I will."

"Y'all better!" Ms. Tonita said. "My husband is the police. And if I have to, I'll have the whole damn school locked up! Including y'all."

We laughed and switched the subject to Bri's and my new school clothes. Although we did not feel like it, they made us model our new clothes. They were more excited than we were.

Chapter Six

*T*hat night when I was about to go to bed, Ms. Alicia knocked on my door. I had to hurry and get out of the shower to stop her from walking in, but I was too late. As I was walking out of the shower with a towel wrapped around me, she was entering my room.

"What's going on with you in that bathroom, girl?"

"Oh, nothing."

"Nothing, my butt." Ms. Alicia smiled. "I kind of wanted to talk to you about what I saw this afternoon."

"What did you see?"

"You! In the bathroom, doing…you know."

"Oh, that wasn't what you thought it was."

"Oh, really?"

"No, ma'am. I mean, no."

"If you're having that much trouble not calling me 'ma'am,' then call me whatever makes you comfortable. Like Tonita said, it shows that you're a respectful young lady." Ms. Alicia folded her arms and paced around my room. "Now, put your clothes on and let's talk, Ms. Shante."

"Yes, ma'am."

I put on my sleeping clothes and crawled into the bed. Ms. Alicia sat next to me on the bed and I prepared myself for our "birds and the bees" conversation.

"What you were doing today is perfectly normal for a young woman. You're curious and you're exploring your body."

"Ms. Alicia?"

"Yes, dear?"

"I had this talk with my dad when I was about ten."

"You talked about touching yourself with your dad?"

"Oh! No, ma'am! We discussed the birds and the bees."

"Well, sweetheart, your daddy may have told you about the birds and the bees, but I'm about to tell you about the flowers and the trees."

"The 'flowers and the trees'?"

"Yes. Now listen up! Women have different ways of being pleasured; clitoral, vaginal, oral, and then there's anal."

"Anal? Yuck!"

"There are plenty of options, Shante."

Ms. Alicia was right. My father may have told me about the birds and the bees, but no one had discussed those damn flowers and the trees she was telling me about.

"Options?"

"Yes, to pleasure yourself."

"I don't pleasure myself, Ms. Alicia."

"Oh-kaaaaay, but anyway, women are capable of reaching their orgasms through either one of these methods of sexual intercourse with a partner. But, women are also capable of achieving very pleasurable orgasms all by themselves."

"I can't believe we're having this conversation, Ms. Alicia."

"Well, I've been waiting all my life to have this conversation with my daughter, and I'm sorry, but you're not going to deprive me of my moment, young lady! Okay?"

"Okay, Ms. Alicia, as embarrassed as I am, I won't deprive you of your 'moment.'"

"Back to the subject at hand…"

Before Ms. Alicia could speak, it hit me all of a sudden that she had just said that I was her daughter. I was so overwhelmingly happy to hear her say those words I had to make sure I heard what I thought I heard.

"Excuse me, Ms. Alicia?"

"Yes?"

"You really see me as your daughter?"

"Of course, I do."

"Oh my God," I wiped tears from my eyes.

"Oh, baby." Ms. Alicia said. "What are you crying for?"

"Because my mother never even acknowledged that I was her daughter, and here you are treating me like I'm your very own flesh and blood."

"That's the past, Shante. Don't focus on the past because it hurts you. Think about how much your father loves you and how Johnny and I love you as our own child."

"This seems too good to be true. You and Dr. Forrester haven't even known me that long and you love me?"

"We've known you long enough to know that you need to be loved and we need to love you."

"You have no idea how much that means to me." I hugged Ms. Alicia. "Thank you."

"You're welcome, baby. I swear you're the only person who cries more than me."

"Okay, I'm ready for our flowers-and-the-trees talk."

"All that I wanted to say was…" Ms. Alicia wiped her eyes and paused momentarily to compose herself.

"Are you crying, Ms. Alicia?"

"Oh yeah, girl, but don't worry about me; I cry at the drop of a dime."

"We're pitiful."

"No, crying is good."

"I do feel better."

"Good," Ms. Alicia said. "Now, can we get back to the flowers-and-the-trees stuff?"

"Yes, ma'am." I laughed.

"Your body is a very precious commodity and it should be treated that way. You're going to have sensations and feelings as you mature, and you're going to want to act upon them. So what you were doing today is perfectly normal for a young woman your age."

"I wasn't doing nothing, though."

God knew I was lying. I knew I was lying. And Ms. Alicia knew I was lying, but for some reason, I could not stop myself from doing it.

"Girl, stop lying!" Ms. Alicia snapped. "It's a natural thing. You just have to appreciate your body and understand that it's not just created for pleasure. It's the essence of your womanhood. And never sacrifice your womanhood for attention, compliments, or anything other than mutual love. I'm not trying to be dramatic. but your body is the creation of life, and should be treated just as precious as a newborn child, because if you do not respect your body, and protect your body, there could be drastic consequences such as pregnancy, STDs, and some could be deadly. But right now, we don't have to deal with that, do we?"

"No, ma'am."

"You sure?"

"Yes, ma'am. I'm not focused on boys right now. All of my focus is on getting through my senior year."

"Good! Well, you get some sleep and if you have any questions, just ask. We have an open-door policy around here, and you can come to Johnny and me about anything, okay?"

"Okay." I smiled.

"Good night."

"Good night, Ms. Alicia."

A couple of days later I started my first day of school at Duluth Christian Academy. I was kind of nervous when I went to my first class. I did not know anyone at the school but Bri, and she was not in any of my classes. I felt like everybody was looking at me strangely. I was the new girl, but the stares I was getting made me feel like a sideshow freak.

I sat in the back of the class trying to take some of the attention off of me. There was a boy to my left and a boy to my right. They were both staring at me. I looked straight ahead and ignored them. I wanted the teacher to speak so badly, say something, anything, to get those boys' attention off of me. God must have heard my prayers because Mr. Thompson, my drama teacher, began to speak.

Mr. Thompson was about six feet tall. He was black, with light skin, a shaven bald head and was pretty cool. He used to be in the military, and as I would find out later, not shy about using his military training to keep us in line.

"Hey, hey, people! Listen up!" Mr. Thompson immediately demanded our attention. "Some of you know me, some of you do not. I am your drama teacher. By the end of this school year, you will know everything it takes to perform a stage production. That will include everything from building a set, selecting your cast and crew, the performance and lastly, post-production. If by the end of this school year, you do not know how to build a set, select a cast and crew, perform your play, and successfully complete your post-production, you will not pass my class. Do you understand me?"

"Yes!" the class answered in unison.

"In this class, you will be graded as a team. There will be two grades, an 'A' for pass, and an 'F' for failure. No 'B', 'C' or 'D'! No curves or midterms! It's either 'A' or 'F.' One way or the other, everybody will receive the same grade. We will either pass or fail as a team. Is this understood?"

I thought to myself, *dude is deep.* Although I knew he was trying to get us to understand the importance of teamwork, I did not want to fail due to someone else's laziness.

I was not the only one thinking that way because somebody had the courage to speak up, someone sitting in the front row. I looked at the kids sitting in my aisle to see who was speaking, and I could not believe my eyes. It was that girl, Asia, from the mall. Out of all the girls in the world, I had to end up in a class with that chick.

"I don't understand, Mr. Thompson," Asia said. "Why do we have to share a grade? What if somebody is lazy or dumb? Why do all of us have to suffer because of them?"

"Well, Ms. Asia," Mr. Thompson said, "if you think that one of your classmates is dumb, you'll have to be twice as smart. And if you think one of your classmates is lazy, then you'll have to work twice as hard."

"My girl Asia is right, though," Valencia said. "Why everybody gotta get the same grade?"

Damn! Not only was Asia in my class, but her friend Valencia was, too. I scanned the room for the third girl, Jheri. And there she was, in the last seat in the second row. As soon as I saw them, I knew they were going to be trouble. I tried to keep my attention on Mr. Thompson and not the mean girls.

"How many times do I have to say this, people?" Mr. Thompson said. "Production is a team effort! You will be a team! You will succeed together, or you will fail together!"

"That's not fair, Mr. Thompson!" Valencia said.

"Life is not fair, Valencia. I'm preparing you for life."

At lunch, I was walking into the café and I saw Bri sitting at a table all by herself, even though the cafeteria was filled with kids. I walked over to her and sat next to her.

"What are you doing over here all by yourself?"

"Just having lunch."

"Where are your friends?"

"I don't have any friends."

"What do you mean you don't have any friends?"

"I just don't have a lot of friends."

"You're a sophomore. You have to have some friends, Bri."

"I know people, but I wouldn't call them *friends*."

"What's up with that, Bri?"

"What's up with what?"

"Why don't you have any friends?"

"Because I don't want any friends!"

"Everybody wants friends."

"Well, I don't!" Bri shouted.

"Look, we're like cousins, Bri. If something's wrong you can just…"

"Nothing's wrong! Just leave me alone!"

Bri jumped up from the table and walked away. She was very upset and it looked like she was crying. I didn't get it. Bri was cute, rich, and smart. I could not figure out why she didn't have one single friend.

The following Saturday, Dr. Forrester and I visited my father in prison. We sat down and I picked up the phone.

"Hey, Daddy," I said.

"How's my Butterfly?" Dad said.

"I'm good. When is your parole?" I asked anxiously.

"It's not too far off," Dad said. "What's up, Doc?"

"What's up, Stone?" Dr. Forrester and my Dad shared a fist pound through the window. "How's it going in here?"

"Same old, same old," Dad said. "Just trying to get up outta here."

"You're going to get out, Daddy."

"That's enough about me, Butterfly. How are things out there with you?"

"I go to this Christian school. It's a little different from public school but nothing major. I'm just trying to fit in right now."

"She's not giving you any trouble, is she, Doc?"

"Oh no, man. She's a nice addition to the family."

"She's not an inconvenience to your wife, is she?"

"Stone!" Dr. Forrester said, "Shante is not an inconvenience to me or anyone else. She and my wife get along like they've known each other all of their lives. She and my daughter get along, too. Brittany even calls her 'big sister.' Everything is fine with us, man. No need for concern."

"I know, but I can't help but be concerned. That's my Butterfly."

"Your Butterfly is fine, Daddy."

"So are we talking college here or what?" Dad asked.

"We'll see. First, I have to get through high school."

"Come on, Butterfly, there's nothing you can't do. You'll be the first one in our family to go to college."

"You got to be kidding me, Daddy?"

"Our family ain't never had no money or no desire to go to college. Yeah, you'll be the first!"

"Oh, man! Why did you tell me that?"

"What's the matter?"

"That only adds more pressure, Daddy."

"Pressure? You ain't got no pressure on you."

"What if I mess up and don't graduate?"

"You control your destiny, baby. Nobody but you! To be able to control your destiny is not pressure; that's a privilege."

"Your father's right, Shante. You are under no pressure. Just go to school, do your best, and everything will be all right."

"I don't know, Doctor Forrester. I don't fit in with those kids at that school."

"That's okay. They don't matter! You're not there for them! You're there for you," Dad reassured me.

"But one of my teachers said we have to work together as a team. So those people do matter."

"That's cool. Your teacher is right. Sometimes in life, we got to work as a team. It's like a chain, and a chain is as strong as its weakest link." Dad placed a sincere look on his face. "Listen to me, Butterfly; never, ever be satisfied with being the weakest link. Always strive to be that link that keeps the chain together. Sometimes that may mean you have to work twice as hard, or suffer twice as much. It may not be a glamorous job, but somebody gotta do it. The important thing is making sure you do everything you can to keep the chain strong. And that's never pressure; that's a privilege."

I think that as far as my dad was concerned, he was only talking in the moment. But for me, his words meant everything. He had absolutely no clue of how much he impacted me that day. He was just talking from his heart out of love, but he filled mine with strength and confidence.

"Okay, Daddy."

"I've been thinking, Butterfly. It's time for us to renegotiate our deal."

"Naw, Daddy, you can't go back on your deal. You said you were going to act right and get out of here. A deal is a deal!"

"I will do exactly what I promised, but I need more from you."

"What?"

"I'll be a perfect inmate if you be a perfect student." Dad put his hand up to the glass window. "I promise I'll get paroled if you promise to go to college."

"I don't know if I want to go to college, Daddy."

"Then you must not want your old man to get out of prison."

"That ain't fair; you're trying to blackmail me."

"Life ain't fair, Butterfly."

"That's what Mr. Thompson said, too."

"Who the hell is Mr. Thompson?"

"That's my teacher I was telling you about."

"Oh. He's a smart man. Listen to him." Dad smiled and stared at me momentarily. "Well, do we have a deal?"

"Okay, Daddy, but you know you ain't right."

"If I was right, I wouldn't be locked up, now would I?" Dad joked.

"Okay, Daddy." I laughed.

"Okay, what?"

"Okay, we have a deal."

"That's what I'm talking about, Butterfly."

My dad had a huge grin on his face like he was the happiest man in the world. I smiled back, but I was not even sure if I was going to make it through my senior year. College was really a stretch. We spent the remainder of our visit laughing and talking about my adjustment to living with rich people. Once again, when it was time for me to leave my dad, I cried.

At school the next week, Bri and I were sitting in the cafeteria minding our own business. Then Asia, Valencia and Jheri came and sat right next to us running their big-ass mouths.

"Snap! Snap!" Asia said as she held up her hands as if she was taking a picture of Bri.

"Shut up!" Bri said.

"Hey, Asia, now that it's a new school year, we got another whole group of people to send that picture to; you still got it?" Valencia asked.

"No, I deleted it; you got it, Jheri?"

"Uh-huhn, it's still in my phone."

"I don't care if you got that picture, Jheri!" Bri yelled.

"Snap! Snap!" Asia said again.

"Why don't y'all just leave me alone?" Bri shouted again.

"'Cause we don't like you," Asia said.

I didn't know what was going on, but I was tired of being caught in the middle of something that did not involve me and I was going to find out.

"Why do y'all keep picking on her?" I asked.

"Because we want to!" Asia snapped. "We'll pick on you, too."

"Hey, I'm not Bri, and I'm not going to keep arguing back and forth with y'all!"

"Well, here I am!"

I should have just sat back, taken a deep breath and then walked away. That is what I should have done, but I didn't. Instead, I leaped across the table and grabbed Asia by her hair and pulled her little ass across the cafeteria floor. The next thing I know, Bri and I were back-to-back swinging and kicking. They got their licks in, but you better believe Bri and I got a lot more licks in than them.

After they pulled us off of those girls, they took us to the office and made Bri and I sit on one side, and Asia, Valencia and Jheri sit on the other. Mrs. Gary, our principal, known for being a hard ass, read us the riot act.

"Okay, ladies, we seem to have a problem that has to be resolved, and it has to be resolved now. So, are there any suggestions?"

The girls looked at each other and then looked back at Mrs. Gary, but no one answered. I raised my hand and waited for Mrs. Gary to tell me to speak.

"Shante?"

"I think we need to find out what happened and then discuss it."

"I agree with you, Shante," Mrs. Gary said. "What happened?"

None of the girls said a word.

"I don't know exactly what happened between you all, but I do know that if you all don't tell Mrs. Gary what happened, all of us are going to be in more trouble than what we're in now." The other girls still said nothing so I continued, "Bri, this is my senior year and I have to graduate. I'm in this trouble because I was trying to help you, now if you're my friend. No, if you're my cousin like we say we are, then tell Mrs. Gary what happened."

Bri looked at me and then she looked at Mrs. Gary. "Okay, Mrs. Gary, last year, I liked this boy named David and I thought he liked me back. He asked me to send him some pictures of me with no clothes on, and since I liked him, I did it. After we had sex the first time, he told me he loved me. We had sex a few more times and then he told me he didn't want to be with me anymore. I was mad, but what could I do? If he didn't like me, he didn't like me."

As Bri was talking, I could not believe my ears. I had to give the girl credit; not only had she fooled her parents, she had fooled me, too. There is no way I would have believed that Bri was not a virgin. She never talked about having sex with anybody to me. We were both claiming to be the last American virgins.

"He started going with Asia and he showed her those pictures of me. I guess he sent them to her phone and she started sending them to everybody at school." Bri looked at Asia as she talked.

"Is this true, Asia?"

"No, Mrs. Gary."

"It's in your best interest to tell me the truth, Asia! *Right this minute!*"

"I'm telling you the truth, Mrs. Gary."

"Jheri? Valencia? Do you know anything about these pictures?"

Jheri and Valencia looked at each other and then Valencia spoke up. "Asia sent the pictures to me, Jheri and a bunch of other people one day at school."

"Is this true, Jheri?"

"Yes."

"Is this David character a student here, Asia?"

"No, he's out of school."

"As in graduated?"

"Yes."

"You two were dating a grown man?"

Bri and Asia looked at each other and then nodded their heads.

"Oh my God, what is wrong with this world?" Mrs. Gray closed her eyes and rubbed her temples. When she opened them, she was through being diplomatic. "All right, we still haven't resolved this feuding issue. Since you can't do it on your own, I'll do it for you. Shante, Bri, Jheri and Valencia, you will receive the manda-tory three-day suspension for fighting. Asia, you will receive five days suspension plus a conference with your parents. And if I ever hear any mentioning of either one of you so much as looking at the other one cross-eyed, you will be expelled for the duration of this school year! And under no circumstances will you be permitted back on these school grounds. Now do I make myself perfectly clear?"

We agreed in unison and Mrs. Gary excused us. I intentionally lagged behind to be the last one to leave. I waited for the others to walk out, and then I turned around to speak. "Mrs. Gary?"

"Yes, Shante?"

"Thanks for suspending us. I think we needed it."

"Wow! That's a first. Nobody has ever thanked me for suspending them before."

"I was thanking you for caring enough to show us how to compromise when we have a problem, instead of just forcing it down our throat. I really do appreciate it."

"With that being said, I'll see you in three days." Mrs. Gary winked at me and smiled.

"Yes, ma'am."

I felt good walking out of Mrs. Gary's office, but I knew it would be short-lived. I still had to go home and explain to the Forresters.

Bri and I had to call Ms. Tonita to come pick us up from school because we had to leave immediately. Boy, did she let us have it.

"Are you two happy now?"

"No, ma'am," Bri answered.

"What about you back there in the backseat?" Ms. Tonita looked at me through the rearview mirror. "You happy now?"

"No, ma'am."

"You got the WWF brawl that you wanted, so what was accomplished?"

Bri and I sat quietly and did not respond.

"Don't get quiet now! A minute ago you were fighting and getting suspended and being all big and bad; now you want to act like good schoolgirls! What did you accomplish?" Ms. Tonita looked in the rear mirror to make eye contact with me and then screamed, *"Answer me!"*

"Nothin', ma'am!" I screamed back out of fear.

"What about you, homegirl?" Ms. Tonita looked at Bri. "You bad now? Did you prove how tough you were?"

"No, Ma, it wasn't like that."

"Then what was it like?"

"We were just defending ourselves."

I don't know where Uncle Mike met Ms. Tonita, but it was not at a debutante ball. I could tell that she was from the streets. She may have been reformed, but the streets were still in her. While she fussed, I sat silently in the back and did not say shit.

"I told you not to take your ass up to that school acting a fool, didn't I?"

"Yes, Ma, but those girls kept making fun of me."

"So! Who cares what those girls think?" Ms. Tonita snapped. "Now I have to take off work to come pick you hooligans up! I'm dropping y'all off over to Alicia's and I'm going to back to work."

"Okay, Ma."

"Naw, it ain't okay. The next time you see outside, you'll be walking across the stage to graduate!"

Ms. Tonita pulled into the driveway, and Ms. Alicia and Auntie Cynthia were standing outside waiting for us.

"Hey, y'all." Ms. Tonita waved and leaned her head out of the window. "Look, Cynt, you already know; if you feel it necessary to take some kind of disciplinary action, you have my permission to tear that ass up!"

"I just might do that, girl." Auntie Cynthia laughed.

Ms. Alicia and Auntie Cynthia stared at us as we walked past, but they did not speak; an obvious attempt to express their disappointment in our behavior. Bri and I stood in the doorway and waited for them to finish talking to Ms. Tonita.

"Just save some of that ass for me for tonight."

"You are crazy, Tonita!" Auntie Cynthia laughed even harder.

"All right, y'all take care."

"You, too." Auntie Cynthia waved.

Ms. Alicia waved good-bye as well. As soon as Ms. Tonita backed out of the driveway, Ms. Alicia looked at me and Bri. "Get your ass in that house!"

They sat us down and we had to repeat the entire story all over again, minus the nude pictures, minus the sex with the grown man, and minus the confession from Bri admitting that she was not the innocent virgin everyone assumed her to be. It probably should not have bothered me, but I had always been looked at as easy, or trampy, and just because these girls had a better life than me, they were looked at as a "good girl."

"What you girls did was absolutely unacceptable! We specifically told you not to get involved with those girls, and you deliberately disobeyed us!" Auntie Cynthia pointed her finger back and forth at us as she paced back and forth.

"But they started it."

"I don't care who started what, Bri! You have a choice to walk away or fight, and you chose to fight. So since you two can't handle the situation, we're going to go to that school and handle it for you."

"No, Ms. Cynthia!" Bri pleaded. "I promise I won't get in any more fights. Just please, don't go to that school."

"You've had your chance to do it your way, Bri, and you blew it."

"Can my daddy go instead?"

"No! Tonita and I will be going together in the morning."

"Ms. Cynthia, you're upset right now. You know how Mama is; she's going to embarrass everybody."

"She's not going to embarrass me. I don't have to go to your school."

"Ms. Cynthia, I promise, I won't get in any fights! I promise!"

"I can't stop your mother from going to your school, and you can't stop me, so stop asking me not to go, okay?"

"Yes, ma'am."

Then it was my turn to hear it from Ms. Alicia. She used a different method. Instead of blaming me and coming hard, she used the understanding and sympathetic approach. They used the classic good cop-bad cop routine on us.

"Shante, you've been through a lot and maybe I can never understand fully the effect it has had on you. But I'm trying. All that I ask is for you to try to meet me halfway, sweetheart. However, I do understand that being a teenage girl nowadays is difficult enough without the pressure of being bullied. In the future, whenever a problem like this persists after you have brought it to our attention, don't think that you have to take it into your own hands because the consequences could be irreversible. Trust me, like you want me to trust you. Okay, baby?"

"Yes, ma'am."

Wow! No sermons! No yelling! No screaming! No threats! Just simple communication between two intelligent people. Ms. Alicia did not have to resort to actions like going up to our school and trying to fight my fight for me.

"So you're not going to DCA, Ms. Alicia?" Bri asked.

"Oh, hell yeah! I'm going first thing in the morning with Tonita and Cynt."

Ain't that a bitch! I thought the speech Ms. Alicia gave was the extent of my discipline, but she played me.

"You are?" I asked.

"Yes, I am."

"But I thought…"

"You thought wrong!" Ms. Alicia interrupted.

The next morning, Ms. Alicia, Auntie Cynthia and Ms. Tonita

went to DCA and had a conference with Mrs. Gary and the mothers of the other girls. To my knowledge, there were no incidents between the women, and if the other girls' mothers laid down the law like our mothers, the last thing any of us wanted to do after that ass-ripping, was fight.

Chapter Seven

O n day three of my suspension, Mr. Forrester, Dr. Forrester's father, who I referred to as Pa-Pa, came in at 4:30 in the morning banging on a pan. It suddenly dawned on me where Ms. Alicia had gotten that method. I got up, showered, and then met him outside. He had a paint bucket and paintbrushes.

"What are we doing out here, Pa-Pa?"

"You're going to repaint my daughter-in-law's gazebo."

"It's pitch-black out here, Pa-Pa."

"Now it's not." Pa-Pa shined a bright flashlight in my face. It was so bright, it lit up the entire backyard.

"Where did you get that flashlight from?" I turned my head away from the light. "'Nam?"

"They didn't even have light when I was in 'Nam. No daylight, flashlight, moonlight, nothing! So no, this didn't come from 'Nam, it came from Wal-mart."

"Didn't you say Bri was coming today?"

"Yes, I did, Private Butterfly. But I can't get her daddy to bring her here any earlier than five a.m., even if it's going to teach her a lesson." Pa-Pa laughed.

"So I have to start all by myself?"

"Yes, Private Butterfly. You can start setting up so that when Private Bri gets here, you can be ready to go."

"Yes, sir," I answered reluctantly.

"Get to work."

"Yes, sir."

"Affirmative!" Pa-Pa walked off with his hands behind his back.

Bri was dropped off around a quarter after five. It was still dark, but day was breaking. As Pa-Pa and I joked around, Bri kept to herself and basically ignored me.

"You have a problem, Private Forrester?"

"No, sir."

"Well, you better put a smile on that face and act like you have a purpose in life."

"Yes, sir."

Bri dipped her brush in the paint bucket but still did not speak to me. Pa-Pa noticed it and took it from there.

"Did I make myself clear, Private Forrester?"

"Yes, sir."

"I don't think I did because you haven't opened that mouth of yours to greet Private Butterfly."

"Hi."

"You can do better than that, Private Forrester."

"Good morning."

"Good morning, who?"

"Good morning, Private Butterfly?" Bri asked as if she didn't know who Pa-Pa was referencing. I wanted to laugh so badly. That damn Pa-Pa was crazy as hell and I loved him to death for it.

"That's right." Pa-Pa smiled and turned to me. "Private Butterfly?"

"Good morning, Private Forrester." I laughed.

"Now, I'm about to go watch television but when I come back I want to see some progress. Do I make myself clear?"

"Yes, sir!" we said in unison.

Pa-Pa walked away again with his hands behind his back. I waited a few minutes before I said something, but eventually, I struck up a conversation.

"Hi, Bri."

"I don't have anything to say to you."

"Why are you mad at me?"

Bri ignored me and kept painting her part of the gazebo.

"*Hey!*" Pa-Pa yelled from inside of the house. "*Heeeeeeelp!*"

We looked at each other and then sprinted inside of the house and upstairs to Pa-Pa's room.

"You all right, Grandpa?" Bri asked.

"Something done happened."

Bri and I looked at each other with confusion. Pa-Pa appeared to be fine, but he was sitting on the bed in an awkward position and would not move.

"What's the matter, Pa-Pa?"

"I done had a bad accident."

"What's the matter?" Bri asked as she started to walk closer.

"Back up!" Pa-Pa screamed. Bri and I froze in our tracks. "I need some towels and I need a bath ran quick!"

"I'll run the bath. Bri, you get the towels."

"Don't tell me what to do."

"I'm not trying to tell you what to do; Pa-Pa is."

"Stop all this arguing and do what I tell you!"

"Okay, Pa-Pa. I'll get the towels and run your bath."

"I'll run his bath!" Bri said.

"Will y'all shut the hell up and get moving!"

Bri went to the bathroom to run Pa-Pa's bath water and I ran to the linen closet and grabbed some towels. When I got back to Pa-Pa's bedroom, he was sitting awkwardly on his side and the smell finally hit my nose. *Damn!!!*

"Pa-Pa!" I shouted. "You stink!"

"It's those damn Ex-Lax! Alicia told me take 'em last night so that I can relieve myself this morning. I didn't know all hell was going to break loose like this!"

Bri walked out of the bathroom shaking her wet hands and making a horrible face. "Whoo! What's that smell?"

"Me! Now shut up and help me get to the bathroom."

Bri stood on one side of Pa-Pa and I stood on the other. We lifted him and wrapped a towel around his waist. He tiptoed to the bathroom, and Bri and I laughed behind his back.

"You know you're looking at your future, don't you, Pa-Pa?" I joked.

"Is that supposed to be funny?"

Bri looked at me and tried not to laugh, but she couldn't help herself. We helped Pa-Pa take off his pants and left him alone in the bathroom to bathe. We grabbed some more towels and cleaned up the mess. We took off his linen and washed them, too. By the time Pa-Pa was finished with his bath, we had everything back to where it was before the minor accident. I took advantage of that opportunity to find out why Bri was so angry with me.

"What's the matter with you? Have I done something I don't know about?"

"No, not really. I guess I'm just jealous of you and Grandpa."

"Why are you jealous?"

"I've always had like this special relationship with my grandfather. Before he moved here, he drank a lot and he was always grumpy. But no matter what, he was never that way with me. And out of all four of his grandchildren, he always gave me his special attention. I was always his favorite and now he's acting all goo-goo-eyed over you, and it's driving me nuts!"

"Are you serious?" I laughed and pushed her.

"Yeah, I'm serious, man." Bri laughed back. "First, it was all the new babies—Alex, then Brittany, then Little Mike—stealing all of my attention and now your old ass come in here, grown as hell, living in the house with him."

"I'm sorry, but we're going to have to share Pa-Pa, Bri."

"I don't think so. You can have Uncle Johnny, but you can't have my Grandpa, niggah."

"Niggah? Look at you talking all ghetto."

"You haven't seen ghetto. You just better stay away from my Grandpa," Bri joked.

"You better stay away from my Pa-Pa!"

"Where did you get that country shit from, anyway?"

"What?"

"That Pa-Pa shit."

"Whoa! Whoa! Where is all this cussing from, Ms. Innocent?"

"I don't knooooow!" Bri whined. "I can't help it! I'm stressing out."

"Over being suspended?"

"I wish."

"What then?"

"Remember that guy David I had sex with?"

"Yeah, why?"

"Well, I..."

"I'm coming out of the bathroom, so y'all get out!" Pa-Pa yelled from the bathroom.

"Okay, Grandpa, we're going to go finish painting the gazebo."

Bri and I went back to the gazebo and continued to paint.

"Now what were you saying about that David guy?"

"Long story short, I'm pregnant, Shante."

"What the fu—"

"Don't make a big deal out of this!" Bri interrupted.

"Don't make a big deal out of this? You're fifteen and pregnant! How can this not be a big deal, Bri?"

"I don't know what to do." Bri sat down and cried.

"Have you talked to that David dude about the baby?"

"Yes."

"And what did he say?"

"He said it wasn't his."

"I want you be honest with me, Bri; is it?"

"Yeah, it's his. I know I lied about being a virgin, but he is the only guy I had sex with."

"So have you told anybody else?"

"Nope."

"How do you think they're going to react?"

"They're going to be disappointed in me."

"So what are you going to do?"

"I don't know." Bri sobbed. "I'm too young to have a baby."

"Talk to your parents, Bri."

"I can't! They won't understand."

"What is there to understand, Bri? You're pregnant."

"I want to tell them, but I don't want to disappoint them."

"This is not like you have a bad grade. You can't hide this for a semester. You're going to have a baby."

"I know, but I cannot tell them, Shante!" Bri shouted. "I just can't!"

I sat next to Bri and put my arms around her. I didn't know what to say or what to do to help her, but I knew I had to do something.

"Bri, whatever you decide to do, I'm here for you."

"Thanks."

"You want some advice?"

"Yeah, silly, that's why I'm talking to you."

"Don't go through this all by yourself. David is just as responsible for this as you are. Make him be a part of this decision."

"I can't make him do anything."

"Oh yes you can."

"How?"

"You can...I tell you what, where that niggah live?"

"Why?"

"'Cause when we get off this punishment on Saturday, we going to pay him a visit."

"I'm not going to David's house."

"Oh yes you are!"

"Oh no I'm not!"

"Hmm, we'll see."

"You're going to make me go, huh?"

"You already know." I wiped Bri's eyes for her. "It's either go, or I'm telling Uncle Mike and Ms. Tonita."

"I don't want him to nut up on me."

"I wish that niggah would disrespect you after his old ass done got you pregnant."

"Damn, I wished this was you in my shoes."

"Why you wishing that on me?"

"Because you could handle it better."

"I'm handling it by not putting myself in that position, Bri. And once we get you out of this mess, you have to promise me you're going to be smarter. If you feel like you have to sex, use protection."

"We didn't have any condoms and we got all hot."

"So! I don't care how hot you got; you know better, Bri," I snapped. "And you can't be depending on no man to protect you, either. You get on birth control. You make sure that you can't get pregnant! Not to mention all the nasty diseases you can catch."

"You fussing just as much as Ma and Dad would have. I should have just told them then if I was going to hear all of this."

"That's what I'm supposed to do. You're like my little cousin and I don't want anything to happen to you. Instead of being pregnant, you could have AIDS or something."

"But I don't."

"But you could, Brimone!" I shouted. "*Damn!* Don't you get it?"

Bri understood my concern and she appreciated it. We were both crying. She wiped her eyes again and then she wiped my eyes. Although the situation was extremely crucial, I loved the sincerity we shared because of it.

"I get it."

"I'm coming to pick you up on Saturday, okay?"

"Okay."

That Saturday before I picked up Bri, I made another stop for some back-up: Keisha, Toya, and the enforcer, Janae. Bri was at her mom's, so when I pulled into the driveway, she came out to investigate.

"Hey, Shante." Ms. Tonita waved as Bri walked off of the porch and walked toward the car.

"Hi, Ms. Tonita." I waved back and then asked Keisha to get in the backseat. "Can you get in the back for me so that my cousin can sit up here?"

"Damn, she putting you in the back, Keisha." Janae laughed.

"Shut the hell up and move your big ass over."

"Hell naw." Janae got out of the car so that Keisha could sit in the middle. "Get your puny ass in the middle."

"I should make you ride bitch, Janae."

"Hey! Stop that cussin', Keisha! Don't you see Bri's mom on the porch?"

"Oops, sorry, Butterfly!"

Once Bri was in the car, I introduced her to my girls. "Hey, Bri, that's Toya, my girl Keisha, and Janae."

"Hey, y'all," Bri said.

"Hey, we heard a lot about you," Keisha said.

"I heard a lot about you, too."

"What you hear about me?" Janae asked.

"I heard you were cool."

"I know she better had mentioned me," Toya said.

"I mentioned all y'all, so just shut up."

"So where this niggah live, Butterfly?" Janae asked.

"He lives in College Park."

"College Park?" Janae lit a cigarette. "Them niggahs crazy down there."

"So you scared?" Toya asked.

"Y'all know I ain't scared of no niggah, Toya."

"Will y'all stop talking so much, so Keisha can tell me how to get to College Park?"

"Hey, take GA-400 all the way to I-75 and stay on I-75 until it split from I-85. When you get to I-285, go west, or north, which-ever one it is." Keisha was drinking a soda and talking at the same time.

"Bri, you know where he lives?"

"No, I just know he lives in College Park. Keisha gave you the right directions, though. You can get off on Old National Highway."

"Oh, okay."

We had no trouble finding David's house. He was sitting on the porch with a girl when we pulled up.

"Didn't he know you were coming, Bri?" I deliberately pointed my finger at him to get his attention.

"Yeah, he knew."

"And this niggah just gon' sit there and disrespect you with that chick like you ain't shit?"

"Let me out!" Janae shouted. "I don't even know you and I want to kick his ass!"

"Don't worry about it." Bri opened the door and got out of the car.

"I'm right here if you need me, Bri."

"No, I got this, Shante."

David walked off of the porch and met Bri at the sidewalk. My girls and I did not say a word to each other because we were trying to hear every word David and Bri said. Looking at the guy, I don't know what she saw in him anyway. He was a scrawny little dude with long braids like a girl. He had tattoos all over his narrow chest and was so skinny his pants sagged more than normal. They talked for a minute and then they elevated their voices. David pointed his finger in Bri's face and then pushed her.

"Oh hell naw!" I screamed. "This fool done lost his damn mind! Pushing on her and he know she pregnant!"

"Pregnant? Let's show this niggah how we do it, y'all!" Janae pounded the back of the passenger seat as she talked.

Keisha and I jumped out of the car and ran full speed toward David. Toya and Janae popped the trunk and pulled out two crowbars. The girl that was on the porch with David ran into the house and slammed the door behind her. I helped Bri get up and then I charged David. He caught me in midair as I was trying to jump on him and knocked me on my ass. I grabbed my lip and there was blood.

"You hit me, niggah!" I yelled.

"Oh you like to hit women, bitch?" Janae swung her crowbar with two hands and hit David in the back.

"Oh shit!" David fell to the ground and grabbed his back.

We continued to beat David until we heard the police sirens and then we ran and jumped in the car. We sped off burning rubber. At first, we were scared as hell, but once we realized there were no police cars in pursuit of us, we laughed and started bragging about kicking his ass.

"Damn, that was fun!" Janae shouted.

"Wow! I can't believe what I just saw." Bri covered her mouth and laughed. "That was wild!"

"Damn!" I hit the steering wheel and sighed heavily.

"What's the matter, Shante?" Bri asked.

"What's going to happen to us when David tells the police what happened?"

"We'll say he pushed me first," Bri said nervously.

"And he hit you, too," Toya added. "That's self-defense."

"Yeah, they're right, Butterfly. We kicked that niggah's ass in self-defense."

"But the police might not think the same way we thinking, Janae."

"Man, I don't give a damn what the police think! This was self-defense, gotdammit!" Janae shouted.

"I'm taking y'all home and putting this car in the garage."

"Why you acting all scared, Butterfly?" Toya asked. "The only thing we did wrong was not kill his punk ass!"

"What did he say to you about the baby, Bri?"

"He told me to get an abortion, and he wasn't going to help me pay for it because he didn't think the baby was his."

"So what are you going to do?"

"I don't know. Why do you keep asking me that?"

"Because you have to have a solution to this problem."

"What can I do?" Bri stared at me, waiting for my answer, but I did not have one. "I don't know anything about an abortion."

We drove for a mile a two and then Keisha said very quietly, "I do."

"You do what?" I looked in the rearview mirror at Keisha.

"I know where she can go to get an abortion."

"Is that what you wanna do, Bri?"

"What other choice do I have?"

"Where is it, Keisha?" I looked at Keisha in the rearview mirror again.

"It's downtown near Auburn Avenue."

"What does she have to do?"

"She can call on Monday and probably make an appointment for Wednesday."

"But won't she have to take a couple of days out of school to recover?"

"No, she can schedule for Friday afternoon when she gets out of school and then tell her parents that she is sick for the rest of the weekend. By Monday, she should be fine."

"But isn't she too young to have an abortion without her parents' permission?"

"Yeah, but we can work around that."

"How can we work around getting her parents' permission for an abortion, Keisha?"

"I can take care of that if Bri wants me to."

"Bri?" I looked at Bri and waited for her answer. "Do you want Keisha to take care of it for you?"

Bri looked out of the window at the highway and then back at me. "Do I have a choice?"

I dropped the other girls off and then I dropped off Bri. On the way, we went over our story to make sure we had everything together just in case the police came to question us. She was pretty calm about the beating of her ex-boyfriend, but she was extremely afraid of having that abortion.

We waited but the police never came to question us about David. They did, however, visit Janae for questioning later that evening. She was not there at the time, so she ran away to avoid going back to jail. The three of us, Janae, Keisha and me, met at Dugan's on Ponce de Leon, to discuss if we should turn ourselves in or just wait it out. Toya was too afraid to show up and wanted nothing more to do with the situation.

"I told Bri not to come because she's pregnant, and it's not even an option for her to go to jail. I'll go to jail myself before I let that happen."

"You really love that girl; don't you, Butterfly?" Keisha asked.

"Yeah, she's a good girl."

"A good girl, huh?" Janae asked. "Good girls don't get pregnant at fifteen."

"Shut the hell up, Janae."

"You shut the hell up, Butterfly!"

"Hey! Y'all stop arguing!" Keisha interrupted. "So what did the police say to your aunt, Janae?"

"Man, Keisha, all that they said was that I'm in some serious trouble. I'm about to go up North to New York and stay with my cousin until this shit blow over."

"How come they're not looking for the rest of us?"

"I think I know that girl that was on the porch with that David dude. And I think she ratted me out, Butterfly."

"Why? Who is she?"

"I'm almost one hundred percent sure she was one of those bitches I fought when I was a fight girl. I whooped her ass; that's why she ran in ol' boy's house that day when she saw me. She thought I was coming after her ass."

"I didn't even get a good look at her." Keisha sipped from her drink.

"Oh, you didn't?" Janae asked. "I did. I know it was that bitch from the West End."

"I been through so much shit in my life, man, I'm tired of this!" I slammed my hands on the table and cried. "Damn! I just want to graduate and get the hell out of Atlanta!"

"Calm down, man!" Janae put her two fingers to her lips and gestured for me to be quiet. "Damn, you embarrassing me and shit."

"Sorry, Janae, but I made so many people so many promises about graduating and going to college, and after this, it ain't no way in hell I'm getting out of this."

Janae held my hand. "I got you, baby."

"What do you mean, you got me?"

"If I have to, I'll turn myself in and put the heat on me."

"Girl, you crazy? I'm not going to let you go down for all of us."

"Why should everybody do time when everybody don't have to?"

"Because all of us were involved."

"Bri was involved, too, but her ass ain't here!"

"Look, I know where you going with this, but it's different."

"It's not different! You and Keisha have a chance to go college and really do something with your lives. You could really be good girls. My shit is over!"

"You're only seventeen years old, Janae. You got the rest of your life, just like me and Butterfly. If you go down, we going down with you."

"Listen to me, Keisha. If I go down, I might do three months tops and then I'm out of there. I can do three months in the juvey in my sleep. Who knows, maybe when I get out the next time, I'll go straight."

"Nope! If you go down, we all go down. That's all it is to it."

"Damn straight!" Keisha added.

"Okay, then. Y'all better get ready to do some time, 'cause we going down."

I had all but conceded to the fact that I was about to go to juvey for a while. It was just my luck that every time my life seemed to be getting in order, something would come along and screw it all up; more times than not, that something was me.

Chapter Eight

Beisha was true to her word and figured out a way to get Bri's abortion scheduled for the following Friday. We paid this girl, Janet Cooper, two-hundred fifty dollars in cash, and she let Bri use her medical cards. We were able to get fake identification with Bri's picture and Janet's information. Yeah, we were committing insurance fraud on the state, but we had to do what we had to do.

Keisha, Toya, and I took Bri to the clinic for her abortion. We tried to reach Janae, but she was on the run, from us, and the cops. We told Bri to pretend to be sick so that Keisha could do most of the talking. She knew Janet's information by heart because she was always using it.

I could not go into the surgery room to get a firsthand account of what went on, but I distinctly remember our conversation on the way home.

"How do you feel?" I asked.

"Tired."

"I was tired when I had my abortion, too. You're probably going to feel sore for like, the next couple of days, but after that, you should be fine." Keisha held Bri's hand.

"What was it like, Bri?"

"Weird, but it didn't really hurt. I was kind of numb through all of it..."

BRI'S STORY:

As I sat in stirrups and the doctor was between my legs, she explained the surgical procedure to me.

"Hi, Ms. Cooper, I'm Dr. Henson and I'll be performing your procedure today. *Dr. Henson was a white, tall and skinny woman. She had short brown hair and wore glasses. She reminded me a lot of an old tennis player named Martina Navratilova. She was very nice, though.*

"During this process, we will end your pregnancy by removing the fetus and placenta from your womb, which is also called a uterus. There are different types of abortions. There is the therapeutic abortion, whereas a woman needs to end the pregnancy for health reasons. And then there is the elective abortion, whereas, like yourself, a woman simply chooses to end the pregnancy. We will be performing what is called an elective-surgical abortion. We will administer a sedative that will help you relax and make you feel slightly drowsy, but you will remain awake throughout the entire process. Because you are further along than fifteen weeks, we're going to have to dilate your cervical canal. Small sticks called laminaria will be placed into your cervix to help it open and then we will insert a hollow tube into your womb before using the vacuum to remove all of the pregnancy-related tissues from your uterus.

"This is a relatively routine procedure, but like all surgeries, there are certain risks involved. In this particular procedure, we run the risk of future ectopic or tubal pregnancies, which is when the child develops in the tube and not in the uterus. There's also PID or pelvic inflammatory disease, which can lead to fever or infertility. Abruptio placentae; it is a condition in pregnancy where the sac holding the baby, or the placenta, tears away from the uterus lining. This can result in extreme and life-threatening bleeding. Women who have this procedure often run the risk of increasing their chance of breast cancer by fifty percent. Do you have any questions, Ms. Cooper?"

"No, ma'am." *I tensed my body because I could feel pressure on my vagina.*

I was under the impression the doctor was trying to scare me out of having the abortion. I had never been a part of an abortion before, but I could not believe that she had to explain the procedure with such detail like that.

"So how do you feel thus far?"

"I'm okay."

"Good, because it's over." Dr. Henson smiled and then slid her chair backward. She threw her latex gloves into a trash can. "You did well!"

"Thank you. That's it? It's over?"

"Yes it is." Dr. Henson washed her hands. "The nurse will be in shortly to explain your outpatient information. Get some rest and have a good day."

Dr. Henson walked out and in a few minutes, a nurse walked in. She was black, light-skinned, with a round shape. Her hair was pulled back in a simple ponytail, but you could tell that she had a very cute shape in her scrubs.

"Hi, Ms. Cooper, how are you feeling?"

"I'm doing okay."

"My name is Connie and I'm going to go over what we need you to do to make sure you're as good as new."

"Okay."

"We want you to make sure you drink lots of fluids. Stay off work for a few days if you can. Make sure you take vitamins, eat healthy foods, and try to get as much sleep as you can. Make sure you take the antibiotics immediately and for the full amount of days. No exercise for two weeks. No swimming or tub baths for two weeks. No lifting anything over fifteen pounds for two weeks. Don't use anything vaginally for two to four weeks. That means no sex, no tampons and no douches, nothing.

"You're capable of ovulating two weeks after you have this procedure, which means you are capable of becoming pregnant again within two weeks of ending a pregnancy. After the two- to four-week period has expired, you should not have sex again unless you feel physically recovered, and *you and your partner have made a planned parenting decision to have a child. Otherwise, you can easily find yourself in this same position.*

"Your body will probably return to its regular menstrual cycle in about two weeks, so if you decide that you want to resume sexual intercourse, make sure you are prepared by having some form of birth control or pro- phylactic. Please be certain that you are healed completely, both physically and emotionally, before resuming sexual activities. We want you to schedule an appointment and come back for your two-week check-up as soon as you can." Connie smiled. "Any questions?"

"Uh, no."

"Okay, you have some friends out there who seemed to be very anxious to see you, so let's get you to them to ease their concerns."

"Okay."

I looked around the small room and wondered how many other young teenaged girls had been in my position, and what did they do to deal with the aftermath?

END BRI'S STORY

"...I don't ever want to go through anything like that again."

"Me either!" Keisha said.

"Ms. Alicia and Dr. Forrester are gone out of town, so it's just you, me and Pa-Pa, Bri. All we have to do is just tell him you're sick and he'll baby you the whole weekend. He won't have a clue."

"Yeah, but we're supposed to be babysitting, Brit, too."

"Oh, Brit won't be a problem. Please, I got her! That's my baby."

"Oh yeah, don't forget I have to stop by the pharmacy and get my prescription, Shante."

"Oh, okay."

We stopped by the pharmacy and picked up Bri's prescription. When Bri came out of the store with the bag in her hand, Toya was excited.

"What you got?"

"What you mean, what I got?"

"What kind of 'scripts you got?"

"'Scripts? What is 'scripts?"

"Your prescription. What kind do you have?"

"I don't know." Bri opened up the bag and pulled out one of the bottles of pills. "I got a hundred and twenty Vicodin pills."

"Vicodin?" Toya shouted. "You done struck it rich, babygirl!"

"What are you talking about?"

"Bri, you won't need all of them pills, girl. I can sell what you don't use on the streets for two or three dollars a pill. And we split the profit fifty-fifty."

"What?" Bri was confused as hell.

"Do you know what you have in your hands right now?"

"Yeah, I got some medicine."

"No, you got a goldmine."

"Don't pay no attention to that fool, Bri." I chuckled for a minute and then kept talking. "She's trying to get you to give her some of that Vicodin, so she can sell them on the street."

"Like a dope dealer?"

"Naw, man, I'm not no real dope dealer. I just sell them to my friends at school and they give me a few dollars for them."

"Look, you got enough to worry about without getting into more trouble with drugs, Bri."

"See, Keisha, you always trying to talk somebody out of doing something."

"And you always trying to talk somebody into something, Toya."

"She ain't talking nobody into nothing 'cause Bri ain't messin' around with that shit! So stop askin' her, Toya!"

"Okay, Butterfly. But I'm telling you, Bri, we can make some money."

"Bri got money!" Keisha snapped. "She don't need to hustle."

"I don't feel good." Bri leaned her head onto Keisha's shoulder.

"We're about to get you home, Bri." Keisha wrapped her arms around Bri's shoulder. "Hurry up, Butterfly."

I drove faster trying to get home as quick as I could. The Forresters were gone and Pa-Pa was playing with Brit outside in the backyard. We snuck Bri upstairs and put her in my bed. Keisha and Toya left and I went outside to play with Pa-Pa and Brit.

"Hey, Pa-Pa." I kissed him on the cheek and then picked up Brit. "How's my favorite baby?"

"Hi, Butterfly."

"Look at what I brought you." I pulled out a lollipop and dangled it in front of her. "You can have it if you give your big sister a great big kiss!"

"Mmmmmmm!" Brit gave me a wet kiss on the cheek.

"Yuck!" I wiped my face.

"Well, she gave you what you asked for," Pa-Pa joked. "Where's Louise, Thelma?"

"She's not feeling good; she's lying down."

"Lying down?" Pa-Pa started to walk toward the house.

I grabbed his arm and stopped him. "She's all right Pa-Pa. It's just like, you know, her time of the month. You know what I mean?"

"If you mean what I think you mean, I don't wanna know what you mean."

"I gave her some Tylenol, so she should be okay."

"That's too bad."

"Why?"

"Because I wanted you two to watch a classic with me."

"What? I'll watch it with you."

"Well, come on!"

I put Brit on my hip and followed Pa-Pa into the house. He put a movie called *Roots* in the DVD player. Pa-Pa sat in his recliner that he had shipped from Michigan and Brit lay on the sofa with me. That was the longest damn movie I had ever seen. Of course I had heard of it, but I had never seen it before. I had no idea it was that freakin' long! The bad part about it is that Pa-Pa and Brit went to sleep ten minutes into the movie and left me all by myself to watch it. Bri came downstairs during the fourth hour with a comforter wrapped around her and lay on the loveseat.

"How you feeling, Bri?"

"I'm sleepy. I keep dozing off."

"You hurting anywhere?"

"No, not really. I'm a little sore, but I'm just sleepy."

"We eating pizza tonight."

"Y'all go 'head, I ain't eating nothin'!" Bri chuckled and then looked at the television. "What in the world is this?"

"It's called *Roots.*"

"Grandpa got you watching this?" Bri looked over at Pa-Pa sleeping in the chair with his head about to fall off. "He's always trying to get people to watch movies with him and then he falls asleep."

"He is knocked out, too, girl."

"Man, take that movie out," Bri whispered.

"I can't. It'll hurt Pa-Pa. He really wanted to share this movie with Brit and me. You, too, but you were sleep."

"Well, your Pa-Pa is sleep," Bri said sarcastically, "so put in something else."

I got up to put another DVD in. "What you wanna watch, Bri?"

"*Avatar.*"

"*Avatar?* I'm not putting in no *Avatar.*"

"I like *Avatar.* It has so many pretty colors."

"Is that why you like it?"

"No. It has a good storyline, too."

"Girl, please! They stole that storyline from that cartoon movie *The Ant Bully* and they know it."

"No they didn't. They're two completely different stories."

"It's the same story, Bri. In *Avatar*, the human becomes an Avatar and have to learn the ways of the natives, which were the blue people. And in *The Ant Bully*, the little boy shrinks and has to learn the ways of the natives, which were the ants. In both stories, they have to prove themselves by going against their own kinds."

"Dang." Bri chuckled. "You're right."

"See, I told you, it's the same story. The only difference is, one was ants and the other was blue people. Now that one blue man was fine, though."

"Oh my God, you are crazy."

"Okay, I found '*ATL*' with T.I. and Lauren London."

"How about N-O-T. I don't want to watch that no more. I've seen that like a billion times already."

"I thought you were sleepy anyway."

"I am, but that's going to keep me up."

"Oh, okay. You better be glad I like you."

"Whatever."

"What you want to watch then?"

"Put in *Beauty and the Beast*. That always puts me to sleep."

"You kidding, right? That's a kid movie, Bri."

"So? After what I've been through today, I want to stay a kid forever."

Bri fluffed her pillow and then lowered her head. I felt so sorry for her. She was truly a good girl who had made some bad decisions. From what I could see, she was doing it just to fit in. Too bad she did not realize that with everything she had going for her, she did not need to fit in with anybody; in time they would want to fit in with her.

"Can I tell you something without you getting all sensitive and sentimental on me, Shante?"

"I'll try, you know how I am."

"Promise me or I won't tell you."

"No! No! I promise! I promise!" I was excited and could not wait to hear.

"I am so glad that you are a part of this family. And there is no way we are ever going to let you leave us. Even though you may not be a blood relative, you are definitely a love relative. You have been there for me ever since we met, and I don't know what I would have done without you today."

"Awwwww." I wiped my eyes.

"See! There you go crying."

"I can't help it."

"I don't understand how anybody can cry that fast? You started crying before the words even came out of my mouth."

"I know! I know!" I sat up and wiped my eyes. "Well, I feel the same way about you. I see you as my little cousin, and I will do anything to protect and defend you."

"Thanks," Bri paused momentarily, "Butterfly."

"Awww." I ran over to the loveseat and kissed Bri. "You called me Butterfly, Bri."

"Oh my God, get away from me, you crazy insane girl." Bri laughed and then playfully pushed me away.

"Muah!" I gave her a big kiss on the cheek. Not as wet as the one Brit laid on me earlier, but I meant it just as much. "I love you, you mean old thang."

"I guess I love you, too."

I went back to the couch and held Brit in my arms. Bri was right;

a few minutes into *Beauty and the Beast* and she was out like a light. I looked down at Brit sleeping in my arms, and then over at Pa-Pa asleep in his old rocking chair and Bri passed out on the loveseat. I thought to myself, *Now this is what a family is all about.*

Keisha and Toya came over on Sunday to tell me some important news. Bri was still on the loveseat sleeping through her medication when they got there. Pa-Pa had taken Brit for a ride, so we had the house to ourselves. We hung out in the kitchen, so that we would not disturb Bri.

"You gon' tell her, or do you want me to tell her, Keisha?" Toya asked.

"You know more than I do, so you tell her."

"Okay, guess what, Butterfly?"

"What's up?"

"You'll never guess where Janae is."

"Where is she?"

"In juvie!"

"In juvie? The police caught her?"

"Nope, she turned herself in and went down for everybody."

"Damn! Why did she do that?"

"I guess she felt like she had less to lose than the rest of us, so she went down for all of us."

"You act like you happy, Toya."

"I ain't happy, Keisha, but I ain't mad, neither. I promise to God, that's the last trouble I'm getting in to."

"We need to go see her," I said.

"For what?"

"For support, Toya!"

"Man, she only gon' get a few months; that ain't gon' kill her. Janae can handle herself."

"Are you kidding me right now? That's your cousin, Toya."

"I know who she is, Butterfly!"

"Y'all don't have to go, Toya. But I'm going."

"I'm going, too," Keisha repeated.

"Let's go tomorrow when we get out of school, Keisha."

"Okay." Keisha turned to Toya. "You going, Toya?

"Don't try to put me on blast, Keisha," Toya snapped, "yeah, I'm going."

Bri walked into the kitchen with the comforter wrapped around her waist and hair all over her head.

"Damn! I didn't look nowhere near that bad when I had my abortion."

"Shut up, Keisha." Bri scratched her head and opened the refrigerator.

"You feeling better?" Keisha asked.

"A little bit. I'm just sleepy."

"That's that Vicodin you taking! I'm telling you, we can make some money off of them thangs."

"No y'all can't." I quickly intervened to keep the conversation off of that nonsense. "I thought you said you didn't want to get in any more trouble, Toya."

"We can't get in no trouble if we just selling it to our friends."

"Fool, that's still illegal," I shouted.

"No it ain't. Bri getting it from the doctor, Butterfly; that's legal."

"So! It's illegal for her to sell prescription drugs. She can get in a lot of trouble for that."

"She won't be selling them; I will."

"Bri, listen to Butterfly; you can get in some serious trouble for that," Keisha said.

"I mean, I haven't said anything. I'm just listening to y'all."

"I'mma text you, Bri."

"No you're not!" I said.

"Watch, bitch." Toya pushed me on the shoulder and laughed.

Ms. Alicia walked into the kitchen as Toya was talking and over-heard her use the *b-word*, From that point on, she never really liked Toya.

"What was that?" Ms. Alicia put her hands on her hips and looked at every single one of us. "Bitch?"

"Hey, Auntie," Bri said with a glass of orange juice halfway to her mouth.

"Hey, auntie nothing! Who said that?"

"I did, Ms. Alicia." Toya sat next to me in a chair. "I'm sorry."

"And what is your name?"

"My name is Toya."

"Toya what?"

"Toya Jackson."

"Like LaToya Jackson?"

"No, just Toya."

"Well, Toya, we don't use that type of language in my house because we don't have any bitches taking residence in my house. So please respect my house, and talk like you have some sense."

"Okay." Toya looked at me as if she wanted me to help her, but it was nothing I could do for her, but pray.

"And what are you doing all wrapped in that comforter, Bri?"

"I got sick on Friday."

"Sick? What's wrong with you?"

"I don't know. I think it was some pizza we ate. I just been nauseated and my stomach hurt."

"You feel nauseated? Did you vomit?"

"Yes, ma'am."

"The only women I know who have those types of symptoms are pregnant women," Ms. Alicia joked.

We all looked around the room at each other. Bri almost spit out her orange juice.

"I don't think you guys have to worry about that from Bri for a long time, Ms. Alicia." I tried to turn the conversation to humor.

"Oh yeah, Bri is a good girl. She probably doesn't even know where babies come from yet."

Bri almost spit up her orange juice again. She was so nervous she choked on some of the juice going down her throat. Keisha patted her on the back.

"You okay, Bri?" Keisha asked.

"Aw, poor baby. You're really sick, aren't you?" Ms. Alicia walked over to Bri and rubbed her on the back.

"Yes, ma'am."

"Girl, go lay down somewhere until your mother comes and gets you."

"Okay." Bri wrapped the comforter around her again and walked out of the kitchen with her glass of orange juice in her hands.

"Well, we'll go outside and get out of your way, Ms. Alicia." I stood up to leave.

"Keisha, you and," Ms. Alicia pointed to Toya, "what is your name again?"

"Toya."

"Can you and Toya wait for Shante at the gazebo?"

"Yes, ma'am."

Keisha showed Toya where the gazebo was and they waited for me outside.

"Have a seat."

Dr. Forrester walked into the kitchen before Ms. Alicia could begin her lecture and interrupted our conversation. It was only a brief stay of execution, but I appreciated it just the same.

"What's the matter with Bri?"

"She's come down with some type of stomach virus."

I thought to myself, *Yeah, a stomach virus called being pregnant!*

"How was your weekend with Pop, Butterfly?"

"Lovely, just lovely," I joked, "Pa-Pa is something else."

"Brit?"

"She was a perfect little angel."

"And you?"

"No problems whatsoever."

"Good." Dr. Forrester turned to walk out and then turned back to Ms. Alicia. "Oh, do I need to take Bri home?"

"No, Tonita is coming to pick her up later this evening."

"All right." Dr. Forrester turned to walk out and then turned back to Ms. Alicia again. "We're going to have to have Alex visit more often since Bri spends so much time over here. I don't want her to feel left out."

"That's fine with me."

Ms. Alicia looked at Dr. Forrester, waiting for him to leave the room so that we could finish our conversation.

"Oh, I get it. This is one of those girl conversations, isn't it?"

"Yes, sir, it sure is."

"On that note…" Dr. Forrester left the room.

"Now who is that Toya girl?"

"She's a friend from my old school."

"I don't like her."

"You don't even know her, Ms. Alicia."

"And?"

"And I'm just saying."

"Saying what? I come into my house and I hear that little ghetto girl using that foul language."

"She only said the *b-word*, Ms. Alicia."

"Only? Do you know how degrading that word is to women?"

"Yes, ma'am, but that's not how we mean it when we say it. We mean it like, you know, like with love for each other. Not in a degrading way."

"Love? How can calling a person an indignant name like *bitch*, ever be about love? Do not use that word in this house!"

"Yes, ma'am, but…"

"But nothing, how do you young ladies expect for people to respect you, if you don't even respect yourselves?"

"I do respect myself."

"Oh really? You speak like you have sense when you talk to me, but when you talk to your ghetto friends, you act like you're from the hood."

"I am from the hood, Ms. Alicia."

"And where exactly is the hood?"

"It's the streets! It's where I come from! It's where black people live. That's where the hood is, Ms. Alicia."

"The hood is a state of mind, Shante, not a place! There are plenty of people who live in poverty who speak well, who act decently, and do not feel like they have to act like they're animals in order to survive."

"Yeah, show me one."

Ms. Alicia walked in front of me and at first, I thought she was going to smack me. I was about to get the hell out of there. But she pulled up a chair and sat directly in front of me. "Me."

"You?"

"I'm from the poorest area of Cincinnati, Ohio, baby, but my mother made sure we understood that our conditions do not define who we are."

I could not believe that the beautiful, classy and elegant Ms. Alicia was raised in poverty.

"How did you get out?"

"Get out of the hood?"

"Yes, ma'am."

"I was never there. My mind was always thinking that my immediate environment was only a temporary situation. I always escaped to the future to a world where I belonged."

"Wow!"

"Wow?"

"Yes, ma'am. That's what I do. That's what my father told me to always do. He told me that I could be a butterfly and I could fly anywhere I wanted to go and be anything I wanted to be."

"And he was right, sweetheart. But you have to want to fly to these places and be these different things."

"I do."

"Then why are you hanging with that girl?"

"She's really a nice girl, Ms. Alicia. You just have to get to know her."

"Hmm, if you say so." Ms. Alicia stood up from the chair and slid it back under the table. "Now, I really like Keisha and I think she's a very nice girl. She's respectful. She's quiet. I don't know what it is, but I have a very bad vibe about that other girl."

"Trust me, Ms. Alicia, she's okay."

"If you say so." Ms. Alicia headed for the den with Bri and Dr. Forrester. "You can go outside with your friends now, but check that Toya girl's pockets for my good China before she leaves out of here."

"Ms. Alicia! That's just wrong!"

I went outside with Toya and Keisha and we came up with a plan for us to get in to see Janae on Monday.

Chapter Nine

On Monday, Bri was still not fully recovered, so she had to stay home another day. It was the Monday before Thanksgiving, so we only had two more days left in the school week anyway, then she could get all of the rest she needed.

Keisha, Toya, Jacqua and I went to see Janae in the juvenile home. We paid Janet Cooper, the same lady who helped us with the abortion, to be our legal guardian. She lied and said that we were all Janae's sisters. We provided identification when we went through security, but other than that, Janet took care of it. She had the hook-up on everything, fake IDs, fake birth certificates, fake death certificates, fake government letterheads; anything you wanted, Janet had it. That was her job, and she was very successful at it because somebody always needed a hook-up.

We had to split up our group because it was too many of us to see her at once. Jacqua and I went in first. I had not seen Jacqua in a while because her mother stopped her from hanging with us.

"What's up, baby?" Janae hugged Jacqua.

"Hey, baby, you doing all right in here?"

"Hell yeah! I'm holding it down in here. You keeping my shit on lock until I get out, right?"

"Oh yeah, baby, this all yours." Jacqua blew Janae a kiss.

What the hell? Jacqua and Janae were together as a couple? I thought Jacqua only did boys, and the messing around we did was just for fun. Apparently, I was way off base. They were looking all goo-goo-eyed at each other, as if I was not even there.

"What do you want me to do to you when I get outta here?"

"I want you to..."

"Excuse me," I cleared my throat. "Y'all don't see me sitting here?"

"Oh, what's up, Butterfly?" Janae gave me a fist pound. "Yo, when my baby around, I can't see nothing but her and that's some real shit right there."

"Wait a minute. You two are together as a couple?"

"Yes." Jacqua smiled and blew another kiss to Janae.

"How come y'all didn't tell me?"

"How come you ain't ask, niggah?" Janae chuckled and put her arms around Jacqua. "Damn, I almost forgot, I can't do that up in here."

"When did you two become a couple, Jacqua?"

"It just happened over time."

"Sheeeeeeeit! I had her ass from the very first time she kissed me up in Keisha's room," Janae said.

"No she didn't." Jacqua smiled and rubbed Janae on the back like she was a boy. "It took us a long time before we actually did anything."

"What? A week?"

"It took you longer than a week, Jay."

"Jay? Who the hell is Jay?" I asked.

"That's what I call my baby." Jacqua kissed Janae on the cheek.

"You can't do that up in here, baby." Janae gently pushed Jacqua away.

"Oh my God, you two are tripping hard." I laughed so hard I could not stop. "Do Toya and Keisha know?"

"Keisha don't, but Toya does. That's why Jay won't let me go around Toya."

"Why can't she go around Toya, Jay?" I asked sarcastically.

"Because she tried to push up on my baby and she knew we were kicking it."

"This is crazy, man!"

Janae and Jacqua secretly held hands underneath the table. Jacqua could not take her eyes off of Janae while she was talking.

"Now, we need to get back down to business!" I asked.

"What business?"

"The business of you going behind our backs and turning yourself in, man."

"Look, it's like this; it didn't make sense for everybody to go down, if we all don't have to go down. This is like church up in here compared to the other juvey I was in. I get three hot meals and a cot. That's all I need."

"Oh, you don't need me?" Jacqua playfully pulled away from Janae.

"Come on now, baby, you that shit."

"Oh God! Y'all about to make me throw up."

"Butterfly, we need to talk, baby."

"What's up, Janae?"

"Hey, look, Keisha is on the real, but you got to stay away from my cousin, man. She ain't shit. I love her to death, but my cousin ain't shit."

"What are you talking about?"

"Man, Toya keep trying to go behind my back and push up on my girl, and I done told her ass to back the hell up. But she keep trying that backstabbing shit."

"Yeah, girl, it's like she always trying to talk shit about Jay behind her back, but when Jay step to her, she like, don't have shit to say then."

"Is that it? That's between y'all, man. I ain't got nothin' to do with that."

"Oh, okay, so I guess you ain't got nothin' to do with Toya trying to get me to snitch on you and your cousin, either?"

"What?"

"Yeah, that's what I thought." Janae sat back and put her arm around the back of Jacqua's chair. "Your girl wanted to go to the cops and snitch on you and your little cousin to keep her ass out of trouble."

"For real?"

"For real, for real, man! Look, I may be a lot of bad things, but I ain't no gotdamn snitch! And that's on the real!"

"Toya was going to let us go down so she could get out of trouble?"

"Hell yeah! Turning myself in, and coming to juvie was the only way she would not go to cop and snitch on y'all."

"Damn, that's dirty!" I could not believe Toya had been smiling in my face all that time and trying to play me behind my back. "I oughta kick her ass."

"For what? So you can end up in here, like me? Don't let that chick bring you down, Butterfly."

"Yeah, but she trying to play me."

"Man, forget that bitch and just do you."

"She better not say nothin' to me when we leave here."

"What you gon' do? Kick her ass? Look, I didn't come here to protect y'all for y'all stupid asses to act a fool and end up in here with me anyway. You got a bright future. You can be somebody, but in order to be somebody, you gotta stop acting like nobody."

"Where you get that from, baby? That was clever as hell." Jacqua hugged Janae quickly and backed off.

"I been writing since I been up in here."

"Writing what? You only been in here a week," I joked.

I was joking, but Janae made a lot of sense. If I wanted to be seen as somebody, I had to stop acting like I was nobody with no responsibilities and no respect for myself. She was essentially saying the same thing Ms. Alicia had just told me the day before.

"They call me Langston Hughes up in here."

"Oh really? So when are you getting out, Langston?" I asked.

"In about six months, if I can make it through without having to whoop somebody ass up in here."

I was surprised that Janae had to do so much time because everybody had always told me she would do no more than three months.

"Six months? That's a long time."

"Yeah, but I need some time to get my head right. I been doing some crazy shit, man. Shit y'all don't even know about. And it's getting out of control. I gotta get back in control of all this shit."

"You like that word don't you, Janae?"

"What word?"

"*S-h-i-t.*" I spelled out the word because I did not want to use profanity.

"Shit yeah, I like to use the word *shit*." Janae chuckled. "Don't you?"

"I mean, I'm trying to stop using profanity so much."

"Profanity? When you start calling cussing, profanity?"

"Since none of your business."

"Forget that, I'm cussing."

"I don't cuss that much anymore, either," Jacqua joked.

"Baby," Janae looked at Jacqua through the side of her eyes, "Don't sit up here and lie in front of Butterfly 'cause she trying to get all religious on us."

"I'm not lying; you haven't noticed?"

"Hell naw, 'cause you still cuss just as much as me."

"Y'all crazy!"

I am not into the lesbian thing, nor can I say I believe that it is right, but Janae and Jacqua seemed to be happy and that was all that mattered.

Our time was up and we were saying our good-byes so that Toya and Keisha could have their time. I hugged Janae good-bye and stood to the side for Jacqua to say her good-bye. Jacqua and Janae hugged, and then rocked back and forth with their eyes closed.

"Uh, we better be leaving, y'all."

Janae and Jacqua continued to rock back and forth in their strong hug. I cleared my throat a couple of times to get their attention, but they ignored me.

"All right! All right! Let's break this up!" I put my arms between them to push them apart. "Let's go, Jacqua!"

I grabbed Jacqua's hand and pulled her away from Janae. She blew Janae a kiss and whispered that she loved her as I practically dragged her out. We passed Toya and Keisha as were going out and they were coming in.

"Can you take me to the mall when we leave here, Butterfly?" Toya asked.

I looked at Toya, and then I looked at Jacqua and we laughed out loud. I did not want to make a scene so all that I said was, "I don't think so, Toya."

Toya looked at us laughing and then followed Keisha into the visiting room. Jacqua and I walked outside and went to the car.

"I can't believe that chick asked me to take her to the mall, Jacqua."

"Don't forget what Janae told you, though."

"What are you talking about?"

"She told you not to react to what she told you about Toya. Despite all that shit she was saying about her, she still loves that girl and don't want you to kick her ass."

"I'm not thinking about putting my hands on that girl. I'm just not going to let her use me anymore."

"I hear you on that."

"All that I'm thinking about is graduating and going to college."

"Can I ask you a question?"

"What's up?"

"Why do they call you Butterfly? You don't look like no damn butterfly to me," Jacqua joked.

"My father nicknamed me that because he said one day, I would grow up to be a butterfly and fly far, far away to anywhere I want to go, and be anything I want to be."

"That's some deep shit."

"Actually, it's not deep at all to me. It's like I believed him. I know he was speaking metaphorically, but I believed him, and I still do."

"I can't believe we're having this conversation, but if you were a real butterfly, and you could fly anywhere you want to go, where would it be?" Jacqua asked.

"That's a good question." I thought about it and I knew where I would want to be. "If I could fly anywhere, it would be to wherever my mother is."

"Um, your mother is dead, right?"

"Not the woman I knew to be my mother, but my biological mother. I would want to know why she gave me up. I would ask her why she didn't love me enough to try and stick it out with me and my dad."

"Of all the places you could go, you would want to go to a sad place like that?"

"That wouldn't be a sad place. That would be a place of resolution. I have a family now. I have people who love me, so I don't really need her love. I need answers."

"But what if she wanted to give you her love anyway?"

"That's another good question."

"Well, what would you do?"

"Well, that's a good question that I just don't have an answer to right now."

"We're at opposite ends of the spectrum, girl. You can't wait to find your mama and I can't wait to get the hell away from mine."

Keisha's parents had a huge fight the day before Thanksgiving and decided not to spend the holiday together. That left Keisha in the middle. Her mother suggested she go to her biological father's house because he had smaller children and she could spend the holiday with family. Keisha wanted to go to Tennessee with her stepfather, but her mother would not let her. Her mother also would not let her go to Florida with her.

I told the Forresters what was going on with her and asked if she could spend the holiday with us. They were such kind-hearted people that they invited her to stay the entire weekend. Thanksgiving eve, Keisha and I stayed up talking almost all night. Everyone else had gone to bed. Keisha and I were the only ones awake. Brit was in the bed sleeping between us so we had total privacy. I found out things about her family that she had been keeping a secret and she found out secrets about mine.

"I can't believe my mother is doing this to our family, Butterfly."

"Doing what?"

"She reconnected with one of her high school boyfriends on Facebook, and at first, she was telling my stepdad that they were just friends, and he believed her. But then he found emails they wrote to each other about still being in love, and how it's going to feel when they get together."

"How do you know all of this?"

"My room is right next to theirs. I can hear everything. And I mean ev-er-y-thing! My stepdad is talking about moving out."

"Wow! It's that bad?"

"Yeah, it's that bad. He is hurt. He really trusted my mom."

"You think he's going to leave?"

"I hope not. I don't want him to go. As far as I'm concerned, he's my real dad."

"Maybe they'll work it out."

"I hope so. If my mother and stepdad split up and my mother makes me go stay with my dad, I'm running away."

"Why would you run away? What's up with you and your dad?"

"I don't like him."

"Why not? Is he mean to you or something?"

"It's worse than that."

"How is it worse?" I knew where Keisha was going with her story, but I wanted her to tell me on her own. "What happened?"

"Just stuff. Stuff a father should not do to his daughter."

"Wait! Wait! Wait! So what are you saying, Keisha?"

"Man, this is so hard." Keisha started to cry. "I ain't never told nobody this before."

"It's okay, Keisha, just say it. Maybe you'll feel better."

"You have to promise me that you will never ever tell anybody else."

"I promise."

"Okay…"

KEISHA'S STORY:

My father is a big fat man. His belly sticks out and he breathes hard. He wears a lot of jewelry and thinks he is a baller because he owns a nightclub. But he looks like an overweight pimp to me! He is very light-skinned. His hair is almost gone on top and he has an itty-bitty ponytail in the back.

When I was young, he lived out of state and he was always in and out of my life for long periods of time until I turned twelve. When I was twelve, he moved back to Atlanta and wanted to build a father-daughter relationship. My mother was excited because he freed up a lot of time for her to do her own things.

I am grateful because she met my stepdad while she was out doing her thing. He wanted children, and did not have any at the time. We were instantly drawn to each other. He stepped in and took over our household. He brought stability, discipline and God.

I used to be so wild. I was out of control. I did not listen to my mother. I did not listen to anybody. My dad thought that by yelling and screaming at me, I would straighten up, but that only made me afraid of him. My stepdad, on the other hand, sat me down when I did something wrong and explained to me what I did wrong. And then he explained to me why he was about to whoop my ass. He had faith in me and his faith in me made me have faith in myself.

I guess since I was not raised with my biological father, we did not have that family connection. And because we did not have that family connection, he did not think that touching his daughter in a sexual manner was inappropriate.

"Hey, Keisha," Dad patted the cushion next to him, "Come sit beside your daddy."

I sat next to my father on the couch. And he tried to hand me a beer.

"Oh, I'm too young to drink."

"It's okay. You're with your daddy."

"I don't think my stepdad would like for me to drink alcohol." I knew that would piss my dad off if I pitted him against my stepdad, but that is what I was trying to do: piss him off!

"Your stepdad? I don't care what that niggah think. If I say you can drink, you can drink, gotdammit!" Dad shoved the beer in my hand. "Here!"

I took a sip and it tasted horrible. I spat it out and my dad smacked me on the back of the head.

"What the hell you doing? That beer cost money!" Dad yelled.

"I'm sorry, Daddy."

"Lick it up!"

My dad grabbed my neck and lowered my head to the table and made me lick up the beer I had just spat out.

"Now, finish drinking the rest of that beer."

My dad handed me the beer can again and watched me drink, swallow after swallow. I was sick! I threw up and he laughed at me. He made me brush my teeth and then sit next to him again on the couch.

"Come here," Dad wrapped his arm around me and kissed me on the cheek. He rubbed his forehead against mine and then closed his eyes. He kissed me on the lips once, and then again and again. I tried to keep my arms between me and him, but he pushed them down to my side.

"I want to go home," I cried.

"You at home!"

"Uh-uhn! I don't want to, Daddy."

I pushed him away and then he pulled me back to him. "We ain't doing nothing. This ain't nothing!"

"But I don't want to, Daddy!"

My father grabbed my hand and placed it inside of his pants. He made me squeeze his hard penis. I turned my head away and squeezed. My father laid his head on the back of the couch and sighed. "See, we ain't doing nothing. This ain't nothing."

He put his hand on mine and made me slide my hand up and down his hard stick. It felt disgusting. I was thirteen freaking years old and that man made me jack him off. I did not know what to do, so I kept holding his stick until it shrank in my hand.

"See, we didn't do nothing, did we?"

I didn't answer. I just sat there and held his stick in my hand and waited for instructions.

"Pass me that napkin." I picked up a napkin from off of the table in front of us and handed it to him. "Now go wash your hands."

I did what he said and washed my hands. He went to his bedroom and washed himself off. I went to the hallway bathroom and washed my hands over and over again. When I went to bed that night, I locked the door to keep him away from me. My mother picked me up the next morning, but I was too afraid to tell her what happened.

I hoped that was a one-time thing because my father was drunk that night. But almost every time I went to his house, he did something to me. Even when he got married, he still did something to me.

When I got a little older and I could stay home all by myself, I rarely spent the night over my dad's. Although I did not want to go at all, my mother still made me. He left me alone most of the time because my little sister and brother were getting old enough to know what was going on when he laid his nasty ass on top of me.

About four months ago, my stepdad went to Tennessee to visit his mother, so my mother took that opportunity to spend the night out, too. She would not let me stay at home alone and made me go to my dad's house. I begged her not to make me go, but all that she cared about was getting out of the house herself.

All of the bedrooms were full, so I ended up sleeping on the living room floor. I thought since I was in an open area, I would be safe, but in the middle of the night, I felt my dad sliding beneath the cover with me. He grabbed me around my waist and pulled me backward and then he started grinding on my butt.

"No, Dad!" I whispered. "Please don't."

"Shh! Be quiet!" Dad whispered back.

He tried to pull my pajamas down, but I kept pulling them back up. He rolled me on my stomach and held both of my arms behind me with just one of his big chubby hands. He was so big and heavy that he almost smothered me. He opened my legs with his legs and that's all that I remember because I blacked out. I don't know if it was from the anxiety of being raped by my father, or the pressure of his big nasty-ass body smothering me. Either way, I passed out.

I woke up with my comforter on top of me and my pajamas around my ankles, but my underwear was nowhere to be found. I slowly stood up and wrapped my comforter around me. On my way to the bathroom, I met my father.

"Nothing happened! You hear me?"

I did not answer I kept going to the bathroom. My father followed me into the bathroom and stood in the doorway. "Did you hear me? I said nothing happened."

I looked at him through the mirror and answered, "Naw, nothing happened."

I took a shower, put on my clothes and then walked all the way home from the West End to Decatur. It took me seven hours, but I made it. When my mother got home, she whooped me for disobeying her and not staying at my dad's until she got home. I wanted to tell her what had happened, but I felt like it would only create more problems. I could not tell my stepdad because my mother did not want him to know that we had been away from the house for the night. Had he found out, he probably would have killed my father with his bare hands! My father thought he was tough and always looked for trouble. He would have loved for my stepdad to step to him, so he could get some of his thugs to hurt him. My stepdad never started trouble, but he sure as hell never ran away from it, either!

Two months after that happened, I got sick and I had a pregnancy test. Sure enough, it was positive. I was not a virgin, but I had not been with a boy in about a year, so I knew he had to be the father. Instead of telling anybody that I was pregnant, I secretly had an abortion and everything went away.

The Monday after that, I was walking down the hall during my lunch period and the secretary called me into the office. She asked me why I was not in the conference my mother was having with Mr. Wilson, my science teacher. Shit, I did not know we were having a conference. She immediately made me go to Mr. Wilson's class. I should have known by the closed door that something was up, but I thought he just wanted privacy for our conference. I opened the door and caught Mr. Wilson having sex with my mother from behind.

She was bent over his desk with her skirt wrapped around her ankles. Their backs were turned to the door, so they could not see me when I walked in. I was completely in shock. I took a few steps toward them calling out to my mother. They were so into it, they did not even notice that I was standing right behind them.

"Mama," I kept walking closer and then I screamed, "Mama!"

My mother and Mr. Wilson looked over their shoulders and finally saw me. My mother reached for her skirt and tried to pull it up. "What are you doing in here?"

"I go to school here, Mama!"

"Keisha, I know this looks bad, but your mother and I are in love." Mr. Wilson bent down behind his desk and hid himself to pull up his clothes.

"How could you do this, Mama?"

I ran out of the classroom and then all the way home. My mother came home and explained to me that she and Mr. Wilson were in love. Mr. Wilson was the mystery man from the Internet. My father was a rapist and my mother was a cheater, and I was the child those evil people produced. Every single night I dream to be a part of a normal family…"

END KEISHA'S STORY

"…But I wake up to the nightmare of the disgusting face I see in my mirror every single morning."

"Oh my God, Keisha! I don't know what to say about your mother, but you have to tell somebody about what your father did to you."

"Tell who, Butterfly?"

"Tell your stepdad."

"If I tell my stepdad, he'll put his hands on my Dad and then he'll be in jail."

"Then tell the police."

"I don't want my daddy to go to jail, either."

"He's not your daddy, Keisha! Your stepdad is your daddy! That man is a rapist!"

"See, that's why I didn't want to tell anybody 'cause people are going to want me to do what they want me to do."

"Well, what do you want to do, Keisha?"

"I just want to forget about it."

"But what if he tries to do it again?"

"He's not going to get a chance to do it again."

"But he raped you, Keisha. He has to pay for what he did to you."

"God will punish him."

"Yeah, but the police need to punish him, too."

"I just want to forget it ever happened and go on with my life."

"Listen to me, Keisha. Bri's stepdad works for the Atlanta Police Department. He can help you."

"I don't want anybody's help. What I want is to be left alone so that I can put this behind me and move forward with my life."

"You're my best friend, Keisha. How can I leave you alone? I care about you."

"If you really care about me, Butterfly, you'll let this go because if this comes out, it's going to hurt a lot of people, especially me. I don't want all of our friends to know that my dad raped me. I don't want people to look and say, 'That girl had sex with her father.' I just want to have a normal life."

"Your life will be normal in time, but you have to deal with what happened in order to get past it."

"You mean like how you're dealing with your mother abandoning you?"

"My situation is totally different from yours."

"What's the difference?"

"I have to deal with my situation in an unresolved manner because I can't deal with my mother directly. But your father is on the other side of town, and you can make him pay for what he did to you."

"We're two different people, Butterfly. You're mad at your mother and you want her to pay for hurting you. You want an explanation! I don't! I don't want to know why my father raped me. I don't want him to pay for anything. I'm not mad at him; I'm afraid of him! I want him away from me...*Forever!*" Keisha yelled and then calmed down quickly. "I'm sorry."

I realized there was nothing I could do to convince Keisha to press charges against her father. She was too afraid that she would be put on trial in the court of public opinion.

"Don't worry about it. They can't hear you in this big old house."

"I just want to have a normal life with a normal family."

"The older I get, the more I'm starting to realize that every family has some type of dysfunctional behavior, Keisha."

"Let me ask you a question, Butterfly."

"Go ahead."

"How are you learning to talk so good?"

"You mean, talk so *well*."

"Yeah, how are you learning to talk so well?"

"It's an environmental thing, Keisha. I'm being pushed to speak properly and it's okay to say a word or sentence the correct way without being criticized by your friends. You know, it's okay to be intelligent."

"It's like you just got smart all of a sudden."

"No, that's not it. I got to a school now where communication is important through dialogue and not through action. And the

Forresters, even Pa-Pa, make sure I'm speaking proper grammar."

"Damn, all that I learn from my house is how to speak biblical terms from my stepdad."

"Wait a minute, don't get it twisted, Pastor Powell is responsible for me having the patience to sit down and listen when someone is trying to tell me some useful information. And he used the Bible to get through to me."

"Oh, I didn't mean it like that. I love the fact that my stepdad tries to teach me about the Bible, but I want to be smart like you."

"I'm no smarter than you, Keisha. It's just that I have a lot of support behind me to excel. I know how you feel. Until I moved in with the Powells, I never had a sense of family. My father did all that he could as a father, but he knew nothing about being a mother. He knew how to survive. He knew how to love me. But he did not know how to teach me how to love myself like a woman should."

"Do you like have resentment, for your father for not being there for you the past eight years?"

"Uh-uhn! Nope! What happened that night was self-defense. He did not go over there to hurt anybody. He went over there to see his kids that he loved. They started it and my father finished it."

"But you don't think that if he would have just walked away, he could have still been in your life?"

"No, I think he did what he had to do."

"What? Are you saying you think he had to murder those people?"

All of a sudden, I had a vivid flashback to that night when the incident occurred. It was in slow motion and my recollection was more synchronized than I had ever remembered. I could see my father on top of the man, but he was not swinging as I had always remembered. He was only trying to restrain the man from hitting him.

Chapter Ten

And as quickly as the image flashed in my mind, it left. But it left behind a migraine headache. I felt this agonizing pain directly behind my right eye that seemed to circulate to the back of my head and throb.

"Aw, my goodness, that hurts!"

"What's the matter with you?"

"I don't know I got this pain in my head and it's killing me! Oh my goodness, it hurts!" I lay on my side and then covered my head with a pillow.

"Hey girl, you all right?"

"Can you do me a favor?"

"Yeah, what's up?" Keisha rubbed my head as I closed my eyes tightly.

"Can you get me some Tylenol out of my medicine cabinet?"

"Okay."

Keisha ran to the bathroom and brought me a couple of Tylenol pills and a glass of water. "Here you go."

"Man, my head is throbbing, Keisha." I sat up and swallowed the pill and then lay back down.

"Just out of the blue, like that?"

"Yes, I don't know where that came from."

"Just lay down and go to sleep then."

"I'm not sleepy." I sat up and laid my head back. "It's kind of going away now anyway."

"So that came out of nowhere when you was—I mean, *were*—talking about your father?"

"Yeah, I don't know what that was all about. But it's completely gone now."

"For real?"

"Yeah, I don't feel anything anymore."

"Man, you need to have Dr. Forrester check your crazy ass out."

"There's nothing wrong with me."

"Oh yes it is. You acting like you just had a damn aneurism or something."

"Now what were we talking about?"

"You told me your father did what he had to do, and I asked you if you thought that your father murdering those people was what he had to do."

"First of all, he didn't murder anybody. It was self-defense and he was convicted of manslaughter."

Again the flashback of that night became very clear in my mind. I could see my father on top of the man holding him down, and Ms. Joyce, my younger brother and sister's mother, running and jumping on my father's back. My father stood up and pushed Ms. Joyce off of him and her boyfriend ran to his car.

"Ah, shoot!" I screamed and grabbed my head.

"Did it happen again?"

"Damn! It hurts!"

"Butterfly, are you all right, girl?"

The pain was so intense, I could not even respond to Keisha's question. It was in the same spot as it was before, directly behind my right eye. My vision was blurry and I was a bit incoherent.

"I'm going to get Dr. Forrester!" Keisha stood up and headed for the door.

"No!" I shouted. "No, don't go get anybody!"

Keisha stopped in her tracks and turned around. "This is not the first time this has happened to you, is it?"

"Damn! This hurts!" I clutched my sheets to absorb some of the pain shooting through my head.

"This is not the first time this has happened to you, is it, Butterfly?"

"I can't talk right now, Keisha! It hurts too bad!" I clutched the sheets again as another intense wave of pain hit me.

"Girl, I'm getting help!"

"No!" I grabbed Keisha's wrist and would not let it go. "Ugh!"

"It's something wrong with you, Butterfly!"

"I'll be fine in a minute; it doesn't last that long!" I dug my fingernails into Keisha's wrist. "Oh my God!"

"Ouch!" Keisha shouted. "Let me go! You're hurting me!"

Keisha snatched away from me and I tightened my body and lifted my head from the pillow. "Sheeeeeeit! It hurts!"

I sat still for a while and then the pain subsided.

"I'm telling Dr. Forrester in the morning about your headaches."

"No you're not."

"Why are you trying to hide this from them? It could be something serious."

"If it was something serious, something would have happened already."

"You don't know that, and if you don't tell the Forresters in the morning, I'm going to tell them myself."

"Please, don't do that! I'm not going to tell anyone your secret, so please don't tell anybody mine."

"No! I'm not making that deal with you. If you want to tell my secret, tell it. Because as soon as I get up in the morning, I'm telling Ms. Alicia and Dr. Forrester there's something wrong with you."

"Do what you have to do."

The next day, the Forresters had a house full of people for

Thanksgiving. There were Auntie Cynthia, Little Mike and Uncle Mike, Pa-Pa, Auntie Tina and her husband, Mr. Curtis; their three kids, Ariel, Kija and Sasha; Auntie Pam, Keisha, Brit and me. They had three tables set up for the adults, the teenagers and the children.

After we finished eating dinner, the men watched football. Dr. Forrester and Uncle Mike were from Michigan, so they were fans of the Detroit Lions. They had to be real fans because who would admit to being Lions fans?

Keisha was enjoying the Thanksgiving activities to the point where she forgot to talk to the Forresters about my headaches. I was glad because I was not in a mood for serious conversation. I wanted to enjoy the moment and not worry about my everyday problems. It was one of those butterfly moments when I wanted to fly away to my perfect world of being with family and friends for a perfect holiday. And that was exactly what happened until…

"We need to talk."

I stopped and turned around. "Yes, sir?"

"When were you going to tell me about these headaches you've been having?"

"Keisha told you?" I asked. "Snitch!"

"That's not important; what's going on?"

"Nothing, they are just headaches that come and go."

"The way I hear it, when they come, they hurt like hell."

"They do, but only for a minute."

"Okay, you have a choice, Butterfly. Do you want me to involve Alicia?"

"No, sir. She will have me in a neurosurgeon's office tomorrow morning."

"Then tell me what's going on, and I want the whole truth."

"Okay, uh, every time I think about the night when my father went to jail, I have this vision or flashback like I'm watching a movie. It's like I'm there all over again."

"And this brings on the headaches?"

"Yes, sir, very painful headaches."

"What is that you see?"

"I see my father and Ms. Joyce's boyfriend fighting and my dad is on top. Ms. Joyce jumps on Dad and pushes him off of her boyfriend. Her boyfriend runs to his car and comes back with a gun and then I wake up with both of them dead."

"Do you ever see your father shoot them?"

"No, I never get that far."

"I think what's happening is that you suffered such a traumatic experience in witnessing the incident, you've somehow blocked out what really happened."

"Is there anything we can do to stop the headaches?"

"We have to get you to confront what happened that night. I think your mind wants to see your father from such a positive perspective that your subconscious has repressed the reality of what happened that night. It's perfectly normal."

"Can we keep this between us? I don't want Ms. Alicia and Ma Powell to be worried about me."

"I'm going to schedule a CAT Scan and see what's going on. If there's nothing abnormal happening, I won't tell them, but if there is, I'm going to have to let them know."

"That's cool."

"Let's get back in the house. I'm missing my game."

"Okay."

"If you have another one of those sudden headaches, I want you to tell me as soon as it happens. You understand?"

"Yes, sir."

I spent the remainder of the semester hitting the books and finished the entire semester with an overall 4.0-grade-point average. My confidence was high and I had actually started to believe that I was going to make it through the school year.

Over the next month, Keisha spent more time with our family than hers. I could see the Forresters' influence in her life. She had become concerned with how she spoke, how she dressed, and her inevitable future. I was proud of her.

She spent Christmas Day with us, but her stepdad took her to Tennessee with him for the rest of the Christmas break. Keisha told me her mother lied to her stepdad and told him she was going to visit her family for the holiday, but she was actually with her schoolteacher at his timeshare home. She often made Keisha lie to cover for her. Keisha hated it!

In January, I was eager to go back to school. Dr. Forrester and Ms. Alicia helped me send applications to major colleges all across the country. Ms. Alicia told me that there was no way I would not be enrolling in a major college in the fall. It seemed like the Forresters were more excited about me going to college than me.

My social life, on the other hand, was quite a different story. I was popular with the girls, but not so much with the guys. Plenty of guys liked me and asked me for my telephone number, but they were busters. I had no interest at all. That was until basketball season and I stayed after school to try out for the spring cheerleading squad. I expected to be cut because I was much taller than the average cheerleader, and the cheerleading coach was the volleyball coach. She had tried to get me on the volleyball team ever since I'd stepped on DCA's campus. I think she had it out for me because I would not play for her.

Anyway, during cheerleading tryouts, I saw this really tall guy that I had never seen practicing with the boy's basketball team.

He was cute, but the way he was dominating on the basketball court was what caught my eye. He was like a man among boys. Everybody was watching him, especially the girls.

"Who is that, Bri?" I pointed to the boy.

"That's Jeremy Winston. He just transferred from New York. You haven't heard of him?"

"Uh-uhn, girl."

"That dude is bad! They've been talking about that boy coming here for months."

"For real? I have never heard of him before."

"You better get your head out of those books and see what's going on out here, Butterfly."

"Yummy!"

Jeremy was tall. I mean really tall. He was almost seven feet tall, as a matter of fact. I think he said he was six-ten or six-eleven, something like that. He was like a pecan color, with a shaven head. His hair was close shaven, but you could still see hair on his head. He had broad shoulders and a small waist. His arms and legs were long, but his torso was short. He had no facial hair which really made him look young, but he had a deep voice which made him sound mature. I had never been so attracted to a boy in my life.

"You like that, huh?" Bri asked.

"Girl, yeah! That niggah is fine!"

"Are you going to say something to him?"

"No, I'm old school."

"Girl, you're not old school; you're no school."

While we were talking, the ball happened to bounce on the bleachers where we were sitting and Jeremy ran over to pick it up. He looked at me and then smiled. He ran back on the court but continued to look at me every now and then.

"I think somebody likes you, Butterfly."

"That boy's not thinking about me."

"Then why is he looking at you right now?"

I looked in his direction and he was staring right into my eyes. I quickly looked away. "Oh my God, he is looking right at me, Bri!"

"Calm down, girl, he's only a boy."

"Okay, I'm calm! I'm calm!"

After cheerleading tryout, Bri convinced me to hang out and watch the rest of the boy's basketball practice. I could not take my eyes off of that boy. During one of their plays, the ball bounced on the bleachers and landed in my lap. Jeremy came over to get it and I tossed it to him. He smiled and then ran back on the court. When the tryout was over, Jeremy came up to me while Bri and I were still sitting on the bleachers.

"What's your name?"

"Shante, but they call me Butterfly."

"Butterfly?"

"Yes."

"I'm Jeremy. I have to talk to Coach before I leave, but can you hang around until I finish?"

"Yeah!" Bri interrupted. "She'll be right here."

"Bri!" I was embarrassed but I composed myself so that I would not look like a big fool. "Jeremy, this is my cousin, Bri."

"Hi, Bri." Jeremy shook Bri's hand.

"Hey, Jeremy," Bri said.

"You're in my Algebra class, aren't you?"

"Yes, I sit two seats behind you."

"Yeah, that's right. I thought that was you."

"A'ight then."

Jeremy looked at me and then smiled. "So how do I get in contact with you after school?"

"What's your email address?" I asked.

"My email address? Email is snail mail nowadays. Got your cell phone on you?"

"Yes."

"What's your number?"

"Four-zero-four, five-five-five, six-two-six-three."

Jeremy dialed my number and then my cell phone rang. I answered it and Jeremy laughed. "Lock me in."

I smiled at Jeremy and said, "I got you locked in. Now what?"

"I'll tell you what, when I talk to you after these tryouts."

"Okay."

"Later."

"Later."

Jeremy jogged back to his coach and they sat down and talked. As his coach talked to him, he kept looking over the coach's shoulder to catch a glimpse of me. And believe me, I was looking right back.

"Later?" Bri chuckled.

"Be quiet!"

"Later? What is this, 1975?"

"Shut up, girl." I laughed. "What's up with your, *'a'ight then.'*"

"I can't believe Jeremy came over here in front of everybody and talked to you like that. I've been in class with him for two weeks and he has never said one word to any girl in that class."

"He didn't just come over here to talk to me; the ball inadvertently bounced on my lap."

"That dude ran past two or three guys to get to that ball because he wanted to say something to you."

"What's the big deal? He's just a boy, that's all."

"That boy could be playing in the NBA next year."

"So?"

"So? You could be dating an NBA basketball star."

"First of all, I may not know a lot about sports like you, but I do know that you have to play at least one year in college before you can go to the NBA. Secondly, he looks pretty good out there, but I don't see pro-ball caliber."

As I was talking, Jeremy shot a long ball from almost half court and then looked as if he was on cue to show me his skills.

"Did you see that?" Bri was so excited.

"I don't care about that stuff, Bri."

"I bet you care when he's drafted to the NBA."

"That's not me, I'm telling you. I'm not into that stuff."

"Whatever, Butterfly."

I did not put my cell phone down the entire night, and guess what? Jeremy did not call the entire night. I was pissed off! I do not like to have an emotional dependency on boys. Ms. Alicia taught me that. She said that I should not depend on the opinion, or the attention, of boys to feel good about myself. I put myself in that position that night I waited on Jeremy to call me.

The next day, he was waiting for me in front of my first-period class. I walked past him as if I did not see him. He stopped me and tried to talk to me, but of course, I was full of attitude.

"Hey, Butterfly."

"Hey."

I was going into my class, but Jeremy reached out for my hand and pulled me to the side. "What's wrong?"

"Nothing."

"Why are you acting funny?"

"I'm not acting funny."

"Are you mad at me?"

"Do I have a reason to be mad at you?"

Jeremy looked around the hallway as if the answer was written on the walls. Then he stared at me like I was going to answer the question for him…so I did.

"I don't like waiting on people to call me, Jeremy."

"Oh, my bad, I wanted to call last night, but my father said I had to study, and he would not let me use my cell phone."

What? The boy was a prospect for the NBA and his father was still telling him when he could, and could not use his cell phone? Under any other circumstance, I would have been proud that his father was making sure he handled his business, but in that case, I wanted him to call me.

"Whatever."

"No, I'm serious. I have to keep my grades up if I want to get into a good college. I'm struggling in two courses: math and history. If I don't pull those grades up, I may not even graduate. I had to transfer to a history class today just to…"

"Okay! Okay! I believe you."

"So can we meet for lunch? That's even better than a phone call, right?"

"I guess."

"I'll pick you up in the front of the gym, okay?"

"Okay."

"Later."

"Later."

What is up with this dude always saying this "later" mess? And why can't I stop myself from saying it? I walked into my first period and Mr. Thompson was on full blast.

"Okay, people, today is the day I hire the producer for the show. I have three final candidates: Ms. Tracy Mueller, Mr. Stephen Glad and Ms. Shante Clemmons. And the producer for our show will be…"

I only had applied for the position of producer because Mr. Thompson forced all of the seniors in the class to do so. I really did not even want to be bothered with being in charge of the production because I felt it would take away study time from my other classes. As Mr. Thompson gave his version of the drum roll, I was silently praying that he would not call my name.

"...Ms. Clemmons. Congratulations, Ms. Clemmons!"

"Thank you, Mr. Thompson."

"Come on up and speak to your production company."

I walked to the front of the class and I did not have a clue of what I was going to say. I looked at the class and then I looked at Mr. Thompson.

"I don't know what to say, y'all." The class laughed and it made me feel comfortable. "I will do all that I can to make sure we have the best production DCA has ever seen. I hope I can get all of your support, so that all of us can get that '*A*' at the end of the year. I'm open to any and all suggestions, but I hope nobody gets mad at me if I don't use them all."

"What do I have to do to be the stage manager?" Asia asked.

"Apply, right, Mr. Thompson?"

"You tell me, Ms. Clemmons."

"Okay, Asia, you can turn in your application and I will give you an interview," I looked at Mr. Thompson, "Is that okay, Mr. Thompson?"

"I don't know, is it?"

"To make this easy, everybody just turn in their application for the positions they want to work, and I'll hire people based on who I think is best for the position and where I think we need the most help. I want you all to know that everybody can't be the director, and everybody can't be the stage manager, and everybody can't be a part of the cast. But everybody can be just as important. That's it!"

"You sound like me up there." Mr. Thompson clapped his hands as he walked back in front of the class. I walked back to my seat. "Okay, everybody listen up. Last semester you were graded on the logistics of running a production. This semester you will be graded on the actual production. I suggest that you give Ms. Clemmons all the support she needs and follow her instructions."

I had never been a leader over anything but myself. I was not comfortable in the position, but I was prepared to do what was necessary to have a successful performance.

My third-period class was history. That was my favorite subject, but my second favorite class behind my drama class. Mr. Thompson be going ham and I liked the way he taught us. But like I said, history was my favorite subject.

My history teacher was Ms. Jamerson. She was white, young and pretty, and all of the boys liked being in her class. She was short, about five-foot two inches tall. She had jet-black, silky hair that was full and bouncy. She had an athletic-type body, and she always wore clingy clothes to accentuate her positive features. A lot of the female student body did not like her because she was so pretty but shoot, I felt like, if you got it, flaunt it.

I liked to get to history class early because we did not have assigned seats. I tried to always sit up front, so that I did not have to deal with the childish playing they did in the back of the class. That day was no different. I went straight from my second period to my third-period class and sat in the front row.

I rarely paid attention when my classmates entered the room. I usually kept my eyes and head forward and waited for Ms. Jamerson to begin class. I sensed something was a little different that day, and lo and behold, when I looked at the door, Jeremy walked through it. I turned my head around quickly and looked at Ms. Jamerson. He walked three rows over to my aisle and spoke to me and then walked to the back of the class.

After class, he caught up with me as I was walking out. I told Bri I would take her to get something to eat because I had forgotten about my lunch date with Jeremy.

"Hey, where you going, Butterfly? I thought we had a date."

"I'm sorry, I forgot about that. I have to take my cousin to get something to eat."

"Does that mean you're standing me up?"

"I'm sorry, Jeremy, but I promised my cousin."

"I can take your cousin to get something to eat...as long as you come with us."

"You sure?"

"Yeah, it's no problem."

"Okay, I'll tell her we'll pick her up in front of the gym."

"Cool."

I called Bri and she met us in front of the gym. Jeremy had a brand-new 2010 Yukon SUV. The truck was beautiful! Too brand-new and too beautiful for a high school student to afford. At first I thought he may have been secretly paid by some college booster looking to improve their alma mater. But actually, his father was a former NBA player and his mother was an attorney, so they had money coming out of the yin-yang! That also explained why he could not talk to me on the phone the night before. His parents knew firsthand the importance of an education and the distractions that could keep him from going to college, or possibly playing in the NBA. But the weekend was ours!

We continued to date and within a month, we were officially a couple. I was selected to the cheerleading squad, which meant I traveled with the basketball team for the away games. It also meant that I got to spend even more time with Jeremy. We sat together on the bus and pretty much kept to ourselves.

I was in love and wanted to know if he was in love, too. I asked him one night on our way back from a game, and he told me that he had wanted to bring up the subject for a long time. I was on top of the world! But whenever you are on top of anything, there is always that chance that you are going to come crashing down.

Chapter Eleven

Valentine's Day was the coming Monday, so Jeremy and I made plans for a romantic dinner. We reserved our dinner for Ruth's Chris on Roswell Road. We had to schedule it for Saturday night, which was actually the twelfth, because that Sunday was the day I had my monthly visit with my dad.

Since we had gotten so serious in our relationship, we decided that it was time to meet the parents. I asked the Forresters if Jeremy could come over for dinner that Friday night to meet them. When I told them who he was, Dr. Forrester was ecstatic! Pa-Pa was beside himself! But Ms. Alicia, she wasn't having it. She thought that Jeremy was too popular to be with one girl and that he was going to eventually hurt me. Thank goodness the men folk were able to convince her to give him a chance.

When Jeremy showed up, he brought Ms. Alicia and me flowers. He sat in the den with Dr. Forrester and Pa-Pa and answered each one of their many, many questions. It worked out well for him that all of their questions pertained to sports and not me. They gave me their immediate approval and then we ate dinner. After we ate, it was Ms. Alicia's turn to do her part of the interview process. She arranged that only she, Jeremy and I would be present when she talked to us.

"Where are you going to college, Jeremy?"

"I don't know yet, ma'am."

"Uh-huhn, do you have any idea?"

"I mean, I have a few choices but nothing definite."

"And they are?"

"My choices?"

"Yes, your choices."

"Uh, Connecticut, Syracuse, Michigan State and uh…" Jeremy looked at me and realized he should be mentioning a nearby school. "…uh, Georgia Tech."

"Any frontrunners?"

"No, ma'am."

"I like you, and I think you're a really nice young man, but I have to be honest with you. I'm concerned about what's going to happen to Shante when you go off to college, or to the NBA."

"Mrs. Forrester?"

"Uh-huhn?"

"Can I be honest with you?"

"Of course."

"I love Butterfly, I mean Shante, Mrs. Forrester. I don't know what's going to happen to me, just like she doesn't know what's going to happen to her. But I do know that I would never try to intentionally hurt her, just like I feel she would not try to intentionally hurt me. My parents have sheltered me to the point where I have almost no friends. Shante is more than just a girlfriend; she's my friend. Over the next three months, my family and I will be making the most important decision of my life. Not just for my basketball future, but for my academic future as well. I want Shante to be a part of that."

"I appreciate your honesty, Jeremy. But just like you have your parents to protect you, I have to do that for my child."

My mind was stuck on Ms. Alicia saying that I was her child. I had been with the Forresters for a little over six months and we had actually become a family. The family I had always wanted. The family I had always dreamed of. But, on the other hand, because of that family connection, my family was ruining my opportunity for the boy I loved.

"I know that you can't foresee what's going to happen, but I want you to promise me that when your life really becomes public, if you are still with Shante, you will protect her," Ms. Alicia said.

Jeremy embraced my hand in his. "I promise, ma'am."

"Okay, good. Shante, can you come with me, please?" Ms. Alicia stood up and I followed her out of the room. She led me to the foyer and then turned around. "I am so happy for you, girl."

"Are you crying, Ms. Alicia?"

Ms. Alicia wiped her eyes. "Yes, I am."

"Why? Stop it! You know you're going to make me cry." I started crying and Ms. Alicia wiped my tears. "Why are we crying?'

"I don't know. I'm just happy for you."

Pa-Pa walked through the foyer and saw us crying and then quickly walked away. "Oh shit, I'm getting the hell out of here."

"Okay, dry your eyes." Ms. Alicia wiped my eyes. "Go back in there and enjoy the rest of your night with your boyfriend."

"So you approve?"

"I approve."

"You don't know how much that means to me, Ms. Alicia."

"Would you stop talking and go back to your company?"

Pa-Pa walked back through the foyer as Ms. Alicia was telling me to return to the living room and then he stopped me.

"Wait a minute now; we want him out of here by eleven o' clock."

"Okay, Pa-Pa." I looked over Pa-Pa's shoulder and Ms. Alicia mouthed the word "midnight" over and over again.

Jeremy and I talked until midnight and Ms. Alicia gave signs to let me know that it was time for Jeremy to go. The next night I was supposed to go to Jeremy's house to meet his parents. It did not go nearly as smoothly as it did with the Forresters.

I was expecting the attitude to come from his mom, but instead, it came from his smothering dad. He suspected that I was trying to be with Jeremy for his money. What money? Jeremy's money was his money, and how in the hell could I get his money from him? From the moment I walked in his house, Mr. Winston was asking the tough questions.

"So why are you interested in my son, Shante?" Mr. Winston asked.

"Because he's nice."

"Is that the only reason?"

"Yes, sir."

"And it has nothing to do with his basketball potential?"

"No, sir."

Mrs. Winston tried to save me by asking questions related to my family background, but she only pushed me out of the frying pan and into the fire.

"My husband played in the NBA," Mrs. Winston said. "I hear your father and uncle played in the NFL, so they have something in common."

"Well, Dr. Forrester is not my biological father, but he did play briefly in the NFL."

"He's not your biological father?" Mr. Winston interrupted. "Are you adopted?"

"No, the Forresters are my foster parents."

"Foster parents? You live in a foster home?"

"Yes, sir, but they're like my real parents."

"May I ask how you came to live in a foster home?"

"I'd rather not answer that question, sir."

"Oh, really?"

"Dad, please, you're embarrassing her."

"I'm not trying to embarrass you, young lady, but my son means everything to me and I don't want him to get into anything that could jeopardize his future."

"Shante is not a threat to me in any way, Dad. She is a good girl and all that we are trying to do is enjoy each other's company with the permission of our parents."

"But, son, you have to realize that there are going to be people to come into your life, and sometimes they are not going to have your best interest at heart."

"He's not saying that you don't have his best interest at heart, Shante; he's speaking generally," Mrs. Winston said.

We sat quietly for a moment or two, and then Jeremy spoke. "We just stopped by for you two to meet Shante, so we're about to head out to dinner."

"Hold on a minute, son. Is this arrangement okay with your foster parents, Shante?"

"Yes, it's okay with my parents. And we don't use the 'foster' word in our house, because for us, it's the love that makes the family, not the titles and definitely not the extracurricular activities."

The room was quiet again. Jeremy looked at me and then patted me on the leg. "Ready to go?"

"Yes." Jeremy grabbed my hand. "It was nice to meet you all."

We stood up and Mrs. Winston followed us to the door. Mr. Winston never even said good-bye.

"You kids have fun!" Mrs. Winston.

"Thanks, Mom."

Jeremy took me to dinner and then we went to a movie. I had a midnight curfew, but Pa-Pa started calling me at eleven-thirty to remind me. When I got home, Jeremy walked me to the door and we were about to kiss, but something told me to back off. I looked in the living room window and Pa-Pa, Dr. Forrester and Ms. Alicia were peeking out at us. I kissed Jeremy on the cheek and pointed my head in their direction so that he could peep them out.

"Oh." Jeremy gave me a hug and returned my kiss on the cheek.

"Good night, Jeremy."

"Good night, Butterfly."

I could see them running from the living room picture window as I walked in. The Forresters got away clean, but I caught Pa-Pa in mid-stride.

"Pa-Pa!" I shouted.

"Ain't nobody spying on you!"

"I never said you were."

"Okay then."

"But what are you doing down here?"

"It's a free country. I can walk anywhere I want to walk."

"Okay, Pa-Pa." I chuckled and wrapped my arms around his. "Come on, old man, let me help you upstairs."

Pa-Pa did not need my help to get upstairs, but I enjoyed escorting the old fart to his room anyway. As we passed the Forresters' bedroom, I knocked and sarcastically said, "You two can go to sleep now."

Ms. Alicia yelled back, "Thank you, dear."

The next day, Dr. Forrester and I went to visit my father. He was in very good spirits that day. We laughed and joked almost the entire time I was there. But, of course, we had our father-daughter moments where we expressed how much we loved and missed each other.

"Guess what, Dad?"

"What?"

"I have a boyfriend."

"I don't know if I like that. Has Doc checked him out?"

"Dr. Forrester, Ms. Alicia and Pa-Pa."

"Who the hell is Pa-Pa?"

"Oh, that's Dr. Forrester's dad. You don't mind if I call him that, do you?"

"Do you love the old man?"

"Yes, sir."

"Do the old man love you?"

"Yes, sir."

"Then no, I don't mind." Dad rubbed his chin. "So tell me about this boyfriend."

"He's tall, he's cute, and he plays on the basketball team."

"Does he have a name?"

"Yes, sir, it's Jeremy Winston."

"Jeremy Winston? The boy that transferred down here from New York?"

"Yes, sir."

"What? My Butterfly is dating the number-one high school basketball player in the country?"

"I guess so."

"Tell that boy he better treat you right, or I'm coming for his kneecaps."

"Daddy!"

"Are you going to spend Valentine's Day with him?"

"For a little while, I guess. We have early curfews during the week, so neither one of us can hang out late. We went out to dinner last night and celebrated."

"Wow! My baby is growing up."

"Where's my Valentine's Day card, Dad?"

"I got your Valentine right here." Dad balled up his fist.

"Whatever, man."

Dad smiled and then abruptly stopped smiling. "Look, I need to tell you something, sweetheart."

"Sounds serious, Dad."

"It is."

"Don't tell me you got in trouble?"

"No, nothing like that."

"Okay, what's up then?"

"Hey, baby, Doc told me what's been going on with your headaches. He thinks it's because of something trapped in your mind and it's trying to get out."

"Bigmouth."

"The doc is only trying to help you, that's all."

"I know."

"I don't even know how to tell you this, baby."

"What's the matter, Daddy?"

"Your mother, or the woman you knew as your mother, was not your biological mother. I met her when you were about a year old. She came into our lives and she loved you as if you were her very own."

"I know, Dad."

"Good, so I hope you're not too disappointed."

"No, I mean I know Mama was not my biological mother."

"You know? What do you mean, you know?"

"I saw my original birth certificate and the woman's name on my birth certificate was not Mama's."

"Why didn't you tell me you knew?"

"Because I was waiting for you to tell me the truth."

"Okay, so now you know."

"Not really. I saw the name on my birth certificate, but I do not remember what the name was."

"That's not important, sweetheart!"

"Maybe you feel that way, Dad, but it's very important for me to know the name of the woman who gave birth to me."

"I'm telling you, you don't want to open that can of worms, Butterfly. Let it go!"

"I can't 'let it go'! I have to know why this woman did not love me enough to keep me! Can't you see how important this is to me?"

"Yeah, baby, but..."

"No, Daddy! I need for you to tell me her name!"

"Why? Why is it so important for you to know her name?"

"I'm going to find her, and I'm going to ask her how she could do what she did to her child."

"It's not worth it, Butterfly. What if she don't want to see you and you end up getting hurt and disappointed even more than you are now?"

"That's impossible, Daddy...I can't get any more disappointed than I am now. So please, tell me her name."

"Okay, baby," Dad lowered his head and then raised it, "Her name is..."

School was really starting to kick my butt. Between cheerleading, the drama club and my studies, I barely had time for Jeremy. But when we did get together, there were sparks flying all over the place. The kissing lessons I'd learned from Toya sure paid off.

And who would have thought that after the way I met Asia, Jheri and Valencia, they would become my biggest supporters in drama class. I was struggling trying to make everybody happy in their roles for the production, but Asia, my stage manager, stepped in and put everybody in their places.

"Hey! Y'all listen up!" Asia clapped her hands together to get everyone's attention. "Hey, listen! The producer has given everybody their roles and positions for the production, so it's time to shut up and get busy! We have six weeks to make this show a success, *so*...like I said, either get busy, or get the hell out!"

"Thanks, Asia."

"No problem, I'm trying to get an 'A' out of this class."

"Okay, everybody, to piggyback off of what Asia said, starting next Monday, we will begin rehearsals. We will spend thirty minutes during class and an hour after class every day, so please tell your parents. If you cannot make it, please contact Asia and let us know in advance. Thank you."

Speaking in front of the class gave me a bit of confidence. I embraced the role of being a leader. The thought of people depending on me was not as frightening as it had been in the past. I skipped lunch with Jeremy to go over the production with Asia, Jheri and Valencia. Bri came because, well, because Bri goes everywhere I go. We decided to meet at the food court in the Discover Mills mall, the place where we originally had our first altercation.

Bri and I arrived first and sat on opposite sides of the table. When Asia, Jheri and Valencia arrived, Valencia sat next to Bri on her side, and Jheri and Asia squeezed in on my side of the table.

"Asia, Jheri and Valencia, I hope y'all don't mind that I brought my cousin with me. The first thing I want to do is clear the air about what happened last semester. Bri is my cousin, and now all of you are my friends. So y'all do what y'all have to do to put this behind us."

"I'm cool with that," Asia said.

"I don't have a problem with Bri at all," Valencia added.

Jheri looked at Bri and spoke directly to her, "Bri, we used to be best friends. Things got all crazy when we got to high school and I'm sorry if I hurt you. We got two more years of high school left and I would much rather you be my friend, than my enemy."

"I can appreciate what all of you are trying to do, but it's still kind of hurts to know my best friends turned on me over a dude."

"David lied to both of us and made us both look like fools. We were young and his old ass took advantage of us."

"Yeah, but even though we liked the dude, I would never post naked pictures of you on the Internet, Asia. Out of everybody, you and I were the closest."

"I know Bri, but I can't change what happened. I'm the one who should be upset anyway. Shit, you beat my ass!"

I had just taken a swallow of my soda, but what Asia said was so funny to me, I spat it out over everybody.

"Damn, that's nasty!" Jheri screamed.

"You spit that shit all over my shirt, Shante!" Valencia stood up and shook the front of her blouse.

"You got me, too, girl." Bri wiped her blouse.

"I'm sorry, y'all." I chuckled. "I didn't mean to. But that was funny as shit."

"Your boyfriend is going to buy me a new shirt when he gets to the pros."

"I don't have anything to do with Jeremy or the money he's going to make, Valencia. I'll get you a new shirt myself."

"Hey, I'll be right back. I have to go dry my shirt off."

"I'm coming with you, Valencia." Bri slid out of the table and went with Valencia.

"I'm coming, too." Jheri climbed from between Asia and me and caught up with Bri and Valencia.

Asia waited for Bri to get out of sight and then told me some rather interesting information. Information that made me mad as hell!

"Shante? I know we have butted heads, but that shit is in the past. I've been hearing some stuff and it ain't cool."

"What's up?"

"Your cousin is messing up."

"What are you talking about?"

"Bri," Asia looked over her shoulder, "she's getting into some foul shit and she's about to get busted."

"Busted for what?"

"She's feeding this chick up in DeKalb County some Vicodin, and the chick got caught up in some shit and now she's about to sell Bri out to save her own ass."

"Who are you talking about?"

"It's a chick named Toya from Decatur. Bri's been selling her some pills and the chick been selling them to other people. Not just kids, but grown people, too! She got out there more than she wanted. I'm hearing they're tight on Bri's ass. She don't even know what's about to hit her. You better let her know."

We paused because we could see the other girls coming. But I made it perfectly clear that I was going to handle the situation myself.

"I know who Toya is, and she's always trying to bail on people. Not this time, though. I'm going to make sure her ass gets what she deserves."

"You know that girl?"

"Yeah, I know her. She's one of my best friends. She went to my old school."

"You better check that chick before she gets Bri caught up."

"Don't worry, I got this. But I need you to do me a favor."

"Yeah, what you need?"

"I need you to keep this zipped until I handle this. I don't want Bri to know anything, all right?"

"Oh, don't worry, I don't know nothing."

"Can you make sure your girls keep that under wraps, too?"

"They don't even know. I just found out myself from my cousin who goes to that school. That Toya girl sold her some pills."

"I can't believe she did something that stupid!"

"Shh! Here they come; you might want to move to another subject."

"Yeah, you're right."

The girls sat back down in their spots and we continued to talk about our production.

I had a conversation with Keisha and Jacqua about a private meeting with Toya. I told her I did not want her to involve Bri in any of her criminal activities, and I meant that. I knew she would suspect something was going on if I called her myself, so I had Keisha set her up.

Keisha invited Toya over to smoke, and no, I'm not talking about cigarettes. I was already sitting in the basement when they arrived. I heard them coming down the stairs; Toya was first, then Jacqua and then Keisha. When Toya saw me, she tried to run back upstairs, but she could not get past Keisha and Jacqua, who were blocking her path. She was moving so fast she slipped on one of the stairs and fell. I grabbed her foot and pulled her back down one step at a time. Her body bounced harder and harder with every stair.

"Come here, bitch!" I let go of her leg and tossed it to the floor. "It's like this; you're going to keep my cousin's name out of your mouth or I'm going to kick your ass!"

Toya started to crawl backward to try to get away. "I ain't said nothin' about your cousin, Butterfly!"

"Yes you did! The police looking for my cousin for selling 'scripts and they said you told them!"

"I promise, Butterfly! It wasn't me!"

"So you're not going to tell the truth, Toya?" I stood over her and she started kicking like a baby to keep me away. "Huh? You're still going to lie?"

"I'm not lying!" Toya shouted.

I looked over my shoulder at Keisha. "Lock the door."

Keisha walked upstairs and locked the door. I pushed Toya's kicking legs to the side and sat on top of her. She was screaming for me to get up, but I put my knees in her chest and I put my hands around her throat. You can believe she stopped all that kicking and screaming then.

"Now," I squeezed her neck even tighter, "are you going to leave my cousin's name out of your bullshit?"

She tried to say something, but I could not understand because I was choking the hell out of that neck. I let go of her neck so that she could speak. She grabbed her throat and tried to catch her breath.

"I ain't told nothing on your cousin!"

"Okay!" I held her face still and I slapped her as hard as I could. "So you're going to keep on lying?"

My slaps turned to punches and my anger turned to rage. Toya was screaming, but I was so spazzed out, I did not even hear her.

"Butterfly!" Keisha screamed.

Keisha and Jacqua tried to pull me off of her, but I pushed them away. I put my hands around her throat and choked her again, waiting to hear what I wanted to hear.

"*Shante!*" Keisha shouted. "*Stop!* You're hurting her!"

I snapped back and realized what I was doing.

"What the hell, Butterfly?" Keisha pushed me away. "I'm going to get a towel."

"Look, you said you just wanted to talk to her, Butterfly. You didn't say nothing about doing no crazy shit like this." Jacqua sat next to Toya and put Toya's head in her lap. "Toya! Toya! Toya, you okay?"

Keisha ran back downstairs with a towel and started to wipe Toya's bloody face. "What's wrong with you, Butterfly?"

"I don't know what happened. I snapped."

"Look at what you did to her."

"Look at what I did to her?" I did not mean to hurt Toya as badly as I did, but it was not like she did not deserve it. "Do you know how many people this girl has hurt with her backstabbing?"

"Yeah, but she didn't deserve all of this."

"I don't believe you, Jacqua! She's the reason your girlfriend is in jail right now! She did not care if either one of us went to jail as long as she didn't! Wait, why am I defending myself?" I pushed Jacqua and Keisha to the side and I slapped Toya lightly on the side of her face. "Toya! Toya! This is my last time asking you; are you going to keep my cousin's name out of your mouth?"

"Yes," she mumbled.

"And are you going to tell the police she had nothing to do with your drug deals?"

"Yes."

"Okay then."

I stood up to leave and Keisha had to throw her two cents in, "But Bri did, Butterfly!"

"Yeah, and I'm about to go handle her ass, too."

I drove to Ms. Tonita's house and I talked to her young woman to grown woman. I loved Bri and I really did not want her to get caught up because she was trying to fit in.

"Ms. Tonita, I need a really big favor." I was anxious and she could tell.

"What's the matter, Shante?"

"Bri's in some trouble with some girls and I need to talk to her."

"What kind of trouble?" Ms. Tonita yelled upstairs for Bri. "Briiii?"

"Please, Ms. Tonita, I need to speak to Bri alone."

"I'm her mother and I…"

I did not mean to be disrespectful but I had to interrupt her. "I know you're her mother; that's why I came to you, Ms. Tonita. But I need you to trust me on this one."

"You're telling me that my child is in trouble and I should let another 'child' handle the situation, and not me."

"What I'm saying is, I love Bri like she is my sister and I know I can handle this if you let me."

"How do you expect for me to sit back and do nothing when my child needs me."

"Because you love her, Ms. Tonita, and you want what's best for her. But this time what's best for her, is not you." I paused momentarily and stepped backward because I did not know what reaction I would get back. "It's me."

Ms. Tonita closed her legs and rocked back and forth in her chair. "Okay, Shante, but this better turn out right!"

"I promise it will."

"It better!"

"Now, I need another favor," I said.

"And what's that?"

"I'm about to take Bri into your basement and I'm going to have a private conversation with her. No matter what you hear coming from that basement, I want you to remember that I love Bri and I would never hurt her."

"What you plan on doing to my baby, girl?"

"Nothing." I chuckled. "But she's not going to like what I'm going to say and there might be some yelling and screaming. Just remember…"

As I was talking, Mr. Robert, Bri's stepdad, walked into the house. He was a detective for the Atlanta Police Department.

"Hi, Mr. Robert."

"Hey, Shante, how are you doing?"

"I'm good."

"Seems like we have a little problem with Bri that Ms. Shante wants to handle on her own."

"Is that right?"

"Yeah, she wants to talk some sense into her about something."

"Wait a minute, and you're not getting involved?"

"I know when to step back sometimes and do what's best for my child without being all up in her business."

"Yeah, right."

"But I don't know about her taking my baby to the basement and telling me to ignore any sounds I might hear coming from down there."

"Will it resolve the situation, Shante?"

"Yes, sir."

"Then by all means, use these handcuffs for precautionary measure." Mr. Robert handed me his handcuffs from his belt. "There you go."

"You better not put those things on my baby."

"I don't know, Ms. Tonita, I might need them." I laughed.

"Okay, hell naw, you're not taking my baby nowhere!" Ms. Tonita snatched the handcuffs out of my hands. "I don't even know what the hell is going on."

"No, Ms. Tonita." I laughed out loud. "I'm not going to do anything to Bri, I promise! I'm just going to scare her."

"Bri!" Mr. Robert shouted upstairs.

"Yes, sir?" Bri shouted back.

"You have company!"

"I'm comin'!"

A minute later, Bri ran downstairs. "Hey, Butterfly."

"We need to talk, Bri."

Bri looked at Mr. Robert and Ms. Tonita and then looked at me. "What's up?"

"We need to talk alone."

"Mama?"

"Y'all go do your little talking. I don't have nothing to do with it."

"Is somebody going to tell me what's going on?"

"I will, Bri. Come downstairs."

Bri followed me to the basement. Mr. Robert's basement looked similar to Dr. Forrester's and Uncle Mike's basements. It looked like a miniature ESPN center with multiple big-screen televisions all over the walls. What was it with men and big-screen televisions anyway?

Chapter Twelve

I waited for Bri to sit down and I wasted no time jumping all over her. "I know about your dope ring with Toya, Bri!"

Bri was cool as a cucumber. "I don't know what you're talking about."

"You don't know what I'm talking about, huh?"

"Nope." Bri rolled her eyes.

"Look, I don't have time for your lies. All that I'm going to say is Toya went to the police on you and they're coming to take you to jail."

"Nobody is taking me anywhere."

"How do you think Mr. Robert is going to feel when he finds out his stepdaughter is dealing 'scripts?"

"I don't know what you're talking about, Butterfly."

For a moment I thought Asia had given me the wrong information about Toya and Bri. If she had, I could never forgive myself for what I'd done to Toya. My instincts, however, were telling me that Asia was right and Bri was lying.

"I'm tired of people lying to me, Bri. I know you sold Toya your 'scripts and I don't care if you admit it or not, I better not ever hear about you doing anything stupid like that again. You hear me?" Bri jumped out of the chair and tried to walk past me. I snatched her by the shoulders and pushed her back down in the chair. "Sit your ass down and listen to me! Whatever little rebellious phase you're going through, it's time for it to stop right now! Too many people that I love, love you, including myself! And I'm not going to let your little stupid ass hurt them, or me!"

"Mama!" Bri screamed at the top of her lungs.

"Mama can't help you. It's just me and you."

"I keep telling you I don't know what you're talking about."

"Yes you do, and you're not leaving this basement until you promise me you're going to leave that shit alone!"

Every time Bri stood up to leave, I pushed her back down in the chair.

"Let me go!" Bri screamed again. "Mama!"

"You know what? You wanna call your mama, call her!" I let her up. "Call her, Bri. Call her and I'll tell her about you having sex with David, your abortion, your stupid-ass dope ring, everything! Call her!" Bri sat in the chair and huffed and puffed, but she did not say a word. "Now shut the hell up and listen! You hear me?"

"Yeah!" Bri rolled her eyes and turned her head to the side. I grabbed her chin and looked her dead in the eyes.

"Why are you doing this?"

"Because it's the only way I can make friends."

"Look, girl, I love you! And I'll be damned if I sit back and let you ruin your life because you don't have as many friends as everybody else. Or, you're not as popular as everybody else! How many times do I have to tell you, Bri, you don't have to fit in with anybody! Don't fall prey to that peer pressure bullshit! Those fools should be trying to fit in with you!"

Bri jumped in my face and screamed, "That's easy for you to say! Everybody likes you! Everybody wants to be around you! And everybody wants to be you!"

I hugged Bri and I kissed her on the cheek. "But Bri, I want to be you. And I want to be around you, because you're my cousin and I love you."

We hugged each other for a minute and then Bri sat down. "Why would anybody want to be me?"

"Because you're cute. You're smart. And you have a loving family that loves the hell out of you. Friends will come and go, but your family is your family, Bri. I'm a part of that family now and I can't let you do this to yourself, or them. So no more, 'trying to fit in with the crowd' stunts?"

"Okay."

"Promise?"

"I promise. But what difference does it make now? I'm going to be in a lot of trouble anyway."

"Don't worry about that. Toya is not going to tell on you. If you want to be done with this right now, you're done with this. So what is it going to be?"

"I'm done!"

"That's my girl." I led Bri upstairs by her hand and she snatched away.

"I'm not ready to face Mama right now."

"She doesn't know anything, Bri."

"You must not know my mother."

"You must not know me! I got it taken care of. Your mom knows we are down here talking, but she said she would let us handle it."

"My mom said that?"

"Yup."

"I don't know about that."

"Come on, girl."

We walked upstairs and as I tried to push the door open, it slammed against something. That something was Ms. Tonita eavesdropping.

"Ouch!" Ms. Tonita shouted.

"Oops! You okay, Ms. Tonita?"

Bri and I walked from behind the door and Ms. Tonita was rubbing her head.

"Ouch, that hurts."

"I told you to stay away from that door, didn't I?"

"Shut up, Rob!" Ms. Tonita walked into the living room with Mr. Robert and we followed her.

"So did your private conversation turn out all right?" Ms. Tonita asked.

"Baby?" Mr. Robert sighed.

"I said I would not interrupt their conversation; I said nothing about asking questions afterward."

"Shante, did you get it worked out?" Mr. Robert asked.

"Yes, sir."

"Great! End of conversation."

"But…" Ms. Tonita tried to speak, but Mr. Robert kept cutting her off.

"End of conversation, baby."

"But…"

"End of conversation, Tonita!"

"Well, if I can't ask my questions, I'm going upstairs!" Ms. Tonita stomped upstairs.

"You girls got everything worked out then?"

"Yes, sir," Bri said.

"You sure, Shante?"

"Yes, sir," I answered.

"In that case, let me go up here and tell your mother I'm taking her to dinner."

"Okay." Bri laughed.

Mr. Robert went to console Ms. Tonita and I went home and took a nap. Keisha called me later that evening and asked me to call Toya, but I couldn't. We spoke a couple of days later and she was the one who apologized for always bailing on the rest of us. Janae put her up to it, but as long as it was sincere, I was cool with it. Her lucky ass also got out of going to juvie, too. They questioned her and then let her go. It turned out that by not snitching on Bri, the police had nothing to tie her to the 'script ring.

In April, the media converged on Jeremy like vultures. It was approaching the time when he was supposed to select the college he would be attending in the fall. Recruiters had begun to camp outside his door on the very first day, waiting for their opportunity to talk to his parents. That meant from April 14 to May 19, the only time I would see Jeremy was through private indoor quarters. I was glad for him, but it was interfering with our relationship. I wanted privacy, and I wanted to spend time with him. Instead of spending my weekends with Jeremy, I was spending every Saturday with Bri, Brittany and Alex, or hanging with my girls.

One Saturday evening when I was folding clothes, Ms. Alicia, who liked Jeremy but still was not a big fan of our dating one another, started to probe into our relationship.

"You feel like taking Brittany to get her some ice cream? I'll foot the bill."

"I may as well. I don't have anything else to do."

"Where's that so-called boyfriend of yours?"

"His dad won't let him out of the house."

"Not even to come visit you?"

"No ma'am, he might get trapped by the media and say something his father doesn't want him to say."

"Does he have a say in any of this?"

"Not really. His father guards him twenty-four hours a day. He doesn't want him to do anything. He doesn't even want him to date me." Ms. Alicia looked at me in a strange way and I knew I had said too much. "Oops!"

"What do you mean he doesn't want Jeremy to date you? Who the hell is he supposed to be that he can't date you?"

"He's just very protective of him, that's all."

"Why does he have to protect him from you?"

"Not just me, everybody. People are trying to get next to him, so they can get whatever they can from him."

"Yeah, but that's not you," Ms. Alicia looked at me, "is it?"

"No ma'am. I couldn't care less about him playing basketball."

"And I don't know who his father thinks he is to even suggest that you are after that boy because he can put a freakin' ball through a hoop!"

"I don't think it's anything personal, Ms. Alicia. I think Mr. Winston doesn't want Jeremy to date anybody, no matter who the girl is."

"He should consider himself damn lucky to have you as his girlfriend."

I didn't respond because she was talking herself into a state of frenzy, and she would only turn anything I said into a negative against Jeremy. She sat next to me and helped me fold a few clothes and then started talking to herself again. I wanted to go to the basement and get Dr. Forrester before she was too far gone because when she got fired up like that, there was no stopping her.

"That man has no right to try to say that you are not good enough for that big-headed boy!" Ms. Alicia folded a few more clothes and then fussed again. "Like he's all that and you're noth-ing! I wish he would say something like that where I could hear it. I'll be right back."

Ms. Alicia fussed all the way upstairs. I did not open my mouth. I could hear her fussing to herself through the ceiling and then all the way back downstairs. When she came back into the room, she had changed her clothes and styled her hair.

"Do you know how to get to this boy's house?"

"Yes, ma'am."

"Come on, let's go!" Ms. Alicia stepped to the side and gestured for me to follow her.

"Where are we going, Ms. Alicia?"

"You know where we're going, come on!"

"Please, Ms. Alicia, don't do this."

"You better come on here, girl, and quit playing with me!"

I stared at Ms. Alicia and then yelled at the top of my lungs, "Doc-tor For-res-terrrrr!"

Ms. Alicia put her hands on her hips and patted her right foot in one place. Dr. Forrester came running upstairs. "What's the matter?"

"You have to help me, Dr. Forrester. Ms. Alicia is going crazy!"

"What's going on?" Dr. Forrester looked back and forth at Ms. Alicia and me.

"Her boyfriend's father thinks his son is too good for her. That's what's going on."

"Is that it?"

"Is that it?" Ms. Alicia snapped. "Did you hear what I said?"

"You have me missing the Final Four for that? The game is on!"

"So that game is more important than Shante, Johnny?"

"No, you know that's not what I'm saying. I just wanna watch my game."

"Do you not understand that we have a crisis here?"

"What is the crisis, Alicia? They're kids, let them be kids and stay out of their affairs! And who cares what Jeremy's father thinks?"

"I do."

"Okay fine, but I'm going back downstairs."

"Dr. Forrester!" I tried to stop him before he went back to his game.

"Yes, Butterfly?"

"Ms. Alicia wants to make me go to Jeremy's house, so that she can tell his father off."

"I don't want to tell the man off. I just want to ask him what the hell is his problem."

"Don't embarrass that girl like that, Alicia."

"Why should she be embarrassed? I'm just going to talk to the man, one adult to another."

"No she's not, Dr. Forrester. She's going to make a big scene. She's going to gouge his eye out or something."

"Stop being so dramatic, Shante." Ms. Alicia pointed her finger at me.

"Sweetheart, will you please stay away from those people?"

"Okay."

"You promise?"

"I said okay."

"Let me see your fingers?"

Ms. Alicia pulled her hands from behind her back and showed Dr. Forrester her hands. "See."

"Okay, now you ladies play fair and stop fighting over boys. I'm going to go watch my game now. Unless it's a fire, or somebody is dying or dead, do not call me. I repeat, *do not* call me. Enjoy the rest of your evening, ladies."

Ms. Alicia licked her tongue out at me as Dr. Forrester went back to the basement. We started folding clothes again and then Ms. Alicia went upstairs and asked Pa-Pa to watch Brit while Dr. Forrester watched the game. The next thing I knew she was pulling me out of the door by my arm.

"Come on, girl."

"But you promised Dr. Forrester you weren't going to go over there."

"Yeah, but I had my toes crossed. Hurry up! Let's go before he comes up here for a snack! Move it! Move it! Move it!"

Ms. Alicia fussed all the way to Jeremy's house. I texted him to see if he was at home. He was, and I gave him a heads-up that we were on our way. Unfortunately, he told me that his father was there, too. I was so nervous I could not think straight. I tried to talk to Ms. Alicia out of it, but she wasn't having it.

When we pulled up, there were a few television and newspaper reporters posted in front of their home. We found a place to park and then walked to Jeremy's door, but before we could answer, Jeremy snatched the door open.

"Hi, Mrs. Forrester," Jeremy looked at me, "Hey, Bae. I mean, Shante."

"Hi, Jeremy, is your father home?"

"Yes, ma'am, come in."

Jeremy showed us to their den and we waited for Mr. Winston. Mrs. Winston was gone. Too bad; I would have much rather preferred her. Ms. Alicia looked around the room for something negative to point out and she found it.

"Um." Ms. Alicia pointed at a piece of African art. "I wonder how much that old ugly thang cost right there."

"Ms. Alicia, shush."

"Don't shush me, girl!"

"You're talking too loud, though."

"I'm talking loud for a reason. I want these people to hear me."

"When Mr. Winston comes in, can you please be nice, Ms. Alicia?"

"If he's nice to me, I'll be nice to him."

"At least try to give him a chance…"

Mr. Winston walked into their den with Jeremy right in his foot tracks. "May I help you?"

"I hope so."

"I, um, my daughter seems to think that you have a problem with her dating your son. And if that is true, I would like to know why."

"It's nothing personal. My son is not your average eighteen-year-old and…"

"And neither is my daughter!" Ms. Alicia interrupted.

"I never said she was." Mr. Winston looked at Jeremy and then looked back at us. "But my son is my responsibility and I have to do everything I can as his father to protect him."

"And what exactly are you protecting him from, Mr. Winston?"

"From the world, Mrs. Forrester."

"You can rest assure that there is nothing about Shante that you have to protect him from."

"Like I said, it's nothing personal. In a perfect world I would like to think that everybody we meet had good intentions for my son, but that's not the reality of his life. People want his spotlight. People want his abilities. People want his money…"

Ms. Alicia stood up and interrupted Mr. Winston again. "Wait a minute! The last thing Shante needs from Jeremy is money! If we don't have anything else, we have plenty of that, Mr. Winston!"

"Ms. Alicia?" I whispered and gently held her hand to try to calm her down.

"I'm sorry you're offended. But I have to do what I have to do to protect my son."

"And I'm sorry, too. I'm sorry that a grown man can get so caught up in the fantastic world of the NBA that he doesn't care if he hurts a young girl's feelings."

"It doesn't seem like Shante is hurt at all. You seem to be the only one upset about this."

"Just because she's not saying it, it doesn't mean that she's not feeling it."

And Ms. Alicia was right. I did not like it any more than she did. But for the sake of keeping the peace with Jeremy, I ignored it.

"I think we've said all we need to say, Mrs. Forrester. I'm missing a very important game, which could have implications on my son's collegiate future."

"Let me tell you something, Mr. Winston…"

"Mrs. Forrester?" Jeremy interrupted. "May I say something, please?"

As much as Ms. Alicia wanted to keep fussing, she let Jeremy speak. "Go ahead."

"Dad, you know I have mad respect for you. And I never talk back to you or anything. But this time, I have to tell you, I think you're wrong."

Damn! My boy was becoming a man! Ms. Alicia smiled and her opinion of Jeremy skyrocketed.

"What did you say?"

"I said I think you're wrong this time, Dad. You judged Shante and you know nothing about her. You don't know that she is the reason why I'm passing history. She tells me to study when I don't feel like it. She is the one that I call for advice when a million reporters are trying to get at me. I hope I say this the right way." Jeremy stood eye to eye with his dad. "Look, Dad, as your son, I understand every single thing you have ever done for me as my father. But as my father, you have to understand that you're not going to be able to do every single thing for me. Does that make sense?"

"It makes plenty of sense to me," Ms. Alicia said sarcastically.

Mr. Winston rolled his eyes at Ms. Alicia and then sighed. Jeremy sat next to me on the couch and held my hand.

"I love playing basketball, Dad. I love practice. I love the games.

I'll even be honest and say I love the attention that comes with it." Jeremy clutched my hand. "But I also love Shante. I know you grown people think we're too young to know what love really is, and maybe we are, but I know how I feel about her right now today. And today is all that matters to me."

"You see, son, that's why you need me to direct you because of that type of thinking."

Mrs. Winston walked into the den carrying some bags and looked at everybody in the room trying to figure out what the hell was going on.

"Did I interrupt something?"

"No, sweetheart, we're about to wrap this meeting up. The Forresters were just leaving."

"The Forresters?" Mrs. Winston shook Ms. Alicia's hand. "Are you Shante's guardian?"

"Yes I am. I'm Alicia Forrester."

"Wait a minute, you look familiar. What's your maiden name?"

"Murray. Alicia Murray."

"Did you happen to attend Spelman?"

"Hold on, please tell me you are not Stephanie Ballard?"

"*Yes I am!*" Mrs. Winston screamed.

"*Oh my God!*" Ms. Alicia yelled back. "*Stephanie!*"

Ms. Alicia and Mrs. Winston started jumping up and down and hugging each other. They were screaming so loudly we covered our ears. How do you go from perfect strangers to acting like long-lost friends? I guess I answered my own question, huh?

"Baby," Ms. Winston shouted, "Alicia is my sorority sister from when we were at Spelman!"

"Oh, damn," Mr. Winston growled as he lit a cigar.

Ms. Alicia was a part of a sorority, Alpha Kappa Alpha, AKA, for short. It seemed like she was always running into one of her sorority sisters everywhere we went. Normally, I would have to wait in agony for her to relive her college days before we could get away, but this time, I was willing to wait all day and all night if I had to.

"For real?" Jeremy nudged his shoulders. "Wow!"

"Girl, sit down and tell me what you've been doing with yourself, Alicia."

"I'm married. I have two girls, Shante and Brit, not through the traditional way, but they're mine just the same. And I don't have to ask you what you've been doing. I know all about ol' Jeremy over there. I'm so proud of him."

I said to myself, *Oh you are?*

Mr. Winston shook his head and walked out of the room. Jeremy grabbed my hand and gave me a quick tour of their house. They had a nice house, but it was not as big as Uncle Mike's. Uncle Mike's house was huge, for real!

Jeremy and I finished watching the rest of the first game of the Final Four and then we watched the entire second game uninterrupted. I really didn't care who won. I was cheering for whoever Jeremy was cheering for. His cell phone rang or he was texted nonstop the entire time I was there. He ignored them, but I could hear his dad's loud mouth talking to reporters, friends and everybody who called, throughout both games. That dude was like, making promises to this school, and then making the same promise to that school. All the while, Jeremy was sitting and listening.

"Don't you want to make some decisions about your own life, Jeremy?"

"I do. That's why you're here now."

"But what about your career?"

"What about it?"

"It seems like your dad makes all the decisions."

"Basically, he does."

"Why? Why can't you make some of the decisions about what you want to do?"

"I make the decisions I need to make. My dad has choreo-graphed my career from the time I was five years old and that's why I'm in the position I'm in today. If it wasn't for him, I'd just be another tall kid."

"No, you have talent."

"You think that's all that it takes is talent? I'm down here because I made a bonehead move and hung out with some guys I had no business hanging out with. They got in some trouble and I was guilty by association."

"What kind of trouble?"

JEREMY'S STORY:

"One night I was walking down the street with four guys from my old neighborhood and we stopped by a liquor store. My friend, Devron, and I stayed outside and my other friends, Bill, Derrick and DeAndre went inside to hustle these older guys into buying us some liquor. While we were standing outside, they were inside robbing the store. They pulled a gun on the cashier and then he pulled one on them and then they just started shooting. We heard the gunshots and then they came out of the store running. When they came out running, hell, I didn't know what was up, so I ran, like everybody else. By the time my friend Devron figured out what was going on, it was too late. The cashier shot him in the back. Now he's paralyzed for the rest of his life, and for what? Nothing!

"The next day, the police came knocking on my door saying one of the witnesses fingered me. It wasn't that hard. I'm seven feet tall running down the street like a runaway slave. I was arrested and charged with armed robbery. I had nothing to do with the robbery, though. I didn't even know they were robbing the store.

"My dad made some moves and the charges against me were dropped. My father knew he had to get me out of New York, so he talked it over with my mom, and she suggested we move down here. The very next day after my fall semester was over, we were packed and on our way to Atlanta."
END JEREMY'S STORY.

"My dad didn't have to do all that for me, but he did because he loves me and he wants what's best for me. He's a hard-ass, and sometimes he comes off as insensitive, but he has invested a lot into my life. Not just with basketball, but with my making sure I stay on the right track. He doesn't want to see me end up another statistic like a lot of those fools in prison."

"My dad is in prison, but he's not a fool!"

"Oh, here we go." Jeremy hugged me. "I wasn't talking about your dad, Butterfly. I don't even know your dad."

"You better watch your mouth, boy!"

"Man, look, I said I wasn't talking about your dad."

"You need to be worried about being more in charge of your own life."

"Okay, Yoko Ono, this is what happened to John Lennon and the Beatles. I'm through discussing my dad."

"So are you telling me to be quiet?"

"Nope, I would never disrespect you like that," Jeremy paused momentarily, "I'm telling you to stop talking."

"Okay, Jeremy!"

I pushed Jeremy back on the bed and then he pulled me on top of him.

"Oh, my mom convinced my dad to let me go to the prom. You wanna go?"

"Hell naw!" I joked.

"What?" Jeremy tickled me.

"I'm kidding! I'll go! I'll go! I hate being tickled!"

His tickling turned to kissing. I slid between his thighs and I could feel his erect stick pressing against me. His big shorts made everything loose, so I started rubbing his legs. We stopped wrestling and began to grind on each other. I raised my head and kissed him on his chest. He turned his head to the side and I kissed his neck slowly. He was moaning louder than I was.

As I kissed his neck, I rubbed his thigh, inching my hand closer and closer to his stick. I grabbed the base and then slowly caressed up and down outside of his shorts. I reached beneath his shorts, so that I could feel the real thing. He opened his legs and I had easy access.

I pulled his stick out of his shorts and then held it in my hand. He was moaning as if we were really having sex. I was like, this dude must be a virgin, for real! His eyes were closed tight and it sounded like he could not breathe. The faster I pumped his stick, the louder he moaned and the faster he moved his hips. He grabbed my head and stuck his tongue in my mouth. We kissed at almost every opportunity we could, but he had never kissed me that aggressively.

Although my hands were getting tired, he seemed to enjoy what I was doing, so I kept right on pumping and he kept right on moaning. His legs began to shake and his stick really got hard. The next thing I knew, a stream of white semen shot from the head of his stick and squirted everywhere, then another stream, and another stream and another stream.

"Shit!" Jeremy pulled me to him and bit into my shoulder blade.

I let go of Jeremy's stick and moved the hell away from him. "Ouch, Jeremy! You bit me!"

"I'm sorry, you all right?"

I pulled my shirt from my shoulder and looked. "You put a mark on me!"

"I'm sorry, Butterfly, but that felt good. You want me to do you?"

"I'm only going to do something like that if you promise that you love me unconditionally."

"Why do I have to say that?"

"Because if I let you touch me down there, I have to know that you are mine unconditionally."

"Okay then, yeah."

"Yeah what?"

"Yeah, I love you unconditionally."

"Okay." I leaned and then sat back up. "What if we get caught?"

"By who? Your mom and my mom are too busy catching up with each other to be worried about us. And my dad, well, you hear my dad. He's too busy trying to be Jerry Maguire."

"Okay. What do you want me to do, Jeremy?"

"Lay back."

"Okay." I leaned back.

Jeremy unzipped my pants and slid his hand into my pants. Just the touch of his hand made me moist. He was lying on his right side, with his left hand in my pants. He raised my shirt and moved my bra out of the way. He lowered his head and kissed my nipples left to right. Then I realized why he was moaning so loudly when I touched him. That shit felt good!

He kept sucking my breasts and sliding his finger closer to my vagina. Even though my pants were unzipped, it was still a tight fit for his hand. He only had room to move his fingers. He was trying to inch closer, but I put my hands on top of his and stopped him. I would let him play with my clit, stop him, and then let him do it again. He kept trying to move his fingers lower, but I kept moving his hand back up to my clit. The faster I moved his hand, the greater the sensation. I moved my hips down into the bed and then lifted them up and grinded on his hands. Wow!

"Oh baby, that feels so good."

"You like that?"

"Keep doing it like that."

"Like that?"

"Stop talking and go faster!"

"Oh, okay."

I could feel my orgasm approaching and seemed like I was about to explode. "Oh Jeremy! Oh, Jeremy! Oh Jeremy!"

I wanted to say more than that, but my mind could not think right. All that I was focused on was the pleasure of having something other than my hand between my thighs.

"Oh Jeremy, I'm coming, baby!" I screeched out a long moan.

I pulled Jeremy on top of me and I bit the shit out of his chest to muffle the sound of my screams. Having Jeremy's body on top of me only intensified the sensation. It felt so good I wanted to cry. But as soon as he moved his hand and climbed on top of me, the sensation went away as well. Damn! I still, had never experienced an orgasm!

"Oh my goodness! That felt good." I looked at Jeremy and he was sitting with his mouth wide open. "What's wrong with you?"

"You bit me like that on purpose."

"I didn't bite you hard, did I?"

"Look at this?" He showed me the mark on his chest. "It looks like I've been bitten by a damn vampire, Butterfly."

"You bit me!"

"But I didn't mean to bite you, though."

"I didn't mean to bite you, either."

"Damn! Ah, that hurts."

"Stop acting like a baby boy."

"Man, my chest hurts." Jeremy rubbed his chest in the same spot.

"Stop it!" I smacked Jeremy's hand down.

"Jeremy?" Mrs. Winston knocked on the door.

"Damn! Zip your pants up!" Jeremy pulled up his shorts and tied them. He jumped from his couch and ran to his door and opened it. "Hurry up!"

I zipped my pants and sat up really quick as if we had done nothing. I tried to straighten my hair with my hands, so it would not look like I had been lying down. Mrs. Winston told me Ms. Alicia was waiting for me downstairs. Jeremy walked me downstairs and then to our car. We said our good-byes and Ms. Alicia made me drive home.

Chapter Thirteen

"I hope that all you and that boy did was kissed."

"Kissed? We didn't do anything but talk."

"Are you sure about that?"

I knew she was up to something, but I did not have time to try to figure it out, so I said the first thing that came to my mind.

"Yes, I'm sure we didn't do anything but talk."

"Okay, so why is that sock hanging out of the back of your shirt?"

"What?" I looked in the rearview mirror as if I would have been able to see my back. "What are you talking about?"

"Girl, you better keep your eyes on the road." Ms. Alicia pulled the sock from out of the back of my shirt and showed it to me. "And I'm talking about this."

"I don't know where that came from."

"It came from that ol' mannish Jeremy."

"I mean, I don't know how it got on my shirt like that."

"I know how! You were lying on your back, that's how."

"I wasn't on my back, Ms. Alicia."

"Girl, stop lying. I've been eighteen before. I know what goes on."

I laughed and then confessed, "Okay, we kissed, but that's it."

"That better be it."

"It is. I promise. I'm a virgin and he is, too."

"If you say so."

"Ms. Alicia, I want to ask you a question."

"Okay."

"Am I too old for you and Dr. Forrester to adopt me?"

"I really don't know. We would have to check into that. Why do you ask?"

"Because I heard you refer to me as your daughter in the heat of the moment with Mr. Winston. I want to make it legitimate. I want to be able to say that you and Dr. Forrester are my real parents."

"I'm flattered, but what about your dad? He's pretty close to Johnny and I don't know if they would be comfortable with that."

"My dad is going to always be my dad and no one will ever take his place. But although he may always be my dad, he may not always be there. I know you, Bri, Pa-Pa and Dr. Forrester, you will always be there."

"As far as I'm concerned, you're already my daughter. But I would love nothing more than to officially adopt you. Talk to your dad and see how he feels about it and then we'll discuss our options."

"I'll do that tomorrow when I go see him."

When I went for my April visit, I was always overly excited to see my dad, but he was unusually excited to see me that day. He was so excited that I did not want to bring up the adoption situation. He knew there was something bothering me, so he asked.

"Look, what's wrong with my Butterfly?"

"I'm cool, Dad, I'm just tired."

"You're not tired. Something's wrong."

"Nothing's wrong."

"I know when there's something wrong with you, Butterfly, so tell me."

"I want to ask you something, but I really don't want to hurt your feelings."

"Hurt my feelings? This must be some heavy stuff."

"Very heavy, Dad."

"It must be important, so ask me."

"Okay, but I want you to know that no matter what happens, you're my father and no one will ever take your place."

"I know that."

"I also want you to know that Mr. and Mrs. Forrester don't have anything to do with this. I don't want you to think they put me up to this and then you end up getting mad at them for nothing. This is coming straight from me, okay?"

"Butterfly, if you don't stop saying okay, and tell me what's on your mind, I'm going to reach through this glass and spank your butt."

"Okay, Daddy. I want the Forresters to adopt me."

"Whoa! That is very heavy right there." Dad sat back and rubbed his head over and over.

I sat still and looked at him. He would raise his head and then drop his head back down. I knew it was really bothering him and I did not want him to hurt. He was already locked up; I did not want him to suffer any more than he had to.

"Don't worry about it, Dad. It was just a thought."

"No, no, no, I'm cool. That was just some heavy stuff."

"Don't worry about it, Dad."

"Look, stop telling me what to do! Okay?"

My father was hurt, but he wanted to do what he thought would make me happy. I was only making it worse by telling him to forget about it when he was trying to give me his approval.

"Okay, Daddy."

"Can I talk now?"

"Yes, sir."

"Okay. I don't know when I'm getting out and I can't do anything for you locked up in here, so if that will make you happy, I'm all in."

"Are you sure, Daddy? They will have all parental rights to me."

"What type of parental rights do I have now?" Dad joked.

"But Dad, I don't want to do this if it's going to hurt you."

"Butterfly, it doesn't matter who the law says is your father, or your mother, as long as we know, that's all that matters. If it was anybody else other than the doc, maybe I would. But I'm fine, baby."

"Thank you, Daddy. I love you."

"I love you, too, Butterfly." Dad put his hand over his heart and pointed to me.

At school, I had several offers for full-ride scholarships to the University of Michigan in Ann Arbor where Dr. Forrester had gone to undergrad and played football; Jackson State University in Jackson, Mississippi, I had never even been to the state of Mississippi in my life, but Uncle Mike went to undergrad there and he said it was a pretty good historically black school; Spelman College, Ms. Alicia went there and it was located in Atlanta, so that was a plus; Howard University, in Washington, D.C., another historically black college; and Yale University in New Haven, Connecticut. Uncle Mike was a Harvard grad-alum, so he despised the notion of me becoming a Yale Bulldog. We considered the curriculums, tuition and of course, the geographical locations. Out of all the schools on my list, when it came to the top two, they were the nearest and the farthest locations, Spelman College and Yale University.

My history teacher, Ms. Jamerson, became my mentor and after Dr. Forrester and Ms. Alicia filled out my financial aid information, I asked them if she could help me make the final decision.

Dr. Forrester did not have a problem with it, but you know Ms. Alicia had something to say. She did not like it, but she let me make my own decision. And I decided to go to Yale.

It was May, I had turned eighteen, I was getting ready for college, everything was going wonderfully, but then like always, the bottom fell out. One morning before class, I heard a horrible rumor about Jeremy. He denied it and initially I believed him. When I got to my Mr. Thompson's class, my girl, Asia, pulled me to the side and told me the same thing.

"Hey, Butterfly," Asia said, "your man is cheating on you."

"I don't listen to rumors, Asia. People are always trying to break us up."

"This is not just a rumor. I saw it with my own two eyes."

"How did you see it with your own two eyes?"

"Look!"

Asia pulled out her camera phone and showed me a video of Jeremy and a white girl on a desk kissing. Jeremy was standing, and she was sitting upright on the desk facing him. She was totally naked and Jeremy's pants were pulled down around his ankles. His shirt was lying on the floor next to the desk. He was inside of her and they were definitely having sex. Her legs were wrapped around his waist and she was moving back and forth. I could hear her moaning and calling his name.

My heart fell to my feet and I almost blacked out. I took the phone out of Asia's hand and leaned against the wall. The two of us watched it for a minute or two, and then Asia asked me a question.

"You don't know who that lady is, do you?"

"No, I can't see her face. She's too busy sticking her tongue down Jeremy's throat."

"Now look." Asia enlarged the shot and froze it.

"That's Ms. Jamerson!" I shouted.

I was literally sick. I ran out of the classroom and into the bath-room. I kneeled over the toilet and vomited. Asia and Jheri followed me and tried to console me.

"You okay?" Jheri asked.

"That was stupid! That niggah's basketball career is over!" Asia shouted. "And that white hoe is getting fired!"

While they were talking, I was sobbing. I could not understand a word they were saying. All that I could think about was, my boyfriend and my mentor were betraying me. How could some-thing like that happen?

"Butterfly?" Jheri lifted my head. "Don't let this shit get you caught up. You only got a few weeks left before you graduate. Our show is Saturday. Do what you have to do to make it through these next three weeks, girl."

Jheri was right. I was hurt. I was sick. I was mad as hell, but I could not afford to let my personal feelings interfere with the promises I had made to so many people. My girls helped me stand up and I went back to class. I still cried, but I did what I had to do.

Ms. Alicia had received the word by the time I got home from school. She was waiting for me to walk through the door. Before I could get both feet in, she went at it.

"I heard about your so-called boyfriend."

"He's not my boyfriend anymore."

"Come sit down, baby." Ms. Alicia patted the spot next to her.

I dropped my book bag right there in the foyer, which was nor-mally a no-no, but on that day, Ms. Alicia understood what I was going through and let me get away with it. I sat next to her on the couch and she put her arms around me.

"Are you okay?"

"No!"

I burst into tears and put my head in Ms. Alicia's lap.

"Don't worry, baby, it's going to be all right."

"Why would he do this to me? Why would he want to hurt me like this?" I cried so hard my face was covered with tears.

"It's all a part of life, sweetheart. You have so much to look forward to. It hurts now, but it will be okay, trust me."

Ding-dong. The doorbell rang and Ms. Alicia went to answer it.

"That's your ex-boyfriend right there."

"*No!* Please, I don't want to talk to him."

"I know you don't, dear, and you don't have to. But you deserve the truth and you're going to get it."

"Please, I can't take looking at his stupid face right now, Ms. Alicia."

"I know how you feel, believe me. I've been there many times, but the sooner you deal with it, the sooner you'll get over it."

Ding-dong. Ms. Alicia answered the door and she came back with Jeremy, and Mr. and Mrs. Winston.

"Good evening," Mr. Winston said.

"Good evening."

"Hey, Alicia, I am so sorry about all of this nonsense."

"It's not your fault, Stephanie." Ms. Alicia looked at Jeremy.

"Say what you need to say, boy!" Mr. Winston nudged Jeremy.

"Shante, Mrs. Forrester, I want to apologize to both of you for my behavior and embarrassing you the way I did. I...I...I know I hurt you, Butterfly, and I know what I'm about to say is not going to make a difference, but the only reason I touched Ms. Jamerson was because she said if I didn't, I wouldn't graduate. I needed that class. I have to graduate, Shante!"

"I saw the video, Jeremy! You looked like you were enjoying yourself to me."

"Is that true, Stephanie?" Ms. Alicia asked. "Did that teacher blackmail Jeremy?"

"Yes, she admitted to it."

"And what are they going to do about it?"

"She's been arrested for misdemeanor charges, but since Jeremy is eighteen and is old enough for consensual relations, the additional charges may not stick."

"Shante?" Mr. Winston said. "For what it's worth, my knuckle-headed son does not deserve a girl like you. I think you're a good girl and if I've ever said anything to suggest anything other than that, I sincerely apologize."

Mr. Winston's apology made me feel much better and throughout my pain, I managed a brief smile. "Thank you, Mr. Winston."

"We just wanted to bring Jeremy over to apologize and let you know all of the details involved, Alicia."

"I appreciate that, Stephanie."

"I hope this doesn't have negative repercussions toward our friendship, Alicia."

"It won't. We're fine. You'll still love your son. I'll still love my daughter and we'll let them figure out how to resolve their situation on their own."

"You're right." Mrs. Winston hugged me. "I'm sorry for all of this, sweetheart. You take care of yourself."

The Winstons left and I cradled myself in Ms. Alicia's arms and cried myself to sleep. She did not offer any more advice. She did not try to get me to talk. She just held me in her arms like a mother, and let me cry.

We often criticized Ms. Alicia for being so dramatically suspicious. But her suspicious nature caused her to check on my college registration paperwork for all of the colleges on my list. It turned out that Ms. Jamerson had been lying the entire time. She never sent off any of my paperwork to any of the schools of my choice. Consequently, it was too late for me to enroll in Yale University in the fall. I felt like a double fool if there is such a thing. Not only did she have sex with my boyfriend, she was so jealous of our relationship, she sabotaged my opportunity to go to college. Luckily, Ms. Alicia being Ms. Alicia, she had sent in all the information I needed for Spelman College behind my back, and not only was I accepted for the fall, I had a four-year academic scholarship!

Jeremy called every hour on the hour trying to get me to talk, but I had nothing to say to him. At school, Bri, Asia, Jheri and Valencia were my bodyguards. They would not let him get close to me. I had to concentrate on our show and that was where I put all of my focus. Everything my drama class had worked on for the entire year was coming down to one day.

The night of the show, I heard a commotion backstage. I ran to see what was going on and I could hear people arguing.

"Man, I wish you would put your hands on me. You'll be pulling back elbows!"

I stopped in my tracks and smiled. "I should have known."

"What's up, my niggah?"

"Girl, you can't talk like that around here."

"These fools trying to tell me I'm not supposed to be back here. I said that's my niggah!"

"So when you get out, Janae?"

"Today!"

"What's up, Jacqua? I haven't seen you in a while." Jacqua had her arm locked inside of Janae's arm.

"Girl, I been hitting them damn books. I'm going to Spelman next fall."

"Me, too."

"That's what's up right there."

"Forget all that school talk. I heard you bagged you a NBA prospect."

"Naw, that's a wrap. We through."

"You don't need that niggah no way."

"Look, the show's about to start in a minute, so I got to run. I have to make sure my people are where they're supposed to be."

"Damn, you the director?"

"No, I'm the producer."

"Oh, okay. I don't know what that mean, but if you're bigger than the director, all I can say is, my niggah!" Janae gave me a fist pound. "Oh, one more thing, though, I know you had to get with Toya over that bullshit, and I ain't mad at you, but she really wanted to come tonight to support you, so I brought her. That's why I came back here to give you a heads-up and shoot you some love."

"That's the past. Tell her I want to holler at her after the show, so we can squash this, for real."

"That's what's up right there."

"I got to go, y'all. See y'all after the show."

"A'ight, my niggah!"

The show went off without a hitch. During the performance, we had great reactions from the audience. It was a huge success. I spoke to my friends after the show, and I apologized to Toya for what had happened between us. She accepted my apology, and then apologized to me again for causing so many damn problems. I was especially happy when I saw Keisha and her date, her stepfather. I had to eat dinner with my family that night, so I promised my girls I would meet up with them the next day to celebrate Janae being released from juvie.

Everybody was there but Keisha. I thought Toya was going to pick her up, and Toya thought I was going to pick her up, so she was left out. I was still going to go get her anyway, but we were way in Conyers at Stonecrest Mall and Keisha didn't want me to drive all the way back to Decatur to pick her up.

That night I spoke with Keisha and she was very upset. Her mother decided that she did not want to work on their relationship anymore. She was moving out of state with the schoolteacher. That meant she was going to have to move in with her father. She was devastated! Throughout the night, we would hang up, she would try to contact her stepdad, he would not answer, and then she would call me again. We repeated that cycle all night long. Keisha thought that if she could talk her stepdad into coming back home or let her come live with him, everything would be fine. I talked to her until it was almost time for me to go to school. Eventually, I got her to calm down and she told me to go to school and not to worry about her.

After school, I went directly to her house to find out if she had reached her stepdad. I knocked a couple of times and then on one of the knocks, the door came open. I could hear Keisha's music blaring from upstairs. I walked up the stairs slowly and then for some reason, I had an eerie feeling. I picked up the pace and ran into Keisha's room. I burst through the door and there she was, hanging from the ceiling fan with a curtain wrapped around her neck, and a chair toppled on its side on the floor.

I screamed at the top of my lungs, "*Keishaaaaaaa!*"

I stood on the chair and snatched the curtain from the almost collapsed ceiling fan. I fell to the floor with Keisha in my arms. I called 9-1-1, and tried to get Keisha to open her eyes, but she wouldn't. When the medics arrived, they tried desperately to revive her, but eventually, they pronounced her dead on arrival.

I helped Mrs. Benson clean up Keisha's room. She put her personal items in a chest and locked them away. I could not believe that everything Keisha had in life was locked away in a small chest, everything but her diary. I slipped it into my pocket and I took it home with me. I read it as soon as I got home and I found out that Keisha only told me half of what that monster had done to her. Word by word, I read each painful page of my friend's horrible life. I did not mention the diary to any of the other girls in our clique. I had to tell someone and that someone was my mother.

Ms. Alicia and I had a long talk about Keisha's diary and her death. That is when I found out that Ms. Alicia had attempted suicide several times as well. She explained to me that was why she was so protective of me. She did not want me to suffer the way she'd suffered with men: the self-doubt, the constant need for approval, and the lack of self-worth, all of the typical symptoms that led to depression. I had issues with wanting to be loved, but not just from boys, from anybody.

Ms. Alicia read Keisha's diary and she cried. She could not believe that my friend was going through so much pain and abuse and no one around her, adult or child, could see it, or stop it. Once her tears stopped, she took the diary to Dr. Forrester to let him read it. He immediately arranged for me to talk to Mr. Robert at the police station.

Dr. Forrester, Ms. Alicia, and I sat in a small room with Mr. Robert and a lady detective named Ms. Sharp. They read some of the diary and were convinced that an investigation into Keisha's father would be launched.

"Did Keisha ever tell you anything about her father sexually abusing her?" Detective Sharp asked.

"Yes, ma'am. She came over for Thanksgiving and that was the first time she mentioned her father had touched her inappropriately."

"When you say 'inappropriately,' what specifically happened?"

"She told me her father started off just touching her. Then he made her make him ejaculate...and then he raped her."

"Did she use the word 'rape'?"

"Yes, ma'am. She described in detail everything he did to her. She was sleeping and he crawled under the blanket with her and held her down and had sex with her."

Ms. Alicia covered her mouth and left the room. "Excuse me, I have to go to the restroom."

Detective Sharp paused until Ms. Alicia was out of the room and then continued, "And she said there was definite penetration?"

"Yes, ma'am."

"Would you be willing to repeat this statement under oath?"

"Absolutely, Detective Sharp!" I could not wait to expose that bastard for killing my friend! "I'll do it right now if you want me to."

"You'll get your chance."

"So what do you think, Detective?" Mr. Robert said.

"Ms. Clemmons' story corroborates the diary. I will definitely launch an investigation and then we'll leave it up to the district attorney."

"Thanks for coming in, Shante. You did good. I'm proud of you."

"Thank you, Mr. Robert."

Keisha's funeral was two weeks before my graduation. I had never seen Keisha's father and I was looking forward to putting a face on the monster. I wanted to see what kind of man could possess such an evil spirit. I was happy to see Mr. and Mrs. Benson sitting together. They were making a serious attempt to mend their marriage. Too bad it took Keisha's death to bring them to their senses. Had they acted like adults earlier and tried to work their problems out, Keisha would still be alive!

Toya was sitting next to me, so I asked her if Keisha's father was in the church. She pointed him out to me sitting in the front row on the opposite side of the church. When I saw him, I automatically tried to slide to the floor. Fear consumed me. I was nervous and I felt like getting up and running out. But I could not do it. The man turned around to casually look behind him and I ducked. I got a good look at him and it was who I thought it was, Mr. Harry.

I was asked to speak prior to her funeral. I was Keisha's best friend and I had to, but I knew by doing that, I would also expose myself to Mr. Harry. When I got up to speak and he finally saw my face, I could tell that he was just as surprised to see me as I was to see him. I went on to tell everyone how much of a good girl Keisha was. How happy and vibrant she was. But I wanted to say was, how much she was tormented. How her father had turned that beautiful caterpillar into an ugly creature inside. How her father had made her believe that she was responsible for the many, many times he had raped her.

Keisha was a good girl, for real, and she did not deserve the life she had been given. The whole situation seemed surreal. It felt like an out-of-body experience. I could not believe my best friend was dead.

I knew it was crazy, but I stepped outside of the church where no one could see me and I dialed her cell phone just to hear her voice. *"Hi, this is Keisha. Obviously I can't come to the phone right now, so if you really want something, you know what to do. 'Cause if you don't leave a message I didn't get your call. Ha! Ha! Ha!"*

I played it over and over. Her loud, crazy laugh put a smile on my face. I tried to remember the funny and witty Keisha, but all that I could think about was her small, precious body hanging from that ceiling fan.

After the funeral, I let Jeremy come over to watch television and talk. I really needed his company. It was uncomfortable at first, but then we loosened up and had the discussion we did not want to have, but we needed to have.

"Are we still going to the prom? We haven't really talked, so I don't know."

"Probably, but not together, Jeremy."

"Oh, it's like that, huh?"

"Yeah, it's like that." I nodded repeatedly.

"Why not?"

"Do you really need for me to answer that question, Jeremy?"

"No, I know why not, but I'm saying, since we've already made plans, why not?"

"I don't know. People are going to think I'm a fool if I go up in there on your arm."

"Who cares what people think?"

"I care what people think!" I snapped. "I don't want people to think I'm some sucker who will take anything from you because you might go pro."

"I made a mistake. I embarrassed you. I embarrassed me, my family…"

"You've already given that speech, Jeremy. I'm immune to it."

"What I'm saying is, I know I was wrong, but I still love you, Butterfly. I try not to, but I can't help it. I love you."

"I love you, too. And maybe if I was another girl, I could forgive you for what you did, but I'm sorry, I can't. And I can't help that."

"I don't understand something, Butterfly."

"What don't you understand?"

"Why is it that you want me to love you unconditionally, but you don't want to love me unconditionally?"

"Our conditions are different."

"But when you say love unconditionally, that means there are no conditions, right?"

"Wrong."

"So no matter what I say or do, you're not going to take me back?"

"Uhn-uhn, I can't do it. I'll take you back as my friend, but not my boyfriend."

"You're just trying to be hard now, huh?"

"I'm not trying to be hard. I've just been through so much in my life, man. You just don't know, Jeremy." I put my hands on my forehead. "My best friend just died. I almost didn't get into college. I just want to have peace in my life. I just want some peace, man!"

"You're only eighteen years old, Butterfly."

"Yeah, but I feel like I've had a hundred years' worth of pain."

"How much pain could you have gone through at the age of eighteen?"

I smiled and said very softly, "A lifetime."

I think when I said that, he got it. He held my hand and gave up trying to convince me into being in a relationship with him. I put my head on his shoulder and he became my friend. My first love was officially over. However, I did agree to go to the prom with him, but as a friend only.

Chapter Fourteen

On prom day, Ms. Alicia, Auntie Cynthia and Auntie Pam took me out for a day of pampering. Auntie Cynthia brought Bri with her, which I gladly appreciated to have someone remotely close to my age. We did the normal spa thing, feet and hands, facial and massage. The adults talked and Bri and I pretty much listened.

"I hear you have a scholarship to Spelman, Shante?" Auntie Pam asked.

"Yes, ma'am, thanks to my mom."

"Ah, she didn't do nothing," Auntie Pam joked. "Don't give her credit for your hard work."

"She don't have to give me anything. I'm proud of my Butterfly."

"You've never called me that before."

"And you've never called me Mom before."

"Oh-kay, here were go," Auntie Pam said. "We're here to have fun, not get all sensitive and crying all over the place."

"Girl, you know I'll cry on you in a minute."

"I know. I'm not in a crying mood right now. I'm in a fun mood, so leave the tears at the house, why don't you?"

"I know her." Ms. Alicia pointed to a woman standing across the room.

"Who is she?" Auntie Cynthia asked.

"I went to college with her! I hear she's this big Hollywood agent now."

"Alicia thinks she knows everybody, Cynthia," Auntie Pam joked.

"She's right, though. I just saw her on TMZ," Auntie Cynthia said.

"Yeah, that's her! That's my girl." Ms. Alicia waved. "Erin?"

The lady looked in our direction and ignored us at first.

"I told you she didn't know that chick, Cynt."

"Shut up, Pam. I do know her." Ms. Alicia waved her over. "It's me, Alicia Murray. I got her in the damn business."

"Alicia Murray?" Ms. Erin clicked her high-heels over to our chairs. "Alicia Murray? Oh my God! How are you, girl?"

"I am wonderful! I see you on television all the time!"

"You do? That's fantastic! Do you still live here in Atlanta?"

"Yes, I'm married with two beautiful kids. My youngest daughter is not with me today, but here is my oldest. Her name is Shante."

"Hi, Shante." Ms. Erin shook my hand. "I'm Erin Philpot."

"Hi."

"And these are my friends, Pam, Cynthia and that is my niece, Brimone."

Ms. Erin shook everybody's hand. She was about five feet four inches tall. Her hair was long and wavy. She was mulatto, but her black features were definitely more dominant than her white features. Her nose was round, her lips were full, but her eyes were bluish gray. She had beautiful smooth skin and a high soft voice.

She told Ms. Alicia that she was in a hurry and she had to go. She had only stopped by the shop to check on a modeling prospect that turned out to be a no-go. She said good-bye to all of us and then clicked her high-heel shoes all of the way out of the door.

"She's a little debutante, isn't she?" Auntie Pam mimicked Ms. Erin's walk.

"Shh! Here she comes again!" Auntie Cynthia said quickly.

Ms. Erin walked in front of us and snapped her fingers. "Stand up!"

We did not know who she was talking to, and she was so authoritative with her voice that all of us stood up at once, even Auntie Pam.

"Not all of you," Ms. Erin pointed to me, "You!"

Everybody sat down but me. We were all confused. Ms. Erin walked around me in a circle, moving my body in certain directions.

"I am the proprietor of the Philpot Modeling Agency. And today might be the luckiest day of your life. Now walk!"

I looked at Ms. Alicia. "You heard her, walk!"

I walked to the door and then walked back.

"Put your hands on your hips and twist those hips from side to side."

I put my hands on my hips and tried to twist my hips.

"Harder!"

I walked harder.

"Faster!"

I walked faster. Ms. Erin put her hands on her lips as if she was contemplating a very serious thought.

"Oh, the camera is going to love you, girlie!" Ms. Erin grabbed both of Ms. Alicia's hands. "Alicia, I have to have her!"

"Um, what does that mean exactly, Erin?"

"That means I need to get her on the next plane to Los Angeles for an audition for the next season of *America the Beautiful.*"

"You're kidding, right?"

"When have you ever known me to kid about modeling?"

"Don't play with me, Erin. You know how I feel about the business. You really think she has the potential to become a model?"

"She has the looks. All that she needs is the attitude. And I have enough attitude for the both of us."

"Now that's something you don't have to convince me of," Auntie Pam joked.

"Be quiet, Pam," Ms. Alicia whispered.

"So, what's it going to be, Alicia?"

"I just don't want her to be disappointed."

"It's just an audition for the show."

"What do you think, Butterfly?"

"I don't know what to say. I'm still in shock."

"You better say yes, if you're interested, because Erin doesn't have all day."

"Yes!" Bri shouted.

"Bri?" Auntie Cynthia gestured for Bri to be quiet.

"I mean, of course! I'm just in shock right now."

"When can you get her on a plane? I need her in L.A., ASAP!"

"She has the prom tonight, and she graduates next Thursday. We can be on a plane Friday morning."

"Friday is too late. I have to have her audition no later than Wednesday."

"Do you have any makeup exams or anything, sweetheart?"

"No, ma'am. I'm done for the year. I'm ready to walk!"

Ms. Alicia looked back and forth at me and Ms. Erin. Ms. Erin pointed to her watch. "I'm late! I'm late!"

"I know there are no guarantees in this business, but how sure are you that she will at least have a shot at this?"

"This is her shot right here! I can guarantee that she will get an audition and the rest is up to her."

"I'll book us a flight for tomorrow!"

"Excuse me, Mom. But I have to visit my dad tomorrow, remember?"

"But this is a once-in-a-lifetime opportunity, hon. I'm sure your dad would not want you to miss out on it."

"I promised him."

"Alicia, let her visit her dad. You can fly out Monday. I'll have my assistant arrange your flight and send you the itinerary. We'll cover your hotel, flight, well, all your accommodations."

"You don't have to do that, Erin."

"I know I don't. Let's just call it an investment."

"Okay."

"And what was the name you called her?"

"Shante?"

"No," Ms. Erin handed me her business card, "You called her something else."

"Butterfly?" I suggested.

"Yes, that's it! Do people call you that?"

"Yes, ma'am."

"Stop with the 'ma'am.' You're about to enter a world where eighteen is a full-grown woman. People will be saying 'yes, ma'am' to you." Ms. Erin chuckled. "Butterfly? I like that. From now on, Butterfly is your name! I'm sorry, people, but I reeeeeally have to catch my plane, so have a good day all." Ms. Erin kissed Ms. Alicia on both of her cheeks and then strutted out of the salon.

"Wow! What the hell just happened in here?" Auntie Pam asked. "One minute we're getting our toes done, the next minute this chick is on her way to L.A. for a damn modeling audition!"

"Our little Butterfly is about to fly away, that's what just happened." Ms. Alicia clapped her hands.

"How do you feel, Shante? I mean, Ms. Butterfly."

"I don't know how I feel, Auntie Cynthia. It seems like a dream and I'm waiting for somebody to wake me up. Stuff like this just doesn't happen to me."

"Well, it has happened and I could not be happier for you," Ms. Alicia said.

"Oh, I almost forgot, Mom."

"Forgot what?"

"I have to meet with Mrs. Gary on Monday morning."

"About what?"

"I don't know, she didn't tell me. She just said it was very important."

"What time?"

"Eight o' clock."

"That's fine. That's only five in the morning, L.A. time. You can do that meeting and then we can get on the next available plane."

"There's still one more thing."

"Now what's the matter?"

"I'm scared to fly."

"Have you ever flown before?"

"No, ma'am."

"Oh well."

"I have an idea, Auntie Alicia," Bri said.

"And what's that?"

"I'm not afraid to fly. If I go with you, I can talk to Butterfly while we're flying to take her mind off of being in the air. It's a delicate situation and I could be a very valuable asset. Not to mention I won't eat much and I can sleep on the floor."

"Actually, I think that's a good idea. But your mom is not going to let you fly to California on such short notice."

"I don't know, Alicia. She may consider it if I go with you." Auntie Cynthia chuckled.

"So everybody's trying to cash in on Butterfly's fame?" Ms. Alicia joked.

"Yup!" they answered in unison.

"I guess it won't hurt to ask."

"Wait a damn minute, if all of y'all going to L.A., I'm going, too!" Auntie Pam said.

That evening, everybody came over to our house to wait for

Jeremy to pick me up for the prom. I wore a long formal white gown. It was fitted until it got to my knees and flared outward. It had spaghetti straps with the back out. In my heels I was about six feet three inches tall. My hair had an Asian-style bang trim in the front and was completely straight and hanging down my back like the way Naomi Campbell wears hers.

Jeremy pulled up in a stretched SUV Hummer. My family and friends took a million pictures of us before we left. I could not believe how Ms. Alicia could not stop crying. I'd had a dream-come-true experience earlier that day with my audition. That night it was Ms. Alicia's turn to live out her dream as a doting mother. If you asked me, I think she was happier than me.

Jeremy and I had fun at the prom. He tried his best to convince me to go to a hotel with him afterward. He said he had already spent a lot of money on the room and if we did not go, it would have been a waste. I told him that he should not have been so prematurely optimistic to assume that we were going to have sex on our prom night. He claimed it was not about sex; he just wanted to have that last night together. I told him two words, "Niggah, please!"

He dropped me back off at home around two in the morning. Pa-Pa was waiting up for me. I was on my way upstairs when he called me into the kitchen. He asked me to turn in circles, so he could see my dress.

"Okay, good!" Pa-Pa said.

"You like my dress, Pa-Pa?"

"Yes, the dress is nice, but that's not what I'm looking for."

"What are you looking for?"

"I'm checking for wrinkles," Pa-Pa examined me thoroughly, "Okay, you good. I can tell by the few wrinkles that it ain't been off of you."

"Pa-Pa?"

"Don't Pa-Pa, me! I know what goes on, on prom night. Things ain't changed that much since I was a teenager. Y'all still do the same thing we did. Your young nasty asses just do more of it!"

"I don't do anything, Pa-Pa."

"If you do, I better not ever get wind of it."

"That's the last thing you have to worry about right now."

"Come here." Pa-Pa reached out his arms. I walked into Pa-Pa's arms and hugged him. "I heard about your audition for that television show."

"Yeah, that's crazy, Pa-Pa. I still don't believe it."

"I am so proud of you!" Pa-Pa hugged me again. "Don't get out there to Hollywood and forget about your people."

"Forget about you? I haven't even had an audition yet. I probably won't even make the cut."

"Don't worry, you will," Pa-Pa let out a long yawn, "It's past my bedtime. I was just up waiting on you because I might not catch you before you go see your daddy in the morning."

"Okay, Pa-Pa, let me put you in the bed."

I grabbed Pa-Pa's arm and we began to walk toward the stairs. "Put me in the bed? I'm a grown-ass man, girl. I don't need nobody to help me get in the bed."

"Shush! Come on, old man!"

I walked Pa-Pa to his room and then I went to bed. I am glad I had the opportunity to say good-bye to Pa-Pa one-on-one that night. I knew I would not get another chance before we left for Los Angeles. We were leaving first thing in the morning to go see my dad and would get back late Sunday evening. We were leaving early Monday morning because I had to meet with Mrs. Gary, and then we were heading straight to the airport from there.

Pa-Pa was not like other old people his age. He did not rise and fall with the sun. He stayed up late watching movies he had no business watching and was always the last one to get up in the morning. I am thankful for our special time together, even if it was at two o' clock in the morning.

During that time, my headaches continued and they began to come more frequently and more severe. Every time I thought about the night of the killings, my head seemed like it was about to burst. Whatever I was blocking in my subconscious was trying its best to break through.

Dr. Forrester finally concluded that the spells may have originally begun from the events that happened on the night of the killings. But he felt that they became more intense because of the recent discovery of my unknown mother. My brain was trying to force my mind to remember my biological mother and until I found something, some memory, to connect our pasts together, the spells would continue. In order to find that connection, I would need my father's help.

On our May visit to see my father, Ms. Alicia went with us to formally introduce herself to my dad. Normally, Dr. Forrester and I visited one at a time for privacy. That day, the three of us sat with Dad at the same time to try to find out what was going on in my head.

"Hi, Mr. Stone, my name is Alicia. I can never thank you enough for so many different things you have done for our family. And I want you to know that we see you as an extension of our family."

"It's a pleasure to meet you, Alicia. And I can't thank you enough for taking care of my Butterfly during my unfortunate incarceration. The doc has told me a lot about you."

"All good I hope."

"Of course."

"Hey, Daddy."

"Hey, baby, so what's first on the agenda?" Dad asked. "I'll let y'all go first because I've been sitting on some pretty heavy news myself."

"Dad, I need to know more about my mother."

"Why do you want to keep bringing up the past, Butterfly?"

"Because I need to know why that woman abandoned me."

Dad paused momentarily. "I never said you were 'abandoned.'"

"What?" I was totally surprised. "I just always assumed that..."

"Your mother did not abandon you, Butterfly."

"What do you mean, Daddy?"

"I don't want you to be mad at me, sweetheart. Not like this. Not when I'm behind these bars like this."

"Why would I be mad at you, Dad?"

"Because your mother did not abandon you." Dad looked at Ms. Alicia and Dr. Forrester and then looked back at me. "I took you from her."

"What do you mean, 'you took me from her'?"

"We were having problems and she threatened to take you from me and go back to Alabama where she was from, and I couldn't let her do that to us. You were the only meaningful thing in my life."

"So what are you saying, Dad?"

"Long story short, the day after your mother and I split up, I picked you up for a visit and I never took you back to her."

"So all of these years you've been lying to me?"

"No. All of these years I've been protecting you!"

"Keeping me away from my mother is not protecting me, Daddy!"

"You don't understand, Butterfly! She was..."

"Don't you call me that!" I snapped. "You lied to me!

"Baby, I had to! She was going to…"

"I'm ready to go, Dr. Forrester."

Dr. Forrester sat quietly and looked at my dad. Without even looking at me, he said, "No, Butterfly. That's not how we resolve issues in this family. I don't know why your father did what he did, but I know he loves you more than anything in this world. There's nothing he wouldn't do for your happiness."

"The doc's right, baby, you don't understand. Your mother was going to…"

All of a sudden, I felt the most intense pain I had ever experienced in all of the spells. My head felt like it was about to explode and I blacked out and collapsed. Usually, I would go back to the night of the killings, but that day it was total darkness. No images, no visions, absolutely nothing. I woke up in the prison's infirmary with Dr. Forrester on one side of me and Ms Alicia on the other.

"Glad you could join us." Ms. Alicia smiled and held my hand.

"What happened?"

"You had another one of those blackouts here at the prison."

"We're still in the prison?"

"Yes."

"Did my dad see what happened?"

"Yes."

"How is he?"

"He's fine."

"I didn't mean to act like that. I'm sorry."

"You didn't do anything wrong." Ms. Alicia ran her hands through my hair. "Just relax, the nurse said you're fine and we can take you home."

"Why do I keep doing this, Dr. Forrester?"

"I don't know, but we're going to figure it out. I promise you that."

They made me lie down for another thirty minutes and then I was allowed to leave the prison. I went straight to bed when we got home. I stared at the ceiling trying my best to focus on that night, that night when my life was turned upside down.

Because of my blackout, Ms. Alicia would not let me fly the next day, so we had to postpone the trip. Ms. Erin pulled some strings and worked it out with the show to let me send an audition video, and if they liked me, I could fly in on Friday. I felt sorry for Ms. Alicia because she was vicariously living out her life-long dream through me. She quickly put me in my place and let me know that being a model should've been my decision because I had to live my own life. She also told me that she would never jeopardize my health for any reason.

My blackout did not stop me from going to school on Monday. Ms. Alicia and I still met with Mrs. Gary for our meeting. We did not know what the meeting was about. We assumed it was about some kind of unpaid balance that I had accrued throughout the year. We could not have been more wrong.

"Good morning, Mrs. Forrester, Shante."

"Good morning, Mrs. Gary," I said nervously. I began to have negative thoughts about the meeting. My life had finally taken a turn for the better and now fate was making her appearance once again to let me know that no matter how far I thought I had come, she was always looming to snatch me back into my world of despair...

"I have wonderful news." Mrs. Gary smiled at me.

...*or maybe not.*

"Thank God." I sighed.

"Mrs. Forrester, I would like you to know that your daughter has been selected as Duluth Christian Academy's 2011 valedictorian!"

"You got to be kidding me?" I held my mouth wide open.

"My Butterfly is the class valedictorian?"

"Yes, she is. You seem surprised, Shante."

I could not answer. I just held my mouth wide open and stared at Mrs. Gary. This was even bigger than the modeling audition. The class valedictorian?

"Why me?"

"One, in terms of your grade-point average, you are rated the student with the highest academic rank of your entire graduating class. Two and three, you have exhibited great leadership and demonstrated the ability to follow directions as well."

"Thank you, Mrs. Gary."

"With that being said, you will be the speaker for the commencement ceremony on Thursday evening."

"Me?"

"Yes, you, my dear."

"I really haven't done public speaking before, except for in drama class. I don't know if I can do that."

"You have four days to practice."

"She'll be fine, Mrs. Gary."

"I'm sure she will." Mrs. Gary folded her hands on her desk. "That's all that I have. Thank you all for coming."

"Thank you, Mrs. Gary." Ms. Alicia shook Mrs. Gary's hand and we left.

I was feeling weird when we left Mrs. Gary's office. I had one of those feelings that something was about to happen. Of course, I suspected the worst. My life was going too well and it was time for reality to set in.

The day went by with no incident so I assumed my intuition was off track. As a matter of fact, it was a very good day. Auntie Cynthia and Auntie Pam came over to help Ms. Alicia with shooting my audition video for *America the Beautiful*. Of course that also meant Bri was there. She was like my assistant.

They hired a professional production company that shot videos for hip-hop artists. It was fun! We shot part of the video out at Lake Lanier, and the other part in the backyard. Ms. Alicia was a little buzz saw running all around, telling the professional production company what to do with their equipment.

She was showing me how to do a runway walk. That woman was throwing those hips all over the place. I tried my best, but my hips did not go the way I wanted them to go. The director wanted me to do sexy, but Ms. Alicia wanted me to do chic. They were battling all night long. The director complained to Ms. Alicia that she was interfering with his creativity, and Ms. Alicia fussed at him that she did not care about him complaining because she was paying him. They compromised between the two concepts, and ended up somewhere in the middle. In the final analysis, they were both very pleased with the finished product.

It was between three and four in the morning when we finished shooting. Ms. Alicia said I was a natural. A natural what, was my question. It was so late everybody just slept at our house that night. While the rest of us were sleeping, Ms. Alicia sent the video, via the Internet, so that Ms. Erin had could have it in front of her as soon as she arrived at her office that Wednesday morning. By the end of the day, she responded and told Ms. Alicia she had forwarded the video to the show's talent coordinator and they loved it! She booked our flight to Los Angeles for the first thing Friday morning.

I slept downstairs with Bri in the den so that Auntie Cynthia could sleep in my room. The older women woke up and fixed breakfast while Bri and I were still sleeping. I woke up to the smell of eggs and bacon and the doorbell chiming over and over.

Chapter Fifteen

"Who in the world is ringing my doorbell this time of the morning?" Ms. Alicia said as she walked to the door. I rolled on my belly where I could see her in the foyer. She peeked through the peephole and whispered, "Who the hell is this?"

"Why aren't you opening the door?" Auntie Cynthia asked. "Who is it?"

"I don't know." Ms. Alicia kept looking through the peephole trying to figure out if she knew the man or not.

Auntie Pam walked in front of Ms. Alicia with a frying a pan in her hand and unlocked the door. "Stop acting so damn scary and open up the door!"

"Pam?" the man said.

Auntie Pam's mouth dropped to the floor. A very angry expression came over her face and she snarled, "You son of a bitch!"

Although I heard what Auntie Pam had said, I was more focused on the man standing in our doorway. I ran to him and wrapped my arms around his neck. "*Daddy!*"

"Daddy?" Auntie Pam looked at me with her hand on her hips.

"Yeah, this is my dad." I held my dad's hand and pulled him into the house.

"Sorry, to impose on you folks so early in the morning, but I could not wait to see my Butterfly."

"I'm sorry, I did not know who you were, Mr. Stone. Come on in and have a seat," Ms. Alicia said.

Auntie Cynthia walked out of the kitchen and shook my dad's hand. "It's a pleasure to meet you, Mr. Stone. I'm Cynthia."

"The pleasure is all mine. And you can just call me Stone."

"Stone it is."

"And Dad, this is Auntie Pam. But apparently you two have already met. She's part owner of Ms. Alicia's PR firm with Auntie Cynthia."

"Pam?"

My dad reached out his hand to shake Auntie Pam's hand, but she walked away and went back into the kitchen. It was an uncomfortable moment, but I was too excited that my dad was home to be concerned with that. I pulled him into the den to meet Bri.

"Wake up, girl!" I shook Bri until she woke up. "I want you to meet my dad."

"Huh?"

"Get up and meet my dad."

"Your dad is here?" Bri sat up and rubbed her eyes. "Oh my God! I have to go put on some clothes!"

Bri darted upstairs with a comforter wrapped around her waist. My dad sat down and Ms. Alicia and Auntie Cynthia joined us. I asked my dad if he wanted something to drink and he said yes. I ran to the kitchen and found Auntie Pam sitting at the table crying.

I tried to ignore her because I was in a hurry to get back to my dad. But I just could not be that insensitive. I did not sit down, but I did stop on my way out of the kitchen to check on her.

"You okay, Auntie Pam?"

"Oh, yes, baby. I'm fine."

"You sure?"

"Yeah, I'm sure. Don't worry about me."

"Okay!" I headed for the door in a hurry, and I swear it hit me like a ton of bricks. I stopped dead in my tracks and took a deep breath. I dropped the glass of water I had in my hands and uncontrollably walked backward. I sat down and stared at Auntie Pam.

"You know, don't you?" Auntie Pam asked.

"Oh my God."

"Come here!" Auntie Pam and I reached for each other at the same time. "My baby! Oh, my baby!"

"This can't be happening!" I tried to stop my body from shaking, but I couldn't.

"I love you! I love you! I love you! I love you! I love you so much, baby!" Auntie Pam kept repeating.

Ms. Alicia walked into the kitchen and saw Auntie Pam and me, crying and hugging. She stood quietly for a minute. I guess she was trying to figure out how getting a glass of water for my dad could turn into the dramatic scene she was witnessing.

"What's going on in here?" Ms. Alicia asked.

"Go get Stone, please," Auntie Pam cried.

"Uh, okay." Ms. Alicia left and came back with my dad and Auntie Cynthia. Auntie Pam and I were still hugging.

"Can you sit down, please?" Auntie Pam asked my dad.

My dad sat down and Auntie Pam dropped in the chair facing him. Ms. Alicia and Ms. Cynthia were watching, but they did not know exactly what they were watching.

"Why?" Auntie Pam asked. "I just wanna know why?"

My dad paused, and for the first time in my life, I saw him cry. "You know why."

"Excuse me?" Ms. Alicia asked. "Why what?"

"This," Auntie Pam held my hand, "this is my baby."

Ms. Alicia sat on the floor. "Wait! Wait! Wait! Wait! Wait! Wait! Wait! What do you mean, she is your baby?"

"This man took my child from me and I have not laid eyes on my child since!" Auntie Pam stared at my dad with fire blazing in her eyes.

"What the hell is going on?" Ms. Alicia looked at my dad and Auntie Pam for answers.

"Like she said, I took Butterfly away." Dad turned his attention to me. "I took you away because when you were born, there was a decision we had to make, and I think you know what I'm talking about. Your mother wanted it one way; I wanted it another. I wanted you to live."

"And so did I!" Auntie Pam snapped. "That is my child!"

"I make no excuses. And I won't pretend that what I did was right, but I did what I had to do to protect my child. And if I had to do it all again…I would."

Nobody said anything for a moment. I was waiting for Auntie Pam to explode, but she didn't. She had every right to be pissed off, and she was, but the joy of seeing me, her own flesh and blood child, superceded her anger for my dad. She didn't shout or scream.

"For seventeen years I have been yearning and crying for my child. I have been mean to so many people because of all of that pent-up anger. And I can't begin to tell you the many different ways I planned on hurting this man for stealing my child from me. But as much as I despise what has happened, I understand why he did what he did. Today, I am so happy and so relieved to know that this child is alive and healthy that I'm not concerned with vengeful thoughts. Nobody knows what this child has been through but Shante, Stone, and me. And despite everything that she has been through, she has literally turned herself into a magnificent young lady! I want to get to know you, Shante, and be a mother figure to you if you will allow me, but only in the current capacity. Alicia is your mother. The bond you two have established cannot, and should not, be broken." Auntie Pam put my hand in Ms. Alicia's hand and placed her hand on top of mine.

"Thank you, Auntie Pam," I said.

"You're welcome, dear."

"Dad?"

"Yes, Butterfly?"

"I love you."

"I love you, too."

I spent the remainder of the day reminiscing with Auntie Pam about her side of the family. She told me that she, too, was a foster care child and that a similar situation had occurred between her and her biological mother. They worked side by side for years but never knew they were mother and daughter until her mother passed away. We decided to keep my being Auntie Pam's child a secret between those who were in the kitchen that morning. It would be too complicated to have to explain to everybody. The aunt-niece relationship Auntie Pam and I had established was satisfactory for the both of us, and we agreed not to mention our mother-daughter relationship publically. I did meet her son, my little brother, Benjamin, but we were introduced as cousins. I felt sorry for Benjamin because if I was him, I would have wanted to know that I had a sister, but what could we do?

My dad was staying in a halfway house downtown near Auburn Avenue. The funny thing is, it was right across the street from the shelter where Janae was living. I stopped by to see both of them Wednesday night and killed two birds with one stone. Joke! Joke! Get it? My dad's name is Stone. Anyway, I visited Janae first and then I walked across the street to visit my dad. I stayed as long as I could and then I left when it was dark. He wasn't supposed to leave the building but walked me safely to my car. What can I say? The man loved me.

The next day was graduation. I slept for a few hours and then got back up. I practiced on my speech for the rest of the morning and afternoon. But no matter what I wrote down, I did not feel comfortable with it.

Dr. Forrester drove me to my graduation. When Ms. Alicia and Brit went to go gather up the rest of our huge group, Dr. Forrester walked me backstage with the rest of my classmates. And there he was...

"Hi, Daddy!" I hugged his neck so tight he could barely breathe.

"You got it from here, Stone?" Dr. Forrester asked.

"If the lady will allow me." Dad raised his left arm for me to take it.

"It will be my pleasure, sir."

"Well, let me go find our party. All that I have to do is listen closely and I'm sure I will hear Alicia's voice."

Dr. Forrester started to walk away and I called him. "Dr. Forrester?"

"Yes, Butterfly?"

"I have another arm and it's lonely." I held up my left arm and Dr. Forrester took my arm in his. He and my dad escorted me backstage where my classmates were waiting.

Jeremy pulled me to the side to talk before we walked out to take our seats. "They could not have selected a better valedictorian."

"You can have it! I have to give a speech and all that I have is a bunch of nonsense scribble-scrabble written down."

"Are you kidding me? You are a walking testimony. Just talk about your life! Your accomplishments! What you had to go through this year alone just to walk across that stage is more than some people experience in a lifetime!"

"Those people don't want to hear about me. They want to hear about a good girl who has lived a good life and that ain't me."

"Well, do it for me then. This is probably the last time we're going to see each other for a while, so do it for me."

"Don't be trying to psych me out."

"I'm serious, say it for me. Forget about everybody else in this school when you get out there and tell me your story. I want to hear it."

"Why?"

"Because I love you."

I smiled and Jeremy and I walked away from each other and filed in line. I led the walk and as I took my place on the stage next to Mrs. Gary, the rest of my classmates took their seats directly below us.

It was a long ceremony. It took some concentration, but I stayed focused and kept my eyes on whoever was speaking. I dozed off a few times, but my eyes were still open, a trick I learned while listening to Reb's sermons. I woke up completely when they called the class of 2011 on stage to receive our diplomas.

I was the last person to receive my diploma. While my classmates were returning to their seats, I went to the microphone to give the valedictory speech. I walked nervously to the microphone. I looked into the section of the audience where my family and friends were, and I had an overwhelming sense of gratitude for all of them.

I saw my dad; my biological mom, Auntie Pam; and my adoptive mom and dad, Dr. Forrester and Ms. Alicia. My Pa-Pa! My uncle and aunts, Uncle Mike and Auntie Cynthia, Auntie Wanda, Uncle Robert and Auntie Tonita, Uncle Curtis and Auntie Tina, Auntie Lisa, Auntie Darsha, Auntie Val, Auntie Susan and Auntie Tazzy. My cousins were there: Bri, Alex, Little Mike and Benjamin. My friends were sitting next to them: Asia, Jheri, Valencia, Janae, Jacqua, and in between them and Toya was a sign with Keisha's name, date of birth and date of death.

I used to think my life was doomed before I ever came out of my mother's womb. But there I stood preparing to speak into a live microphone before a congregation of folks waiting to hear my story. These would be the most important heartfelt words I had ever said in my life. I was nervous. My heart was beating fast. But I had to put my fear to the side, as I had done my entire life, and do what I had to do. Well, without further adieu went…

"Good evening. My name is Shante Clemmons and I am the valedictorian of Duluth Christian Academy's class of 2011. As I stand before all of you as representative of my class, I also stand before you as a daughter, a granddaughter, a sister, a niece, a protégé, and a friend."

I kept my eyes locked on Jeremy and I continued to talk.

"I have read and heard many times the adage, 'It takes a village to raise a child.' If I had not been surrounded by people who felt that way, I would not be standing in front of you today. I'm not just speaking academically; I mean that literally. Through the nurturing love of others, I have completed the metamorphosis from caterpillar to butterfly. All that is left for me to do now is spread my wings and fly.

"I have been friendless! I have been homeless! I have been food-less! And I have been clothes-less. I have been less of almost anything you can imagine. But for every less I have suffered, I have been rewarded abundantly. Because I have been very fortunate to be blessed with so many people who care so much about me.

"I wanted to get up here and talk about my grades and my accomplishments, but in my heart, I know that everything I have accomplished was the result of someone else offering me their time and love. I am a living example of what happens when the entire village treats each child as if it was their very own!"

Led by Ms. Alicia and my fan club, the entire audience stood and clapped. I waited for the ovation to stop and then continued to speak.

"For the class of 2012, I can only hope that you are as blessed and as fortunate as I am to have people around you to care enough to say 'yes' when you need to hear yes, and 'no' when you need to hear no. With that being said, on behalf of the class of 2011," I threw my cap in the air and then my classmates followed, "*We outta here!*"

We screamed and jumped up and down. I walked off of the stage and my family and friends greeted me with opened arms.

Ms. Alicia suggested I ride home with Jeremy and my friends, and not with the family. That should have been a clue, but I had no idea that she wanted Jeremy to take me home to give her time to execute her plan. When we turned the corner onto our block, I saw all the cars and then I realized I had been duped!

Ms. Alicia had planned a surprise graduation party for me, and the first person I saw when I walked through the door was Sparkle. I pushed through the crowd to get to her.

"Come here, girl!" Sparkle hugged me and we rocked back and forth. "Oh my God, look at you! You've grown about six inches."

"Look at you, Sparkle, you're so beautiful!" I said. "Where have you been?"

"I went to California and married my first and only love. I've been keeping an eye on you, though."

"Keeping an eye on me? Why haven't you been keeping in contact with me?"

"Because you needed a clean break from the life, just like me."

"You're married? Where's your husband?"

"He had to stay in California, but he sent a gift to give to you."

"What gift?"

"Me!" Ma reached out her arms and laughed.

"*Maaa!* Oh, my God! Ma!" I closed my eyes and hugged Ma as tight as I could. "I love you so much, Ma."

"I love you, too, baby."

I pulled away from Ma and looked at Sparkle, "Hold on, what do you mean your husband gave me a gift? Ma, are you the gift? Wait a minute! That means…"

"Yes, I'm married to Stanley!"

"No you're not. I don't believe that." I shook my head no. "Nope! Ma, she's lying, huh?"

"No, she's my daughter-in-law."

"Then why haven't you contacted me?"

"I keep telling you, I did not want to bring Harry to you. He knew nothing about my past relationship with Stanley and the Powells, so you were safe. But that man is a monster without a conscience. He would have hurt you if he found out where you were."

"I guess I understand."

"But I have been around. I saw you at Pastor Powell's funeral."

"You were there?"

"Yes, I flew in and flew back out without anyone knowing. I had to say good-bye to that old man. He changed my life in more ways than one."

"I would have been so surprised to see your face in that church that day."

"Speaking of surprises," Ma Powell said. "We have another surprise for you, Shante."

"I'm so excited, I don't know if I can handle any more surprises."

"I think you're going to want to handle this one."

"What is it?"

"Go in the kitchen and see."

"Okay, come on, Ma."

I grabbed Ma's hand and went into the kitchen. When we walked in, Dr. Forrester and my dad were already there.

"This is kind of a surprise for you and Stone, Butterfly."

"What's going on, Doc?" Dad asked.

"Bring them in, honey!" Dr. Forrester called out to Ms. Alicia.

Ms. Alicia walked in with the two kids and then walked back out. Dr. Forrester put the kids on either side of him and put his hands on their shoulders.

"I have two people who would like to introduce themselves to the both of you." Dr. Forrester urged the girl to speak first. "Go on, sweetheart."

"Hi."

My dad sat in a chair and put his head in his hands. He knew immediately who they were.

"How are you?" I asked.

"I'm fine."

"And what's your name?"

"My name is Natalie."

"Natalie?" I began to cry. "Oh, your name is Natalie?"

"Yes."

"Can I have a hug, Natalie?"

"Yes."

I held out my arms and she ran to me. She spoke kind of child-like, but her body was very mature. She was a teenager and she looked like a teenager. She was only two years older than Alan, but she was so much taller than him. She reminded me so much of myself when I was her age.

"Oh my goodness! I can't believe this! Do you know who I am, sweetie?"

"Yes, you're my sister!"

"Come here!" I pulled Natalie into my arms again, and gave her another hug. "And you must be Alan?"

"Yes."

"Can I have a hug, Alan?"

Alan was shy and slightly hesitant to come at first, but he walked over slowly and gave me a hug. They looked so differently from the last time I had seen them. But then again, they were only five and three.

My dad was apprehensive to talk to them. I could not even imagine what was going through his heart and his mind.

"Do you know who that is, Natalie?"

"Yes, I remember him. That's my father!"

Natalie ran to Daddy and squeezed his neck.

"You remember me, baby?" Dad asked.

"I remember everything about you. I remember the last time I saw you. I remember everything."

My dad had a special but different bond with each and every one of his children. Whatever he had with Natalie, even when she was at a very young age, was strong. I used to be jealous of their relationship because for the first five years of my life, I was my daddy's little girl. And then all of a sudden, Natalie came out of nowhere and *bam*, she stole his heart. Of course she eventually became my baby doll, and now my baby has become a young lady.

"Do you remember me?" Natalie asked.

"I remember everything about you, too, sweetheart." Dad touched Alan's stomach. "Do you remember me, little man?"

Alan nodded his head yes.

"Now somebody please tell me how this happened?" I asked. "Wow! How did you find them?"

"It took some research and a lot of resources, but as you can see, we did it."

"After what happened, I can't believe their grandparents let them come."

"Their grandparents forfeited custody years ago. They were placed in foster care, like you. Thank God they were living in the same foster home."

"So what does that mean, Doc? Does that mean I can get my kids back?"

"Not exactly." Dr. Forrester did not want to bring up my father's criminal activity in front of the children. "Considering your current circumstances, you probably can't get them right now. But we're working on it."

"Come with me, kids." Ma held Natalie's and Alan's hands and led them out of the kitchen.

After Ma walked out, Dad asked, "Then what happens to them?"

"This was an unofficial visit, Stone. They have to go back."

"Will I ever see them again?"

"Of course. Stanley is working with the state of California to see what we can do to get your kids back to Georgia."

"How long do you think it will take?"

"I have no idea, brother. But we're going to be working as fast as we can."

"Eight long years, man. And all I get is one day?"

"Actually, they don't have to be back in Los Angeles until Sunday evening."

"I guess this is better than nothing."

"Don't worry about it, Daddy. We'll get them back. But for right now, let's just enjoy the time we have with them."

"Yeah, you're right, sweetheart." Dad smiled and began to leave the room. "I'm going to spend every waking second with them."

"I think that's a good idea, Stone."

After my dad left the room, I asked Dr. Forrester again, "How were you able to pull this off, Dr. Forrester? I need details."

"Stone gave me information on the grandparents in Los Angeles and then I contacted Mrs. Powell for help. She told me her son was an attorney and I gave the information to him. He tracked down the grandparents and we found out that after they took the children to Los Angeles, they never assumed legal parental authority. They turned them over to the State of California, and like you, they were passed around from foster family to foster family. Luckily for them, we found both of them in the same home."

"Be straight up with me, Dr. Forrester. Is there any possible way we can get them back?"

"It will take some time, but sure, you're going to get them back. Their situation is not as simple as yours. First of all, you were sixteen and that's a legal age for a foster child to decide on their own where they want to live. Secondly, they're in an entirely different state where the laws are slightly different. But, Stanley specializes in family law and he's confident that it's not a matter of if, but when."

"Thank goodness! I can't wait to have all of my family together in the same city; my dad, my siblings, you, Mom, everybody."

"You will, Butterfly."

"Thank God."

"I have some more news."

"Oh really? And what is that, good doctor?"

"They arrested Harry Warren yesterday on the charges of prostitution, extortion, rape, child abuse, and molestation, contributing to the delinquency of a minor, and contributing to the death of a minor."

"Thank you, Jesus!"

"They may not get him on everything, but they have enough to keep him behind bars for the rest of his miserable life."

"All of that from Keisha's diary?"

"No, his wife."

I was leaving the next morning, so I took some private time to spend with Natalie and Alan. Natalie's memory was very keen. She remembered things she and I did together that I did not even remember. I guess I was the same way after meeting my dad in prison. I never knew I missed my siblings so much until they were brought back into my life. I had to leave the next morning, but I stayed with my little sister and brother until they fell asleep.

Ma Powell, Sparkle and I talked in my bedroom for a little while before they went back to their hotel. I told them about my modeling opportunity and they were ecstatic! It was mostly because the modeling would be in Los Angeles and we could spend more time together. Knowing that I would see them in Los Angeles in a couple of days alleviated the sadness of saying good-bye.

Jeremy and I hung out in my bedroom, too, but we did more than talk. We kissed and fondled, and he tried once more to get me to be in a relationship with him. I was down with kissing, but the boy cheated on me and I cannot speak for all girls, but there is no coming back from that. I just wished my heart understood that philosophy.

After everyone had gone, Ms. Alicia, Auntie Pam and I decided to clean up the kitchen before we left for L.A. My dad boldly walked in to talk to my Auntie Pam.

"Can I speak to you privately, Pam?"

"About what?"

"Just…talk."

If I had not been in the kitchen, I am sure Auntie Pam would not have taken the time to talk to my dad. And I would have understood, but she did not want to hurt his feelings in front of me.

"I'm about to leave anyway, so I guess you can walk me out to my car."

"Okay."

"But don't try to steal it," Auntie Pam joked.

"That's cold." Ms. Alicia tried not to laugh but did not do a good job at it. "I'm sorry, Stone, but that was funny."

Dad stepped to the side to let Auntie Pam walk ahead of him. "That's all right, Alicia. Pam got her little joke in, but he who laughs last, laughs best."

"Hold on, what you plan on doing?" Auntie Pam looked back over her shoulder at Dad.

"Don't worry about that."

Dad and Auntie Pam left out of the kitchen. Ms. Alicia and I were so exhausted that we just relaxed for a minute and did not speak a word. I dozed off momentarily and when I woke up again, Ms. Alicia was asleep. She must have felt me watching her because she opened her eyes.

"What are you looking at?"

"I'm just thinking."

"Thinking about what?"

"I did it, Mom."

"You did what, sweetie? You've done so much."

"I graduated. And I'm going to college."

"Yes you are, sweetie." Ms. Alicia stood up and stretched. "Let's get some sleep."

"I need some."

On our way upstairs, Ms. Alicia noticed a car was still outside of our house. She cracked the door to see who it was.

"Who is it, Mom?"

"Your daddy and Pam are out there hugged up."

"You lying!" I stood behind Ms. Alicia and we spied on them. "I can't believe this."

"Wow!" Ms. Alicia covered her mouth.

"My dad is putting his mack down!"

"Wow!"

"Okay, I've seen enough."

"Well, I haven't."

"Come on, Mom, let's go."

"Give me a minute."

"No, come on." I pulled Ms. Alicia away from the door and we went to bed.

Chapter Sixteen

We had to get up early to catch our flight. Our plane departed at 7:45 in the morning which meant we had to be there at 5:30 a.m. Dr. Forrester drove Ms. Alicia, Auntie Cynthia, Bri and me to the MARTA Doraville station where we met Auntie Pam. We caught the train to the airport. We had fun on the way making fun of each other for having so many pieces of luggage for only a weekend trip.

When we got to the airport. there were not a lot of people there. We got our boarding tickets and then went through security. They made us take off our jackets, our shoes, and run it through this conveyor. We had to put all of our money, coins. and all other metallic objects in a tray with the rest of our items we were carrying on board and that went on the conveyor belt, too. They had security look through something that looks like an X-ray machine to see the inside of our suitcase. It was nothing to them, but it was my first time and I needed some instructions, shit.

We waited for like an hour-and-a-half to board the plane. I was nervous, but after waiting for so long, I just wanted to get it over with. We went through the tunnel, which led to the opening of the airplane's doorway. There was a flight attendant to greet us at the door and direct us to the aisle. The first thing that caught my eye was, this thing was a lot smaller than it looked on television. I had a sudden realization that I was indeed claustrophobic.

Bri sat by the window, Ms. Alicia sat in the aisle seat, and I sat in the middle seat. Auntie Pam and Auntie Cynthia sat behind us in the middle and aisle seats. We sat on the plane for about thirty minutes before it moved away from the gate. It was like moving on a big bus. It was not bad at all. And then we turned onto the runway. The plane was still moving rather slowly and then it took off! We were going so fast, I thought we were already in the air. It was shaking and bouncing and then all of a sudden, we left the ground for real. Whoa!

The plane seemed to be going up at an angle, which made my body press backward into my seat. I stopped getting on the amusement rides at Six Flags because I was afraid and that takeoff was worse than any ride I had ever ridden in my life. I clutched Bri's and Ms. Alicia's wrists as tight as I could as we climbed higher and higher.

"You okay, Butterfly?" Bri asked.

"No, I am not. I want to get down. We're up too high, Bri."

"No! No! No! It's fine. Once we get leveled off, the ride will be comfortable."

"What is 'leveled off'?"

"When the plane gets to the height where the pilot wants, it just flies straight ahead and you don't get that nauseated feeling like you're on a roller coaster."

"I hope he hurry up and level off."

"Okay, let's talk about something else. I can't wait to go to Disneyland, Universal Studios, Magic Mountain and take a picture at the Hollywood sign." Bri tried to get my mind off of the flight.

It worked. We talked until I fell asleep. I woke up when I heard the pilot say that we were descending into Los Angeles.

"Wow! We're here already." I nudged Bri. "Wake up, girl."

"What?" Bri said.

"We're here."

Bri sat up and raised the cover on the window. We were still above the clouds.

"I thought the pilot said we were descending. We're still in the sky."

"It's still going to take another fifteen or twenty minutes before we land."

"Cally-for-ni-a! Here we come!"

"California Love!" Bri broke into a serenade of Tupac and Dr. Dre's "California Love" and I joined in. *The track hits ya eardrum like a slug to ya chest. Pack a vest for your Jimmy in the city of sex.*

"Whoa! Whoa! Whoa! What the hell?" Ms. Alicia playfully covered my mouth. "I bet y'all better watch your mouth!"

"Oops! My bad, Mom."

Ms. Alicia leaned around the back of her seat to Auntie Cynthia. "Can you hear these hussies up here?"

"No, what did the hussies say?"

"They're talking about sex, and jimmies and slugs to your chest."

"Who?"

"Bri and Butterfly."

"Not my Bri?"

"Yeah, your Bri."

"Stop it!" Auntie Pam laughed. "That's Tupac and y'all used to dance to it when it came out, so stop acting like you're disgusted."

"Shut up! We're moms now." Auntie Cynthia laughed out loud.

We were still laughing when the plane touched down and then my nightmare was all over. It was only nine o'clock in the morning there. I asked Ms. Alicia how could we be in the air for four hours and only lose an hour-and-a-half of time? I forgot about California was in the Pacific Standard Time, which was three hours behind us. I had to adjust to the time difference.

Ms. Erin had a limousine pick us up from the airport and took us to our hotel. We shared adjoining rooms. The elders had the main suite, and Bri and I shared the smaller room. They laughed about stealing our large room, but the room we were in was more than big enough for us.

Auntie Cynthia and Bri went on a private tour of the hotel. Auntie Pam was in the bathroom, and Ms. Alicia and I were going over the itinerary that Ms. Erin had placed in the main suite. She arranged events, which covered almost every waking moment from the time we arrived to the time we were scheduled to leave. None of the activities on the list included Disneyland, Universal Studios or a trip to Magic Mountain. This was all about business! I thought it was going to be a one-day thing and then I could enjoy the rest of my weekend.

"I thought we were going to be able to have some fun."

"Welcome to the world of modeling, dear," Ms. Alicia said.

"Is it going to be like this all the time?"

"No, it's going to get worse."

"Worse? I may be in the wrong business then."

"You may be. And before a lot of people invest a lot of time and money into you, you need to be sure that this is something you want to do, Butterfly."

"I'm sure."

"Hey, wait a minute, come here." Ms. Alicia sat me down and then sat next to me. "I don't want you to think you have to do this for me. I want you to do this for yourself, baby. This is a very strenuous, strenuous job. There is a lot of traveling with long, long days. You have to be disciplined in your diet, which sometimes lead to eating disorders.

"There is an underworld of drug addiction and sex slavery. Everybody wants something from you, and they will make you seem like you're the greatest thing since the invention of the wheel.

And by the time you're twenty-five years old, those same people will turn their backs on you and your career will be over.

"But sweetheart, this business is also like any other thing in life. There's good, there's bad, and then there are the choices you make. If you stay focus on your career and not allow yourself to be caught up in the extracurricular activities surrounding it, it could be a rewarding lifetime experience, filled with excitement, adventure and international culture. Not to mention it pays out the gazoo!"

"And just how much is a gazoo?" I joked. "I don't know what being a model entails, but I know that I'm prepared for whatever lies ahead. And it's not about the glamour, or the fame. Like everything else in my life, it's about the challenge. I've never been referred to as beautiful before and it's difficult for me to accept. The challenge is not to prove to the world how beautiful I am, but to myself."

"I want you to think about this and make up your mind quickly because if we go further, Butterfly, these people will be very upset if you quit on them."

"Believe me, I won't quit. I'm ready! I want this! And I want this for me!"

"Okay, baby."

Auntie Pam walked out of the bathroom and Ms. Alicia quickly took her place. I took advantage of the opportunity of being alone with Auntie Pam and asked her about my dad.

"I know you may be upset for what my dad did, but he really is a good man who has made some unfortunate bad decisions."

"I'm not upset with your dad, Butterfly."

"It's obvious you guys didn't have a great relationship, but I would still like to know what it was like when you two were together."

"I have moved on from that period in my life, Butterfly."

"Please?"

"Okay," Auntie Pam said, "At times, your dad and I had a very volatile relationship. But that was only when we were mad at each other. Most of the time we laughed, had fun; we were like best friends."

"Did you love each other?"

"Yes, I think we did. I know that I loved him. We were young at the time and we really didn't know how to deal with our issues, especially parenthood. I had a career objective, and your dad was just about living for the day. We didn't know how to compromise and it got ugly."

"So, are there any sparks flying, Auntie Pam?"

"I don't think so, sweetheart. What your dad and I had was a long, long time ago."

"He still cares about you."

"And how do you know this?"

"Because I know my dad."

"I think I need a little more evidence than that."

"Well?"

"Well, what?"

"Well, my dad is single, and you're single, soooooo…?"

"So, stop trying to be a matchmaker and we'll see what happens."

"That's cool with me; for right now anyway."

"You are your father's child."

"Auntie Pam?"

"Yes?"

"Do you remember the first day we met?"

"Sure do."

"When my mom introduced us, we both said to each other that we looked familiar. Do you remember that?"

"Yes, and I guess now we know why."

"Do you think that I could have remembered you from that early age?"

"Stranger things have happened."

"I guess some things just can't be explained." I smiled and then went back to my room.

Chapter Seventeen

*T*he limo was scheduled to pick us up and take us to the studio at noon, so we only had time to shower, get dressed, and grab a quick bite to eat. When we pulled onto the studio's lot, we were greeted by a security officer in a booth. Ms. Alicia gave him our names and we were allowed on the grounds. He directed us to Studio B where they shot *America the Beautiful.* The studio property was much larger than it appeared from the street. I was in awe.

Ms. Erin met us in the studio's lobby. She showed me how to sign in and from there, it was like enrolling in a new school all over again. There were like a hundred girls scrambling from room to room answering questions and filling out forms. I had two interviews about my modeling background. Ms. Erin answered most of the questions. After my third interview, we had another meeting where I was officially welcomed to *America the Beautiful: Season Five.*

They explained the premise of the show in full detail. There would be twenty girls living in one house together for six weeks. The show was going to record our modeling competition as well as our daily activities behind the scenes. The winner would get a modeling contract, $100,000 and a Cadillac Escalade. I really did not need the money or the Escalade, but I was not going to turn them down, either. We were scheduled to film for six weeks during the summer. Each week would be an elimination round until there were two remaining finalists. The final episode would air live with the announcement of the winner of *America the Beautiful: Season Five.*

I had to sign contracts about the confidentiality and integrity of the show. If we were eliminated, or even if we were among the two finalists, we were legally bound not to discuss any of the details of the show prior to the announcement of the winner.

Ms. Alicia was by my side through every meeting. I was proud that she was able to control her emotions and not directly get involved while the staff was talking to me. You can bet, though, she did not hesitate to advise me right there on the spot when she felt it was absolutely necessary. Auntie Pam, Auntie Cynthia and Bri watched and sat from afar.

By the time we were finished with my first day, it was after nine o'clock. Ms. Erin treated all of us to a late dinner, and she and Ms. Alicia had a great time telling their old college stories. She was an AKA like Ms. Alicia. I never knew that Auntie Pam was a Delta Sigma Theta, or that Auntie Cynthia was a Zeta Phi Beta until that night. Auntie Pam and Auntie Cynthia never talked being in a sorority, but Ms. Alicia constantly bragged about being an AKA. To be honest, I did not know the difference between a fraternity or a sorority until Ms. Alicia explained it to me my senior year.

The four of them lobbied for Bri and me to join their respective sororities when we went to college. I did not lean toward either one of them, but knowing me, I would not join any sorority at all. I loved my family and friends, but as far as the adolescent camaraderie of college unity, I could do without that.

We got back to our hotel room around eleven-thirty that night, which was two-thirty in the morning our time. Everybody took their clothes off and went straight to sleep. We had to get up at six in the morning to be ready for our limo at eight. Auntie Cynthia, Auntie Pam and Bri had had enough of the modeling life. They slept in, and planned a trip to Disneyland first, and then they were going to go to Hollywood to see the Walk of Fame and take their picture in front of the big Hollywood sign. That Hollywood sign thing was all Bri's idea. They wanted to take a celebrity tour bus to see the celebrity homes, too, but there were only so many hours in a day. Our plane did not leave until ten Sunday night, so they scheduled a tour for the afternoon.

While they were having fun, I was being told to sit like this, sit like that, walk faster, walk slower, smile, don't smile, stick your ass out, stick your ass in. What bothered me the most was when I kept hearing, "Nibble on this for right now, and you can eat when we are finished."

Around seven o'clock, they gave me a break. I sat in a high chair and reached for a bottle of water.

"Here." Ms. Alicia handed me a sandwich.

"Oh my goodness, thank you, Mom!" I bit into that sandwich like a starved savage. "I am so hungry I could eat a bear!"

"Not so fast, girl, you're going to choke."

"I don't care. I'm hungry."

"So how do you feel?"

"I'm sleepy."

"Is this too much for you?"

"Are you kidding me? This is nothing. I'm ready for some more." I finished my sandwich and then jumped out of my chair.

"Look at you." Ms. Alicia smiled. "That's my tiger! But save some of that energy for tomorrow, sweetheart."

"Oh thank goodness, I'm about to pass out!" I slumped down in the chair and kicked my legs out.

"Get your butt up." Ms. Alicia laughed.

"I can't!"

"Let's go, your carriage awaits." Ms. Alicia pulled me out of the chair.

I grabbed my duffle bag and stumbled outside to the limo. I stretched out on one of the seats and put my head in Ms. Alicia's lap. When I woke up, we were in front of our hotel. I hobbled to my room and lay across my bed.

"Don't you want to catch up with our posse?" Ms. Alicia joked.

"No ma'am." I mumbled with my face stuffed in my pillow. "And please, could you not use the word *posse* ever again in that context?"

"Girl, go to sleep!" Ms. Alicia laughed and went into her room.

Bri came in later, wanting to know what I had done all day. She also wanted to tell me how she had spent her day. I turned over and faced her, but I kept dozing off. She was so excited, I don't think she even noticed that I was unconscious. I paid attention as much as I could, but I dozed off on her one time and the next thing I knew, it was six-thirty in the morning and Ms. Alicia was shaking me.

"Get up! Get up! We're late!"

"Huh?"

"Get up, girl! It's six-thirty! We overslept!"

"Oh my goodness!" I jumped out of bed and ran to the shower.

I threw on a warm-up suit and some shades and waited on Ms. Alicia, who was not going outside without her makeup under any circumstances. She did a rush job, but you could not tell by looking at her. She was still gorgeous! When the limo pulled up, we were standing outside and ready to go.

I took more pictures later that morning. During the afternoon, I was zoomed away to read in a commercial. Somehow, Ms. Erin got the gig for me. It was only a small part, but I got paid for it. And it was going to be seen nationally. Once we finished the commercial, I had another meeting with Ms. Erin.

"So what do you think so far?" Ms. Erin asked.

"I love it."

"Great!" Ms. Erin opened up a folder and pulled out a stack of paper. "I want to offer you a contract to represent you exclusively for the next three years. I can go on and on about telling you all the things I can do for you, Butterfly. But that's not how I do things. That's why I brought you and your family here this weekend to show you what I can do for you. When you board that plane tonight, you will have a complete portfolio filled with beautiful pictures. You will have a commercial where you are a principal actress. And you will be a contestant on one of the most popular reality shows on television. If I can do all of this for you in just one weekend, imagine what I could do for you in three years."

Ms. Erin handed me the contract, and Ms. Alicia made me read every single word, line by line. She explained to me what each item meant. She was used to handling entertainment contracts with her PR firm. It took a while, but we finally finished it.

"Wow! I don't know what to say." I was speechless. I turned to Ms. Alicia for guidance. "What do you think, Mom?"

"This is your decision, baby."

"Can I ask why you are doing all of this for me, Ms. Erin?"

"Because I love what I do. I love molding new talent and turning it into something beautiful. I believe in you, Butterfly, and now I ask you to believe in me."

"Okay, I want to sign the contract."

"You sure, baby?" Ms. Alicia asked.

"I'm positive."

Ms. Erin handed me an ink pen. "Young lady, you're on your way to being a star!"

Ms. Alicia smiled and watched as I signed my contract. Ms. Erin sent a limo to pick up the rest of our party, including Ma Powell, Sparkle, Stanley, Natalie and Alan to celebrate. We had a ball! And no matter how I tried to make it a family event, everybody made sure I was the center of the attraction.

Our flight left at ten o'clock Pacific Standard Time, and we arrived in Atlanta at six in the morning. We caught the train back to the Doraville MARTA station where Dr. Forrester, Brit and Uncle Mike were waiting for us. Auntie Cynthia and Bri rode home with Uncle Mike, and we dropped off Auntie Pam on our way home.

I had two weeks before I had to fly back to Los Angeles and I wanted to make the most of my remaining time in Atlanta. I felt like I had been neglecting Brit over the past month, so I took her for a drive to get some ice cream. We were only a mile or two from our house when Brit told me she was going to miss me when I left.

"I'm going to miss you, Butterfly."

"I'm going to miss you, too, little girl."

"Are you coming back?"

"Of course, why do you ask that?"

"My other mommy left and she never came back."

"That's because she went to heaven."

"I know. That's what my new mommy said."

"But I'm only going to California. I'll be back in a little while."

"You promise?"

"I promise."

"Can I take a picture with before you leave? I want to hang it up on my wall by my bed, so I can see you every day when I..."

Slam!!!

As Brit was talking, a speeding car went through a red light and smashed into my driver's side door. I recall the initial impact, and then I was immediately knocked unconscious. I remember waking up to medics asking me questions that I could not answer and then I blacked out again.

SHANTE'S STORY:

I do not remember a lot about my mother, but I know that she took care of me very well. I remember, even at that young age, a life of stability and security. After my mother died, my father had to take care of me all by himself and at that time, he simply was not mentally equipped for the task.

My father thought we needed a change, so we moved from Raleigh, North Carolina to Atlanta, Georgia. My father was from the streets, so when he moved to Atlanta on the West End, he went back to familiar surroundings, the streets!

I was my father's pride and joy, and as a single father, he did all he could to provide for me. But as far back as I can remember, he never had a real job. He sold drugs or had multiple part-time jobs that paid next to nothing. I was not ashamed or anything, that was all I knew. I thought everybody's father sold drugs for a living. I didn't know any better.

When DFACS found out, I was frequently being left at home alone. They started snooping around our apartment. My father tried to slow down after that. He tried to find a real job and stop hustling. He was barely making minimum wage working real jobs. But in the streets, he could have made thousands of dollars a week. So what do you think he did? He went back to the streets.

He met this lady named Joyce when I was six. She was from Los Angeles. She was kind of like from a rich family. She was not rich, but her parents were, and she expected my father to provide the same luxuries as her parents. He had two kids by her: my little sister, Natalie; and my little brother, Alan. Natalie was two years older than Alan.

After they were born, my father left the streets alone and found some pretty decent jobs. He and Ms. Joyce got along fine until her spoiled ass started to put pressure on him to make more money. No matter how hard my father tried, he could not please her. Eventually, they broke up and went their separate ways.

When my sister, Natalie, was four, she told my father that Ms. Joyce's boyfriend had showed her a burn mark near his genitals. My father tried to talk to Ms. Joyce about it, but she got mad at him and stopped him from seeing Natalie and Alan altogether. My father was mad, too, but he did not retaliate.

In the State of Georgia, if the father is not married to the mother when the child is born, he has no legal rights to the child. Ms. Joyce took advantage of that stupid law and used it against my father. She placed a restraining order against him to stop him from seeing the kids. And because she had the restraining order against my dad, he could not have a paternity test to legitimize my brother and sister. He was caught between a rock and a hard place.

After a year of not seeing Natalie and Alan, he woke me up in the middle of the night to put an end to it. He put on my clothes and told me we were going to see my little brother and sister. He couldn't take it anymore. He had to see them.

I was still kind of sleepy when we pulled into their yard, but I could hear him and Ms. Joyce fussing. When I sat up, I could see my father on top of Ms. Joyce's boyfriend, whose name was Jamie. My dad was holding him down and they were screaming at each other.

"You ain't got nothing to do with this, man!" Dad yelled. "I want to see my kids!"

"She said you can't see yo' kids, now what, niggah?" Jamie yelled back. Ms. Joyce ran out of the apartment with a bat and hit my father in

the back. *He fell over and Jamie ran to his car. He snatched open his car door and reached into his glove compartment. He pulled out a gun and held it in the air. He pointed at my dad and walked toward him.*

"Let's see how bad you are now, niggah."

My dad was lying on his back. He crawled backward as the man walked on top of him with the gun in his hand. I jumped out of the car and ran to my dad. He pushed me out of the way and stood up. Ms. Joyce swung the bat at my dad again, but it slipped out of her hand. Dad picked it up and held it in his hand. I stood between my dad and Jamie.

"Shoot his ass!" Ms. Joyce screamed.

"Naw, I want him to beg before I blast his ass."

My dad put me behind him. "I don't beg to no niggah!"

"Shoot him, Jamie!"

Jamie took his eyes off my dad to look at Ms. Joyce and my dad charged him. He knocked Jamie to the ground and the gun fell out of his hand. Ms. Joyce ran for the bat and I ran for the gun. My dad and Jamie were tussling on the ground. Ms. Joyce raised the bat in the air and was about to come down on my dad's head and I fired!

Dad and Jamie released each other. Jamie saw Joyce lying on the ground and rushed me. I still had the gun in the firing position and when I saw him coming toward me, I fired at him. And then I fired again! And again! And again!

"Baby, no!" Dad screamed. He ran toward me while I was firing at Jamie and tackled me. By that time, I had emptied the gun. "What have you done, baby? Oh God! What have you done?"

I collapsed in my dad's arms and when I woke up, Ms. Joyce and Jamie were dead. My dad was in the backseat of a police car. They would not let me talk to him. They asked me questions about what happened, but I could not remember anything. I was taken to a shelter that night and turned over to the State the next morning."

END MY STORY:

The next time I woke up, I was lying in a hospital. My dad, Ms. Alicia and Dr. Forrester were standing by my bedside. I screamed loudly and reached for my dad.

"Daddy!" I grabbed my dad and hugged him.

"You okay?" Dad asked.

"Thank God, you're all right." Ms. Alicia held my hand.

"Please." I could barely breathe. "I need to talk to my father!"

"You've been in an accident, sweetheart. The doctor needs to check you out first before you engage in…," Dr. Forrester said.

"No! I need to talk my dad!"

"Honey?" Ms. Alicia tried to rub my hand and I snatched away.

"*I have to talk to my father!*" I screamed. "*Now!*"

"Okay, just calm down!" Ms. Alicia said softly.

"We'll get a doctor, Stone." Dr. Forrester and Ms. Alicia left the room.

"Daddy? I killed those people!" I hyperventilated as I was talking. "I…I…I…killed those people!"

"Butterfly!" Dad tried to make me relax. "Calm down, baby! You didn't kill anybody! You're confused, baby! It wasn't you; it was me! Remember?"

"No! No! No! It was me! I remember! It was me! I shot those people!" I sat up and tried to get out of the bed.

"Baby! Baby!" Dad gently grabbed me and held me down. "Shut up! Baby, please, shut up!"

"I killed those people, Daddy!"

My dad ran to the door and called Dr. Forrester into my room while Ms. Alicia went to get a nurse. I was still yelling and screaming incoherently about Ms. Joyce and her boyfriend. The nurse gave me a sedative that knocked my ass right back out. I was out for a few hours and when I regained consciousness, I was in a much calmer state. I opened my eyes and my dad was staring right at me. He was the only person in the room.

"What are you looking at?" I joked.

"You."

"How come you never told me, Dad?"

"Why would I tell you something like that, Butterfly?"

"Because I cost you eight years of your life."

"No, you saved my life. I was a man with no direction. I was just surviving out there on them streets like I was an animal. I did what I had to do to protect my child. That's what a father does."

"You knew that's what I've been blocking in my mind all of this time, didn't you?"

"No, I didn't know for sure. Maybe I did and I just didn't want you to remember."

"Dad, why can't I have a normal life? I just want to be a normal teenage girl. But we both know that can never happen, don't we?"

"What's normal, baby? Look at everybody around you. The doc, me, Alicia, Pam, you may not know what we're going through, but every last one of us is going through something that makes us ask that question: why me?"

"But none of you are like me. None of you have two different..."

"Butterfly! You are who say you are! That's all that matters."

"But I don't know who I am, or don't even know what I am."

"You're a beautiful young woman; that's who you are."

"Thank you, Daddy."

My dad grabbed my hand in his and then squeezed lightly.

"You ready for me to send in the clowns?" Dad joked.

"As ready as I'll ever be."

Like always, my father unselfishly stepped to the side to share me with other people that I loved. Dad walked out and Ms. Alicia walked in. But on that day, he was all that I wanted, and needed. But Ms. Alicia was not a bad alternative.

Chapter Eighteen

"Hey, baby."

"Hi, Mom."

"I uh, I spoke to Pam and she told me why your father took you away from her."

"She told you everything?"

"It took some urging and physical threats, but yes, she told me everything."

"So now you know."

"Yes."

"Do you still want to be my mom?"

"Even more so." Ms. Alicia started to cry.

"Can't we have just one conversation without us crying?"

"I don't think so." Ms. Alicia hugged me tightly, and kissed me on the cheek several times.

"Me either." I joked while I wiped my eyes.

"Hey! If you're up to it, I have something for you." Ms. Alicia was hiding something behind her back.

"You know I'm just like you." I chuckled. "I gotta know what's behind door number three. What are you hiding?"

"Lookie at what I got." Ms. Alicia opened a padded envelope and pulled out some photographs. They were pictures from my Los Angeles photo shoots.

"Wow! Is that me?" I went through them one by one.

"Yeah, that's you."

"How did they get the camera to lie like that?"

"That's the real you, sweetie. The camera just captured pure beauty in motion."

"Wow! These pictures are amazing."

"Art imitating life."

"More like a fantastic photographer turning an ugly duckling into a swan."

Ms. Alicia found a small sitting mirror and put it in front of me. "I want you to repeat after me, all right?"

"All right."

"I am beautiful."

"I am beautiful," I repeated.

"Beauty is not just a pretty face, or a slim body; it's a state of being. If you feel beautiful, then you are beautiful. Now I want you to keep those words, 'I am beautiful,' inside of you, and remember this precious face that is in front of you."

"All right." I smiled.

"I love you."

"I love you, too."

I recovered from the accident without any physical scars or damage. Two days later, I was on an airplane, heading back to Los Angeles all by lonesome. I was terrified, but I manage to compose myself. I read my Bible from takeoff to touchdown. If I could not tell you "what Jesus would do" before I boarded that plane, I certainly could by the time we landed. I did not sleep one wink.

Ms. Erin had her assistant, Tara, meet me at the airport. She was a thin white girl, with a thin nose. Her head was long and skinny and she needed some sun badly. Her hair was straight and blonde. She was tall with long, skinny legs. She talked a lot, but she was nice. Basically, she was a white replica of me.

I still had a week before the show actually began, so Ms. Erin wanted to squeeze as much experience into those 168 hours as she could. I stayed with her in her Malibu home on the beach. My first morning was spent drinking tea and watching the night turn to day. The sunrise scenery was unbelievably beautiful. However, it was short-lived. Ms. Erin let me enjoy my tea and then it was off to work.

I worked from sun-up to sundown! Outside shots, inside shots, summer wear, winter wear, underwear, just about every damn wear you could think of, I wore. By the time the first round of elimination came for *America the Beautiful*, I was worn out. I think the only way I got through it was those brief evening phone calls with my family and friends.

I was kept up to date on what was going on in the ATL by Keisha... My bad, I meant, Toya. I guess my girl Keisha was still on my mind like that. Anyway, Toya told me some news that made my jaw drop. Jacqua, who was supposed to be totally into girls, and who I heard say out of her own mouth, that she would never be with another man for as long as she lived, was pregnant! So I do not have to tell you that the baby was not Janae's, huh? That was wild. I heard Janae went looking for the guy with a gun.

But I did not get caught up with that drama back home, or that bullshit those girls were doing in the house. I stayed focused and did what I had to do to make it to the next round of elimination. I was courteous to everyone, but friendly to no one. And as each week passed, and I remained on the show, my confidence grew. Not just as a contestant on *America the Beautiful*, but as a woman. I never thought I would make it out of the first round, but I did, and I made it all the way through to the final round.

In the final episode when the winner was announced, all of the women in my family flew in from Atlanta. They came to support me in my victory, or in my defeat. It was like my graduation all over again. I was still under contract to stay in the house, so I could not see them until after the final live episode was shot.

It came down to me, and the only girl I considered to be my friend. It was a bittersweet situation for me. Out of all those crazy maniacs in that house, Melinda was the only person I liked, or respected. She was pulled into a few altercations but nothing too dramatic. I liked that about her. Unfortunately, though, it was down to her and me.

The final competition was the catwalk! It would be both of our first time in front of a large audience that was not associated with one of the challenges of the competition. We had on high-heels, bikinis and a thong with our asses out. Out of courtesy, she wished me luck before the cameras started to roll. Out of pity, I wished her luck because stilettos and nakedness was right up my alley, literally! It was like being back in the strip club. I was so into it, I almost climbed up a pole. It felt natural to me. Let's face it, I was an exhibitionist! Needless to say, when they announced the name of the winner of *America the Beautiful: Season Five*, it was Butterfly.

Afterward, Melinda was a sport about losing. She told me I looked like I had been doing that all of my life. Well, maybe not all of my life, but for a year at Emerald City, yeah, I was the shit!

After almost two months of not seeing any of my family, we finally reunited at Ms. Erin's house for a Southern barbecue. I invited Melinda, and a few of the girls that I had not heard from since they were eliminated from the show. We discussed some of the things that went on in the house that we knew nothing about. We also revealed some of the things that we did know but never made it on air. All in all, we had a ball. We let our hair down and for that one day, we ate like pigs.

I flew back with my family for a couple of days for rest and relaxation. I did everything but rest. All of my friends wanted to see me and I did not want it to seem like I had changed, so I drove all over Atlanta to see different people. I met up with Janae and Toya and they had me laughing, talking about how Jacqua was scared to tell Janae she was pregnant.

"So you don't talk to Jacqua at all now, Janae?"

"Hell nawl! That bitch better be glad I didn't break her damn jaw like I did to that niggah."

"Whose jaw did you break?"

"That fool that jacked my girl from me."

"You got in a fight with that dude, Janae?"

"Not really." Janae laughed and gave Toya a fist pound. "I just whooped that niggah ass. I had that niggah crying like a little bitch."

I laughed so hard my stomach was tightening up. "Did she?"

"Butterfly, when she say she whooped that niggah ass, she whooped that niggah ass. Janae rolled up on the hoop court while them niggahs was in the middle of playing ball and parked her shit! She got out of the ride with her pistol in her hand and chased that niggah against the fence where he couldn't run."

"I ain't ask that niggah no questions. I just commenced to beating his ass with my gun. This niggah was crying in front of his boys, begging me to stop whooping that ass."

"Yeah, but what Janae is not telling you, is that him and his boys put the word out that they're going to come back for her."

"They're going to shoot a girl?" I asked. "Those are some punk-ass niggahs!"

"Those dudes don't see Janae as no damn girl. They see her as a niggah."

"I ain't studdin' them fools, Butterfly. They gotta bring some ass to get some ass."

"You're not worried about that guy coming back?" I asked. "I am!"

"Hell nawl, niggahs like that ain't nothin' but talk. If he was a man, he wouldna ran in the first place; he woulda took his bullet when I got out the car."

"Girl, you better watch your back."

"When it's my time to go, it's my time to go. It ain't nothin' I can do about it."

"There is something you can do about it. You can stay the hell out of trouble!"

"I'm trying, but niggahs keep coming at me and I ain't backin' down to no niggah! That's all it is to it."

"Y'all have to let this go."

"Naw, I'm a'ight! I gotta be grown style now. I'm eighteen. If I catch a case now, I'm going to be tried as an adult. It's time to lay low."

"Okay, girl, I don't wanna be hearing about you getting caught up in no more of this street-type activity."

"Naw, I'm good, though."

"Toya, watch this chick for me. It's just us now. Keisha gone, Jacqua's not a part of the clique no more. I can't lose any more of my girls."

"Imma try, girl."

"Get outta here with that bullshit. You probably met all kinds of new niggahs out there in L.A. We saw you on television every week fronting like you one of them runway hoes."

"Fronting my ass! You saw me doing what I needed to do to win that hundred grand, Janae."

"Don't get it twisted; I'm proud as hell!" Janae said hitting the table slightly with her fist. "I was like, my niggah gon' win this shit!"

"I recorded it every week on my DVR and watched it whenever I wanted to."

"I didn't even know y'all watched reality TV, Toya."

"I didn't, until you got me into that shit." Janae laughed. "Now I watch everything, *Tiny and Toya*, Keisha Cole, Atlanta housewives, Monica, all of them niggahs!"

"You mean all of the people from Atlanta reality shows?" I joked.

"All of them niggahs here in Atlanta?"

"Yeah, fool."

"Damn, shit, I didn't even know."

"Hey." I was very sincere. "I want you to make me a promise, Janae."

"Man, you know I don't do promises, Butterfly."

"You got to this time."

"Come on, man, don't make me do that. I'm not good at keeping promises and you know it."

"Janae?" I poked my lips out and raised my eyebrows.

"What, Butterfly?"

"I'm serious."

"Aw, man, damn. What is it?"

"I want you to promise me to stay out of trouble."

"Come on now, you know fools are always coming at me, man. I can't...I can't back down to nobody, man. Half of the battle on the streets is your rep, baby. I can't promise that."

"Okay then, come out to L.A. with me."

"Fool, you crazy."

"No, I'm serious. Both of you." I looked at Janae and Toya. "Come out to L.A. and stay with me and just start over."

"How are we going to live in L.A. all by ourselves when we're barely making it in Atlanta with our families?" Toya asked.

"I got y'all, don't worry about that."

"Naw, that's your money, Butterfly. We move out there with you and we'll go through your money like it ain't shit. Do you, don't worry about us."

"Speak for yourself, Janae," Toya snapped. "I want to get the hell out of here! I want to start over. It ain't no future in Atlanta for me."

"What you gon' do out there in California, Toya?"

"I don't know. Get a job, do something."

"Get a job where, niggah? They got McDonald's here."

"I can be your personal assistant, Butterfly. I'm good with computers, Word, Excel, PowerPoint, all that shit."

"I don't need no personal assistant."

"You will. Your ass is about to blow up."

"I don't know about no blowing up, Toya."

"Niggah, everybody in this whole country know who you are now." Janae pounded the table again. "Niggah, you won the *America Beauty Queen* show."

"It was *America the Beautiful*, fool." Toya chuckled.

"Whatever it was, my niggah won it!"

"Okay! That's enough! I can't take it no more!" I pointed my finger at Janae.

"What?"

"I can't take the way you use the n-word."

"What you talking about, niggah?"

"That! Everything is niggah this, or niggah that. Stop using that word so much."

"A'ight. I didn't know it bothered you so much, niggah."

"You still saying it!" I shouted.

"Damn! I did? That word just run in my family. It's hereditary."

"That word don't run in your family. You just so used to saying it, it just comes out automatically. I mean you use it as a verb, noun, adjective, everything, man. And let me tell you what else you need to stop saying."

"This niggah is trippin'." Janae laughed out loud.

"I'm serious. Stop calling women bitches and hoes so much."

"Shit, I call niggahs bitches and hoes, too."

"Well, stop calling them those names, too."

"Wait a minute." Janae lit a cigarette. "We've been through this before. I can either cut back on saying niggah, or bitches or hoes, but ain't no way in hell I can do all three at one time."

"Okay, cut back on using the words 'niggah' and 'bitch,' for right now."

"A'ight, my niggah." Janae took a puff on her cigarette and blew it out.

Toya was laughing so hard her head was leaned back over the seat, and her face was pointing straight to the sky.

"Toya, back to you." Toya stopped laughing and sat straight up. "How much are you charging to be my assistant?"

"I don't know. How much they normally charge?"

"I ain't never had no assistant before."

"How about forty dollars an hour?"

"How you gon' go from making eight dollars an hour working at Rally's to making forty dollars an hour doing some shit you ain't never done before in your life, Toya?"

"You ain't got nothing to do with this, Janae."

"I got this, Janae," I said. "Keisha…"

"Keisha gone, baby," Toya interrupted. "I'm Toya."

"Dang, did I say Keisha again?"

"Yeah, you keep calling me Keisha, girl."

"I'm sorry, I meant Toya." I paused momentarily and reminisced over the times Keisha and I had hung out at Dugan's. "Toya, why do you think you deserve forty dollars an hour?"

"Okay, thirty dollars an hour then."

"Why you drop ten dollars like that?"

"I don't know."

"Okay, let's do this. I'll pay you five thousand dollars less than what the average personal assistant makes, plus, you can move into my apartment with me when I get back out to L.A."

"What do your apartment look like?"

"I don't have one yet. My agent is looking for one now. But it should be big enough for all three of us."

"I don't know if I could make a big jump like that. I know Atlanta, man. I know what to do and how to do it up in here."

"But everything you know is self-destructive, Janae. You have to break that cycle, girl."

"Butterfly is right. What are you going to do here besides go to jail?"

"Y'all don't get it, man!" Janae was frustrated. "I fit in here! I can be what I want to be here."

"They got lesbians out there in California, Janae," Toya joked.

"This ain't just about that. I like the way I look! I like the way I dress! I don't want to go nowhere, where I can't be me! People in California is all about trying to be skinny, and pretty, and that ain't me."

"They have a place called West Hollywood that you need to visit, Janae. You would be considered conservative out there. It's not what you think. Los Angeles is loaded with freaky, weird people! Just give it a chance. If you don't like it, come back to the A-T-L, a'ight?"

"Come on, Janae," Toya urged. "Come out there with me."

"You sure your modeling friends won't be whispering in your ear?"

"Don't worry about them. Y'all family."

"Okay then, cool."

"I'm leaving the day after tomorrow, so y'all need to be ready to go."

"I can be ready today if you want me to. I'm ready to get the hell up outta here." Toya was so excited.

"We driving?"

"Hell no, Janae!" I said. "Okay, y'all, I have to go pick Bri up, so we can go to my little sister's dance recital."

"A'ight, I got to go get with this chick before it gets too late anyway." Janae stood and gave me a fist pound. "I'm out."

"Me, too."

We left Dugan's and I picked up Bri. She was acting strange, kind of distant, so I had to find out what was going on.

"Okay, what's going on, Bri?"

"What do you mean?"

"Why are you acting strange like that?"

"Like what?"

"Stop answering a question with a question."

"I don't know what you're talking about."

"Oh, man, here we go." I sighed heavily. "Why aren't you talking to me?"

"Okay, if you want me to tell you, I'll tell you."

"I'm listening."

"You come home from California and you act like you can't hang with me. It's all about your friends."

"Bri, come on now."

"I'm serious. We haven't done anything together since you been here."

"If you wanted to do something, why didn't you just call me?"

"Okay, whatever, Butterfly! Forget it! Just go be with your friends."

"Bri? Look, my friends have problems. Serious problems and I'm trying to help them. You're my family. No matter how much time I spend with them, it's always going to be me and you, and you know this…maaaaaaan!"

"That's not funny." Bri chuckled.

"All right, look, you, me, and Brit, tonight, we're having a sleepover."

"Can I ask if Alex can come? I haven't seen her in a couple of weeks."

"Yeah, I haven't seen her since I've been back."

After Brit's recital, Uncle Mike picked up Alex and brought her over to our house and we had a sleepover. I enjoyed my cousins tremendously, but I was also sad. There was still a missing pillow in the room that could not be replaced. When everybody had fallen asleep, I placed Keisha's picture on my pillow next to me, and then I cried myself to sleep.

I promised Jeremy we could hang out the next night. Since he announced that he was going to stay home and attend Georgia Tech, Jeremy had been all over the local news, ESPN, talk shows, everywhere. The Yellow Jackets were an underdog to get him, but in the end, he went with the home team. I understood why; they were not a national powerhouse and his talent would flourish. His light could shine brightly for the one mandatory year he had to spend in college and then he would be on to the NBA. I know it was his father's idea. Jeremy would be the only star on the team, but more importantly, he would still be near his daddy.

We decided to go to the movies at Lenox Square mall. On our way out, Jeremy was holding my hand and brought up the subject of us getting back together again.

"I really think you need to reconsider my PowerPoint proposal I emailed you about getting back together."

"You're nuts!"

"Did you get it?"

"Yeah, I got it and you are crazy, boy."

"I'm going to keep bugging you until you give in, so you can save us both a lot of time if you just said yes right now."

"You can't love me the way I need to be loved, Jeremy."

"What are you talking about? I do love you unconditionally. I'm practically begging you to come back to me."

"That's an ego thing, not an unconditional thing."

While we were talking, two goofy teenagers, one black and one white, walked in front of us and stopped. The young black girl mustered up the courage to speak and nervously reached out a piece of paper.

"Oh my God! It's you! Can I have your autograph?" The girl's hand was practically shaking like a leaf on a tree.

Jeremy, who was used to signing autographs at that time, reached into his front pocket and pulled out an ink pen. "Who do I sign it to?"

"Oh, I'm sorry, I meant Ms. Butterfly."

"What?" I looked at Jeremy and then back at the girl. "Excuse me?"

"Can I please have your autograph, Ms. Butterfly?"

"You want my autograph?"

"Yes ma'am! You were terrific on *America the Beautiful!*"

"Thank you." Jeremy handed me the pen and smiled. "Who do I make this out to?"

"Keisha."

"Keisha?" I stopped writing and looked the girl in the face. "That's a very pretty name, Keisha."

"Thank you, Ms. Butterfly."

"You're very welcome, Keisha."

"I want to be a model when I grow up. Do you have any advice for me?"

"Yes." I held her face in my hand. "I want you to repeat after me, okay?"

"Yes."

"I want you to say, 'I am beautiful!'"

"I am beautiful!"

"You see beauty is not just a pretty face, or a slim body; it's a state of being. If you feel beautiful, then you are beautiful. Now I want you to keep those words, 'I am beautiful,' inside of you, and remember this precious face that you wake up to every day. Okay?"

"Okay, Ms. Butterfly."

Her friend handed me a piece of paper and then I signed an autograph for her. I stared at them when they walked away. Jeremy knew I was trapped in my thought and that it was about Keisha.

"Hey, you okay, Butterfly?"

"Yes, I'm fine."

"Sure?"

"Yeah, I'm fine."

"Okay." Jeremy held my hand and we began to walk toward his car. "I can't believe I'm holding the hand of Butterfly, the super-model, superstar!"

"I'm not a superstar."

"You are in my book. And I'm quite sure that little girl feels the same way."

"You're the superstar. You have women, grown women, eating out of your hands."

"And you have me eating out of yours." Jeremy kissed me on the hand.

"Okay, Romeo, dial it down."

"Butterfly." Jeremy kissed me passionately. "I love you."

"I love you, too."

"If we love each other, then why can't we be together?"

"You know why, Jeremy."

"Because of my mistake?"

"I don't want to talk about it."

"I do."

"I love you, Jeremy, and I probably always will. But I can't forget what happened. I've tried, but I can't. I wanted you to be the first boy to make love to me. I really, really wanted that. I know I was naïve, but I thought that's what you wanted, too."

"That woman seduced me and manipulated me, Butterfly."

"That may work with your mama and with your friends, but it doesn't work on me, Jeremy. You were twice as big as Ms. Jamerson. If you didn't want to have sex with her, you didn't have to have sex with her. But you did."

"So are you going to hold this over my head forever?"

"I'm not holding anything over your head, but you know how I feel about it, yet you keep putting yourself in the position to be rejected. Like I said, I love you, but after what happened, I can't be with you."

"What about in a year or two?"

"There's no telling how many girls you will have by then."

"If I'm with another girl, it's because I can't have you."

I kissed Jeremy on the cheek. "Have fun, baby."

Jeremy drove me home, and of course, Pa-Pa was waiting up for me. He told me Toya had stopped by to see me. She never came over unannounced, so I knew exactly what she wanted. She wanted to nag me about our California trip. She was anxious and ready to go. I was looking forward to having my girls out there in L.A. with me. Toya was a little hustler, so she was just trying to solidify that job of being my assistant while it was still on my mind.

It was my last night. Bri and Pa-Pa were waiting for me to come home. Pa-Pa talked to me about the dangers of living in a big city. When he finished, Bri and I stayed up talking about the show and my modeling career. That nagging Toya blew my phone up all night long. I did not answer because there was no such thing as a short phone call with Toya. I was with my family, and no matter how excited she was, I was not going to answer. The next morning, I woke up to my phone vibrating next to my head. It was Toya.

"Girl, what is your malfunction?" I had my eyes closed while I was talking.

"*They killed her!*" Toya screamed into the phone.

"What?" I sat straight up and put the phone closer to my ear.

"They killed Janae, Butterfly! They killed her!"

"Who killed her?" I screamed back.

"Those boys! They set her up! They killed Janae!"

"Toya! Are you trying to tell me that Janae is dead, girl?"

"*Yeah!* She's dead!" Toya's voice was so high, I could barely understand what she was saying.

I paced back and forth in my room. It finally hit me and I screamed loud and long. "*Noooooooooooooooooooooooo!*"

I fell to my knees and pounded my phone on the floor.

"What's the matter?" Bri kneeled beside me and rubbed my back.

Pa-Pa rushed into the room and stood me up. "What's wrong with you?"

I collapsed in Pa-Pa's arms with what was left of my phone, still in my hand. "They killed Janae, Pa-Pa!"

"Your friend Janae?"

"Yeah, Pa-Pa!" I sobbed.

Ms. Alicia ran into the room. "What's the matter with you?"

"Her friend was killed." Pa-Pa held me in arms.

"Who? What friend? Keisha?" Ms. Alicia thought I was releasing pent-up grief from Keisha's death.

"No, the big girl."

"Janae?" Ms. Alicia ran to me. "Sweetheart? Something happened to Janae?"

"She's dead, Mom."

"Come here." Ms. Alicia took me out of Pa-Pa's arms and sat me on the bed next to her. "It's going to be all right, sweetheart."

Dr. Forrester stood in the doorway but did not say a word. Bri sat on the other side of me and cried just as hard. She knew Janae well. Janae had spent time in the juvie for the both of us. My life was too good! It was only a matter of time before fate evened the score with me. But I had no idea it was going to come back so damn hard! How many more people in my life were going to die before fate left me the hell alone? I knew the answer before I asked the question, but I asked it just the same. What had I done to bring so much tragedy into my life? I was born!

I met with Toya the next day, and she told me the girl Janae was supposed to be hooking up with that night, was actually setting her up. She was the baby's mama of the boy that had threatened Janae.

Apparently, the girl had flirted with Janae to get her to come over. When Janae knocked on the girl's door, that boy and two of his friends opened the door and aimed their guns in Janae's face. They were only trying to scare her, but one of the guns accidently went off. They were locked up. Three sons, three brothers, three friends, three nephews, three fathers, three lives...gone! And my girl, oh, what I would have given to hear her use the n-word one more time. R.I.P. Janae!

I had to delay returning to L.A. until after Janae's funeral. Ms. Erin had set up some photo shoots and a few fashion shows to keep me active. She was afraid that I may be too emotionally distraught after Janae's murder and did not trust me returning on my own, so she came to Atlanta to get me. She visited me at our house, and although Ms. Alicia sat in the room with us, she promised me she would not get involved.

Everything was going fine until we had a conversation about Toya moving to L.A. with me and becoming my assistant. Ms. Erin felt that it was in my best interest to leave Toya back in Atlanta.

"I realize you're grieving right now, Butterfly, but it's a huge responsibility to have someone depend on you for everything when they move to a new city."

"I know that, Ms. Erin, but she cannot stay here in Atlanta."

"I understand that, but your career is taking off and you don't need any setbacks."

"My friend is not a setback."

"What happens if you bring her out to California and you have to fly away to Milan, or Amsterdam?"

"She'll be fine."

"I'm going to have to insist that you leave her behind, Butterfly."

"I can't do that." I sighed, and thought about what I was about to say. I wanted to say the right thing, the right way. "Ms. Erin, I have done everything you've asked me to do. I haven't questioned you. I haven't resisted you. I have done nothing but trusted you. Now I'm asking you this one time to trust me, please."

"I can empathize with you Butterfly, but..."

"I hate to interrupt." Ms. Alicia looked at Ms. Erin. "But I would like to say one quick thing if I may?"

"Sure."

I prepared myself for the "you have to do what you have to do" speech from Ms. Alicia, but she was not a teacher that day. She was a mother.

"I understand what you're saying, Erin. But Shante has been through an awful lot this past year. And I am proud of what she has accomplished and I appreciate what you have done for her. However, right now, what she needs more than a modeling tiara, is a friend. A friend who understands the pain she's suffering. If her friend moving to Los Angeles means that she can no longer pursue her modeling career with you, I'm afraid it is time for Shante to find her a new representative because her sanity is much more important than her vanity."

"I think my point is being taken out of context here. I want what's best for Butterfly as well. If that means her friend coming to Los Angeles, I'll buy the damn ticket. You know the situation better than I do. She's your child, Alicia. If you like the idea, I love it!"

"So Toya can come?" I asked.

"If that's what you want," Ms. Erin said.

"Can she be my assistant?"

"If you're the one paying her, she can be whatever you want her to be."

"Thank you, Ms. Erin."

"So we're all good here?" Ms. Erin asked.

"Yes," Ms. Alicia answered.

Ms. Alicia walked Ms. Erin to the door and they said good-bye. Ms. Alicia came back into the den to give me some advice.

"Butterfly?"

"Yes ma'am?"

"Sit!" Ms. Alicia waited for me to sit down and gave me some advice. "In this business, you are the commodity, not your agent, nor your agency. You! You are not an up-and-coming model any-more. There's a demand for you. Erin knows this. And so does everyone else."

"Okay."

"Now, in Erin's defense, she was right."

"How was she right?"

"I commend you for being loyal to your friend. But you can't bring yourself down trying to bring someone else up. It won't benefit either one of you. And, no matter where Toya is, until she decides to get her life together, she's going to always have prob-lems. And I don't want her problems to become your problems."

"I won't let that happen."

"I'm sure you won't."

"Thanks for having my back, Mom."

"That's what a mother is for."

Chapter Nineteen

We flew back the same day as Janae's funeral. The first time Toya saw my apartment was the first time I saw my apartment. It was huge and spacious. It had three bedrooms downstairs and four-and-a-half baths. It had an upstairs with a one-bedroom suite and a gigantic bathroom. We were like children running around that apartment. I stopped running and almost cried when I found out how much it was going to cost me.

Ms. Erin wasted no time getting back to work. I had two important photo shoots the very next morning. Over the next couple of days, I was in two more commercials, but I had no dialogue in either one of them.

As soon as I finished the second commercial, Ms. Erin, Tara and I flew to San Francisco for a show where there were going to be big-time international designers. Two other girls from the agency flew ahead of us for fitting. Since I was new, Ms. Erin wanted to coach me through every step of the process. The three of us were in first-class. I paid for Toya's ticket, so she had to fly in coach. That's my girl, but first-class?

I was still nervous about flying but not as much as I was on my first two flights. Maybe it had something to do with flying first-class, or maybe it had something to do with Tara running her mouth so much I did not have time to think about being in the air. At one point she was getting on my nerves so bad, I almost asked the pilot to fly the damn plane into a mountain just to shut her ass up!

"You are going to be a star in this business, Butterfly."

"Thank you, Tara."

"Like, how old are you again?"

"Eighteen."

"That's close to my age, I'm twenty-one."

"Really?"

"People tell me I look younger than that, but it's true. I'm only twenty-one."

"Oh, okay."

"And where are you from again?"

"Georgia."

"Is that near Atlanta?"

I wanted to scream, *Yeah you ignorant heffa, now shut the hell up!* But instead, I smiled and said sarcastically, "Yes, Georgia is near Atlanta."

"I've never been to the South before. I want to go someday."

"Okay."

"I've been to New York, though."

It pissed me off when people from New York and Los Angeles talked like they were the only two cities in the entire United States. I was born in Raleigh, North Carolina, and I was raised in Atlanta, Georgia, and I did not give a damn where anybody else came from.

"I'd never left Georgia until I came here."

"Wow! This is like a true American rags-to-riches story."

"Not exactly. I'm not coming from rags."

"I'm sorry. I didn't mean to offend you."

"I'm sorry, but you did. Every black girl in this business is not modeling because we're looking for a meal ticket. Some of us do it because we know that we're beautiful."

"That's beautiful."

Tara stared at me and then turned around and talked to Ms. Erin. After that, I was able to get a power nap before we landed.

Once we arrived at the arena, Ms. Erin asked Toya to come with her, while Tara took me backstage. Ms. Erin made sure I did not eat any bread or pastries from the time we arrived in Los Angeles until after the show. She wanted me to look thin and shapely without any bulges. In my mind I was already paper thin. Why in the hell did I need to be thinner than that?

I found out as soon as I stepped backstage. I was four hours early just for the rehearsals and there were already five models preparing for the show. They were as tall as me, or taller, and thin as hell. Even their feet and hands were thin. Two of them were the girls from Philpot's Modeling Agency. I knew I was going to have to step my game up when I found out they flew all the way in from Paris. They had arrived a full day before me and I was only flying in from Los Angeles. Tara introduced me to them and they welcomed me to the team. Their French accent was very apparent.

"Hi, Sophia, this is Butterfly. She is now a part of our Philpot family."

"Hi, Butterfly." Sophia hugged me and then kissed me on the cheek. "What an unusual name."

"Hi, Butterfly." Bridgette kissed me on both cheeks. "I am Bridgette."

"Nice to meet both of you."

I had grown another inch my senior year, bringing my height to a statuesque six feet one. Sophia was about an inch or two taller than me, perhaps six feet two, or three inches tall. She wore short, jet-black hair that was cut evenly at one ear, and then longer all the way to the back of the neck, and then all around to her other ear. She had broad shoulders which led to a V-shaped, slender waistline. Her hips were almost even with her waistline and they barely spread as they met with her thighs. The woman had no hips. But she was wearing the hell out of that tight mini-dress.

Bridgette was about the same height, with red hair. It was pinned up. She was thin, but she had slightly more hips than Sophia. She was wearing an elegant, long dress that went all the way to her ankles. Her four-inch heels were skimpy, but cute.

"Nice shoes," I said. "I hope a designer fits me in a pair of shoes like that."

"Oh no." Bridgette chuckled. "These are not the designers' clothes. These are mine."

"What?" I felt like a fool. "You dress like that every day?"

"But of course." Bridgette pulled me close to her and whispered in my ear. "Do you know whose clothes are in this show?"

"No."

"Jean-Claude Francois."

"Who?"

"You are such a baby into this business."

"Okay, but who is this Jean-Claude Francois again?"

"He is only the most fantastic designer in all of the world. That is why we arrived so early. We want to convince him that we are best for his work."

"You do not know who Jean-Claude Francois is?" Sophia asked.

"No! I just found out who Jean-Claude Van Damme is."

"Jean-Claude Van Damme? Yum-Yum!"

"Maybe back in the day, he was yum-yum, but now he is more like, oh-noooo!" Neither Sophia nor Bridgette understood my joke. "My bad, it was a bad joke; forgot he was one of your native Frenchmen."

"No, he is not from France at all. He is Belgian."

"Belgian?"

"Enough of this talk!" Bridgette interrupted. "Have you been fitted for your designer?"

"Not yet, I just got here."

"You better get that fanny moving."

"Moving where?"

"To be fitted, of course."

"Come!" Sophia snapped her fingers at me. "Follow me."

I was like, *wait a minute, chick. Do not snap your fingers at me like I am a dog.* I was going to say something out loud, but she walked away so fast, I had to shut up to try to keep up. We went to a room where there were naked bodies all over the place. Women were scurrying from one person to another.

"Hi, Chanel," Sophia said. "This is Butterfly. Is she with your designer?"

"No, I don't know anything about a Butterfly."

We trotted over to another area and she asked the same question. "Hi, Patty, this is Butterfly. Is she with your designer?"

"Not that I know of, no."

"Come on." Sophia quickly trotted off.

She took me to two other designers' stations and both said I was not wearing their clothing. Sophia continued to simultaneously walk and talk extremely fast.

"There is only one designer remaining and there is no way—" Sophia stopped abruptly in mid-sentence and stomped away until we stopped in front of a very feminine-looking man. "Rene, we seem to have a problem. I am trying to have this model fitted for her wardrobe, but we can't seem to find her designers. Can you help me?"

"What is her name?" Rene asked without even looking at us and slinging pieces of clothing from one place to the next.

"Butterfly."

"Butterfly?" Rene stopped what he was doing and looked at me. "This is Butterfly?"

"Yes."

"She is mine! Come with me!" Rene rushed off with Sophia and me following in his footsteps.

Sophia whispered in my ear while we were speed walking behind Rene. "This is impossible!"

"What's impossible?"

"That you are wearing Jean-Claude's line."

"Is that a big deal?"

"That is the biggest of deals! Everybody wants to model Jean-Claude's line! Everybody!"

"Then why did he pick me?"

"Because you were on television! Everybody in this business watched that television show and you won."

"So it's not about me being a real model then? It's about that damn television show."

"Of course you're a real model, sweetheart. But models are not born; they are made."

"And here we are." Rene stopped in front of two large doors. "The dressing room."

We walked in and there were people working like they were on an assembly line. They were coordinating each designer's line to a certain area. Sort of like a controlled chaotic situation. If it was that frenzied before rehearsal, I did not want to imagine what it was going to be like in real time.

"Listen up! This is Sophia." Rene pointed at Sophia. "She will be modeling some of Jean-Claude's pieces today. And this is Butterfly! She will be modeling Jean-Claude's masterpieces today!"

Jean-Claude had five handpicked dressers for his line. Dressers are the people who assist the models in putting on the designer's wardrobe before they hit the runway. All five dressers came toward me for fitting. Rene cut them off at the path and stood between them and me. He held both of his hands in front of them. "Wait a minute, you piranhas! You will not devour her. Back up! I said, back up!"

The group backed up a few feet and waited for instructions. Sophia put her hands on her hips in frustration.

"I do not believe what I am seeing here." Sophia pouted.

"Listen up! All of you! I refuse to let you people send me to a mental institution today! Jean-Claude wants two of you to work with Ms. Butterfly and he wants her to be immaculate! And what Jean-Claude wants, Jean-Claude gets!" Rene put his finger on his lips and then contemplated which of the five he would select. "Okay, you and you! Get to work!"

One man and one woman took my hands and led me to a full-body mirror. They took my measurements and then handed me piece after piece of clothing. They somehow made each piece fit my body perfectly.

I was rushed onstage for the rehearsal. It lasted over three hours. I thought we were going to have time to leave and come back before the show, but that was a no-go. I was fitted for the designers in segments one and five, Ria Ramone of Italy, and of course, Jean-Claude Francois of France. Some models were in each segment. They would be dashing in and out all night long.

Rene met with me after rehearsal and prepped me for the show. He had to leave briefly to make sure everything was going accordingly and I relaxed. When he returned, it was on and poppin'!

"Is there going to be anyone else modeling Jean-Claude's new line?"

"You are a star, my dear, but you are not the only star. We have three of the top models in the world introducing his fantastic pieces."

"Oh." I was embarrassed. "I didn't mean it like I wanted to be the only model. I was saying it because I *didn't* want to be the only model."

"That's neither here nor there."

"We still have an hour or so before the show. Is there anything I need to do?"

"Yes. Sit down."

"Okay." I sat down and Rene sat next to me.

"I don't exactly know how you got to where you are so quickly or why Jean-Claude wants you so badly. And frankly, my dear, I don't care. Those quaint fashion shows you've done are not comparable to what you are about to experience tonight. I know Ms. Erin has taught and prepared you very well. But if you're going to be in my show, we have to give you a crash course in Fashion 101."

"Okay."

"Are you aware of the term, 'fresh face'?"

"Yes, it means no makeup."

"Did you bring nude and black thongs?"

"Yes."

"Are we shaven in all of the proper areas down there?" Rene pointed between my legs.

"Yes."

"Raise your arms." I raised them above my head and Rene looked closer. "No residue under there? Good!"

Rene sniffed my neck and then my entire body to smell if I was wearing perfume or body lotion. He gestured for me to get up and follow him. Sophia, who was getting a last-minute adjustment, playfully stuck her tongue out at me on our way out. I smiled and stuck my tongue out at Rene behind his back. Sophia laughed, and was accidentally poked by one of the dressers.

"Shit! That hurts!" Sophia snapped.

I followed Rene to another huge room they called the hair and makeup room. They had four chairs and six mirrors for the hairdressers on one side and four mirrors and four chairs for the makeup crew on the other side of the room. Bridgette was sitting in one of the chairs when I walked in. She waved at me and I waved back. They sat me in a chair next to hers and started putting on my makeup. We were sitting at an angle where our backs were turned to one another, but we could see each other in the mirror.

I had never participated in such a large fashion show where the world was watching. I was accustomed to relatively small shows and everybody being in one spot, certainly nothing as extravagant as that. It was nothing for Bridgette, though. She had modeled all around the world and nothing seemed to surprise her—nothing but Jean-Claude selecting me to showcase his new line.

"Which segments are you in?"

"The first and the last."

"The last? That's Jean-Claude's line?"

"Yes."

"How did that happen?"

"Erin."

"You are her pet."

"I don't think so."

"I have been in this business for seven years and I have never seen an amateur move so high up as quickly as you."

"What can I say? I have a good agent that really knows what she's doing."

"I have the same damn agent!" Bridgette chuckled.

"I know." I laughed.

"Take advantage of these people who are taking advantage of you. You are a hot commodity because you won that title on that television show. But from what I hear, you have what it takes to stay on top for a long time."

"You think so?"

"Absolutely. The other four winners of that show gave up on their careers to become movie stars. And where are they now? They're on other American reality shows trying to get famous by being famous. But you, you are putting in the work to become a real supermodel."

"Thank you. That was so sweet, Bridgette."

Suddenly, Rene burst through the door and came directly to my chair. He seemed like he was about to go into cardiac arrest.

"Jean-Claude is on his way in here to speak with you, Butterfly."

"About what?"

"About his masterpiece."

"Oh-kaaaay."

"I want you to tell him you love his line, especially his master-piece."

"Okay."

"I must go, but, remember," Rene whispered as he walked back-ward out of the room, "You love it! You love it! You love it!"

When Rene disappeared through the doors, Bridgette gave me more advice.

"Butterfly?"

"Yes?"

"Never let anyone put you in a piece that does not feel comfort-able on you. Take it from me; you and the designer will regret it."

Jean-Claude walked through the door with a small entourage. He was flamboyant and stylish. He wore big shades, heels, and a long feathered scarf that touched the ground on both sides. He also had on flared pants with a flared-sleeved shirt. His hair was cut like a woman, shaven on the sides and the back, and curly on top. He had on eyeliner with long eyelashes.

"Bridgette?" Jean-Claude bent his wrist like a girl and shook Bridgette's fingers. "How are you, my heart?"

"I could not be better. I missed you in Paris."

"And I, you."

"This is Butterfly." Bridgette pointed to me.

"Aw!" Jean-Claude covered his mouth and then kissed me. "You are more gorgeous than I imagined, my chocolate Butterfly."

"Thank you, Mr. Francois."

"Mr. Francois?" Jean-Claude chuckled as he looked from side to side. "Is my father in the room? Call me Jean, or Jean-Claude."

"Okay...Jean."

"Are you completely comfortable with my ensemble? Your attitude will emanate the essence of my piece. If your attitude is uncomfortable, it will reflect through your walk, your smile, your twists, and your turns, everything you do. If you feel like my line is a part of your soul, that, too, will be reflected to the audience."

"I feel comfortable."

"Are you certain?"

"One hundred percent."

"Good!" Jean-Claude walked off with his entourage standing to the side until he passed them, and then they followed him out of the door.

"Wow!" I chuckled.

"He likes you. That means a lot. He doesn't like anybody."

"It seems like he likes you."

"That means nothing. He would just as much as called me a bitch, as sweetheart. He's moody, but he likes you, so stay on his good side."

"I'll try."

After my makeup, they fixed my hair. Things picked up in a hurry after that. In the first segment with Ria's line, I had two pieces to wear. On my first run, I was dressed by two women. That was fine, but then there was a man doing something right beside us. I was timid to undress in front of the man. I was trying to find an area to shield myself from him while the girls helped me into my piece.

"What are you doing?" Sophia asked.

"That guy is standing right there and I have to slip into my swimwear."

"And?"

"And?" I was surprised Sophia was so casual about undressing in front of a man. "And I don't want him to see me."

"You better take off your clothes and slip your skinny black ass into that swimsuit if you ever want to work again."

"But what if he sees my goodies?"

"Who cares? Here!" Sophia handed me a bottle of lotion and asked me to put it on one of her legs while she put lotion on the other.

I helped her with her lotion and she showed me how to put bronzer between my breasts to enhance the look of my cleavage. She also put the bronzer on the bony part of my shoulders to enhance their look as well. And then I was off to the races!

I stepped onto the runway and I immediately took control of the audience. I strutted down the aisle with the grace of a gazelle. It was such a rush when I felt all of the eyes in the room were on me.

After my first walk, I went backstage and then quickly changed into another swimsuit. I was so high on the moment, I did not care who was looking at me. I did not give a damn if I had on clothes, butt naked, or whatever. I just wanted to get back on that runway as quickly as possible. My adrenaline was pumping!

At the end of the show, everyone was waiting for us to reveal Jean-Claude's new line. I could hear the *oohs* and the *aahs* from the audience as the girls pranced their way onto the stage. I thought to myself, if they reacted that way to them, I was going to bring the damn house down. I was the final model, and I rocked the hell out that piece!

Sophia and Bridgette were waiting for me when I walked backstage. They hugged me once I was out of sight of the audience. I was out of my mind with excitement. Jean-Claude came backstage with Ms. Erin and he was in seventh heaven. Ms. Erin stood aside and absorbed the moment. She had made me a star, even if it was only for one night.

Jean-Claude and Ms. Erin pulled me into a private room, and I was invited to model his line in Europe for the entire month of September. It would begin in Paris, and then I would go to Portugal, Milan, Berlin, Amsterdam, Oslo, London, and it would end in the desert of the beautiful Dubai. I was so excited I allowed myself to get too caught up in the moment. I signed the contract on the spot without considering my scholarship to Spelman.

Ms. Erin had two limos waiting for us after the show. I thought it was strange that she, Toya and the other Philpot girls piled into the first limo, but Ms. Erin instructed me to get into the second one. Again, I was hyped from the show and was not thinking straight. I stepped into that long, stretch limo and I could not believe my eyes. Jeremy was sitting all alone with a dozen roses in his hands.

"You were absolutely beautiful."

"Oh my goodness! What are you doing here?"

"I'm here to show you how much I love you, Butterfly."

"This is amazing! How did you get here?"

"I flew, and your friend Toya did the rest."

"What?"

As I was asking Jeremy a question Toya texted me: *Have fun, you deserve it. Your PA, Toya Laury!*

"Your friend Toya called your mom, and your mom called my

mom, and my mom asked me if I wanted to forget about basketball for a weekend and enjoy being a teenager."

"She let you fly out here all by yourself?"

"I did not say all that! She and your mom, oh, and Bri, too. They're all here in San Francisco. They came to see you at your fashion show."

"They were there?"

"Screaming like they were at a sorority party."

"Oh, wow! This is an unbelievable night."

"I know. I can't believe I'm here with you. I love you, Butterfly."

"I love you, too, Jeremy."

"I want to ask you…"

As Jeremy was speaking, my mom called my cell phone. "Hi, Mom."

I immediately told my mom that I had committed to a European tour. She told me the decision was mine to make, but she advised me to take advantage of the opportunity to see the world. She told me the opportunity to go to college would be there when I returned. I asked her about trading in a dream for reality. In that case my dream was modeling, but my reality was a college education. She told me I should never trade in a college education for a dream. But she reminded me that modeling was no a longer dream; it was a reality and I had the contract to prove it. I told her I loved her, I would see her in October, and then I hung up my phone.

"I need to call one more person, and you will have my undivided attention."

"Okay." Jeremy sighed and sat back in the seat.

I called my dad and told him I was going to Europe, and I would not see him again until I returned. He wanted to see me, but he was excited that his little girl was fulfilling her dream. I told him I loved him, I would see him in October, and then I hung up my phone.

"Okay, I'm all yours. What's up?"

"Ever since…"

My cell phone rang again. It was Ma Powell.

"Sorry, Jeremy, this is my grandma. It will only take a minute."

I chatted with Ma for a few minutes and told her about my European tour. She was so excited she asked me if I needed her to buy me some underwear for the trip. I told her I was okay in the underwear department and she told me she loved me. I was going to spend plenty of time with Ma before I left for Europe, so our conversation was not as bittersweet as when I had spoken to Ms. Alicia and Dad.

"You just heard everything I said to my parents, right?"

"Yup."

"What do you think about me not going to college this fall?"

"I think school will always be there, but this opportunity won't. I saw you on that stage tonight. I won't lie. Maybe it's because I love you, but you seemed like the star of the show. All of the women were beautiful, but all of them didn't electrify the stage like you did. I was looking at people, looking at you. They were just as amazed as I was."

"Wow!"

"Butterfly, I love you." Jeremy held my face in his hand. "Go to Europe, baby."

"Hold on, if you love me so much, why do you want me to leave the country?"

"Because it's time for you to really do what you have to do."

"But I could be at Spelman and you could be at Georgia Tech."

"Yeah, but if it was about me wanting what's best for me, I would be playing ball at a D-1 powerhouse, like Duke, U-Conn, or Michigan State. My dad didn't make me stay in Atlanta to go to school. I stayed because I wanted to be near you."

"Jeremy, stop talking to me like that. I'm going to start to believe you, boy." I turned my head and looked away.

Jeremy turned my face back toward him and kissed me on the lips. "It's true! I wanted the chance to get you back, and once I found out you were going to Spelman, and not Yale, that was my chance."

"Do you realize what you're saying? We're too young to be talking like this."

"Everybody is filling our heads with us being too young. But what if they're wrong, Butterfly? What if we were meant to be together? I don't have to sow my wild oats to know that I only want you."

"Yeah, that ship has already sailed, huh?"

"Okay, I made a mistake! How long are you going to make me pay?"

"I'm not trying to make you pay for anything, Jeremy. You cheated on me! I just can't forgive that. I'm sorry."

"Not this time. I'm not accepting no this time. I love you, Butterfly."

"I love you, too, but we can't undo what you did. And I can't forget it."

"You're right, we can't undo anything. Just like we can't undo when we were in that basketball gym and we first laid eyes on each other. Or we can't undo the first time we kissed. Or we can't undo the first time I held your hand. We can't undo any of those things, Butterfly. Nor can we forget them. You wanna know why?"

"Why?" I said softly.

"Because you still love me, and I never stopped loving you." Jeremy kissed me.

"I want to believe you, Jeremy, but I'm scared. I'm scared as hell!"

"I'm scared, too! But I'm even more afraid of losing you."

"Okay, Jeremy," I sighed.

"Okay, what?"

"Okay, I'm yours. I'm going to trust you with my heart. Please don't break it."

"I won't…I promise."

Jeremy and I stayed up all night talking on the beach. We revealed our most vulnerable secrets, but in a healing way, it was therapeutic. We hung out as much as we could for the remainder of the summer and became even closer.

In September, I finally fulfilled my dream. I had become what I always wanted to be. Not by becoming an international model and traveling all over the world, but by enrolling as a freshman at Spelman College in Atlanta, Georgia. I'd be lying if I said I didn't "like" being a model. But the truth of the matter is, I "loved" being a Butterfly!

About the Author

Born in Saginaw, Michigan, Sylvester Stephens was introduced to the arts by the entertainment era of his elder siblings. He is the author of *The Nature of a Woman*, *The Nature of a Man*, *The Office Girls* and *Our Time Has Come*. He lives in the Atlanta area. He is the CEO/owner of "The DEN" (THE DIVERSITY ENTERTAINMENT NETWORK), a new and entertaining network of drama, situation-comedy, talk, and music! The "DEN" premieres August, 2013. Visit sylvesterstephens.com

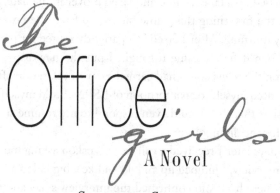
After my insensitive and cruel termination I set out to prove that in corporate America, women would behave in the same manner as men if given the same circumstances. I was pissed off and I blamed every woman on the planet earth for me being fired. My anger sparked me to expose women in all of their glory. I would resurrect my literary career by writing a tell-all book about the corporate battle of women's sensitivity versus men's logic, that in the grand scheme of things, women's sensitivity and men's logic don't mean shit! Money and power produce the same result with any gender or any race; greed, selfishness, and cruelty. But before I could do that, I had to find a job that would allow me the research. I needed a female guinea pig that worked in corporate America.

I bought a Sunday newspaper and half-heartedly browsed through the classified ads, mostly to prove to myself that I was at least making an attempt to get started with the book. I looked back and forth, and back and forth. As luck would have it, I saw an advertisement for a position in an office setting. The ad took up half of the page as if God didn't want me to miss it. It read, ***"Upskon Hiring! Claims Dept. Please fax resume to Jaline Dandy."***

I fell on my knees and shouted, "Thank you, Lord!" I wanted sweet revenge and God seemed to be telling me that vengeance is on the way! I typed up a fake resume and faxed it over immediately. I wanted it to be the first thing this Jaline picked up from the fax machine on Monday morning. After I faxed it, I patiently waited for the confirmation. When it finally came through, I put the newspaper down and turned on the television. I had earned a day of relaxation after all that, and I treated myself to an afternoon of ESPN. I told myself that it was a long shot that they would even respond to my resume so I prepared myself for the disappointment.

Two days later I received a call from Upskon asking me to come in for an interview. I jumped up and down like a big kid in a candy store. I called them back and confirmed the interview's day and time. I will never forget my interview. That day started the beginning of my new life, my new life with the office girls of Upskon.

Jaline Dandy didn't look anything like I imagined. I imagined her being an old white woman with white hair, with wrinkles around her mouth. Perhaps with a Southern dialect, even though I knew she was from the Northwest. But instead, she was a young-looking, middle- aged woman, moderately attractive, and very articulate.

"Good afternoon, Mr. Forrester. I'm Ms. Dandy."

"Good afternoon, Ms. Dandy."

"Any trouble finding us?"

"No problem at all."

"Well, you're a Harvard man, huh?"

"Yes, yes, I am."

"Why would a Harvard man want to work in a small claims department?"

"Harvard men have to eat, too," I said jokingly.

"I like that attitude."

"Thanks."

"Well, Mr. Forrester, your resume is quite impressive. And, the position is available. But I must say that with your credentials you are well overqualified. But as you say, you have to eat, too."

"I sure do."

"Can you start on Monday?"

"No problem."

"Okay, we'll see you Monday."

"That's it? I got the job?"

"If you want it, you do."

"Sure I do. Thanks, Ms. Dandy."

"Welcome aboard," Jaline said, shaking my hand.

"Thank you, Ms. Dandy."

"Stop with the Ms. Dandy, call me, Jaline."

"If you say so, Jaline."

"All right, our business here is done," Jaline said, standing and walking around to the front of her desk. "Tazzy, your supervisor, will meet you on Monday and show you around. That's it. Guess I'll see you on Monday."

"First thing."

I walked out of Jaline's office, and as I scanned the office with my man radar, all I could see was desk after desk of women. I knew immediately that in order for me to fulfill my mission, I would have to deny the dream of every red-blooded, straight American male. And that is to be the only man on an island of women. This may not have been an island intrinsically, but it was the next best thing.

I showed up for work on Monday bright and early as promised. I didn't have a badge so I had to wait until Tazzy showed up. It didn't take long before she came strolling up to the door with her arms full of bags. We greeted each other very cordially, and I took the bags out of her arms.

Tazzy was a petite young lady, who looked as if she was straight out of high school. She was slightly short of five feet tall and a hundred pounds soaking wet. She had beautiful smooth caramel skin. Her hair was short, but cut very neatly. She showed me to my desk and informed me that a lady named Cynthia would be training me. She then showed me to the break room and told me to relax until Cynthia came to get me. One by one the office girls started to arrive for work.

"Hey, how are you doing?"

"I'm fine, how are you?" I responded.

"I'm fine. My name is Virginia. It's a pleasure to meet you."

"It's a pleasure to meet you, too."

"And your name is?"

"Oh, excuse my manners. My name is Michael Forrester," I said, standing to shake her hand.

She shook my hand with the grace of an angel and the elegance of a queen. There was something insouciant about this lady. She was middle-aged, maybe late fifties to early sixties. Her hair was white, but her face looked young. She showed no signs of wrinkles on her face. She reminded me of a jazz singer named Nancy Wilson. As she left the break room I couldn't help but stare.

Susan, the assistant supervisor, a white lady, came in the break room next and fixed a cup of coffee. Susan had blonde hair, blue eyes, and a thin, tight body. She was about five feet five inches tall, with a high-pitched, squeaky voice that bordered on the verge of annoyance.

"Hey, are you the new guy?"

I was tempted to say, *"What does it look like, fool?"* But instead I courteously replied, "Yes, I'm the new guy."

"My name is Susan, and I'm the assistant supervisor here in the office. If there's anything you need, just let me know."

"Thanks."

"Not a problem," Susan said, walking out of the break room.

I sat twiddling my thumbs for a while when Darsha, Valerie, Lisa and Alicia walked in. They were in full gossip mode. When they saw me sitting at the table they stopped talking and looked at me.

"Do you work here?" Lisa asked.

"Yes. Today is my first day."

"I'm Alicia. Hi."

"Hi, Alicia," I spoke.

Alicia was a very attractive light-skinned woman with a perfect thirty-six-twenty-four-thirty-six frame. Maybe even better! She had long golden hair that was pinned up. Her eyes were big and light brown, very welcoming. She was definitely in the wrong business.

There was some modeling agency missing a star! It was all I could do to keep from asking her to marry me on the spot. For the life of me, I could not figure out her nationality. Black, Hispanic, biracial, I couldn't pin it down.

"Hi, my name is Valerie."

"Hi, Valerie, I'm Michael."

Valerie was quite tall with long legs, a nice round butt, slim waist and nice pert breasts. Her hair was about shoulder-length and curled underneath. She had a nice dark-brown complexion. She was quite attractive. She was dressed in a man's suit, which looked very neat on her and business-like. She probably had men lining up to date her.

"Hey, what's up? I'm Darsha."

"Hey, Darsha, I'm Michael."

Darsha was about twenty-two or twenty-three years old. Judging by her attire I could tell she was an active member of the hip-hop culture. That made me wonder what kind of business would hire such a young, inexperienced person. I would find out later that she was very mature and responsible for her age, probably more than I. She was fair-skinned, slim with slender hips, strange-looking eyes, and humorous.

"Hi, I'm last, but definitely not least. I'm Lisa. How are you?"

Lisa was what we black people call high-yellow, light-skinned, with short hair, broad shoulders, and broad hips. She was gentle and soft-spoken.

"I'm fine, Lisa. I'm Michael Forrester."

"Who's training you?" Lisa asked.

"I think Tazzy said it was someone named Cynthia."

"Okay, good to meet you," Lisa said. "Later, Michael."

"Uh, later," I said.

They cleared the break room and then Wanda and Pam walked in.

"Hey, man, you the new dude?" Wanda said, without even looking at me.

Wanda was tough-looking, with a tough voice. She had big bulging eyes, a deep voice, and a presence, which demanded respect, or she'd kick your ass. She was about five feet six inches tall, a little husky, with a delightfully friendly smile.

"Yes, I'm the new dude."

"I'm Wanda. And that's Pam," Wanda said, pointing at Pam.

"Wanda, I don't need you to introduce me," Pam said. "I'm Pam, how are you?"

Pam was an attractive woman with an athletic build, dark-brown, smooth skin. Nice muscular legs. A protruding round buttock that extended from her body at least twelve inches. Her hair was cut perfectly to match the sculpture of her face.

"I'm just fine. Good to meet you."

Pam and Wanda walked out together. I played with the salt and pepper shakers until Cynthia finally came to get me.

"Michael?" Cynthia asked, as she peeked her head through the door.

Cynthia was short, about five feet three inches tall. She was pretty, but in a homely type of way. She wore a long skirt that had to be handed down by her grandmother's grandmother. It revealed no form of human shape within its wrapping. She wore big glasses that she looked over, instead of through. But despite her outward appearance, she was warm and inviting. Upon our first introduction I had a feeling that I knew her from somewhere, but I couldn't quite place her.

"Yup, that's me."

"Let's go, man. You got a date with a computer."

I stood up and followed Cynthia back to my desk, passing everyone else in the office along the way. As I got closer to my desk, I saw Alicia's beautiful face. Her desk faced directly in front of mine. I smiled at the thought of having her picture-perfect view from the time I came in the door, until I clocked out to go home. Maybe my life of recent mishaps was taking a turn for the better. Once again, I reminded myself that no matter how attracted I became to any of the women in the office, I would maintain my objective and keep the project of researching first and foremost. As I sat down, I noticed there was also a vacant desk on my right. I found out later that my neighbor was out sick.

Before Cynthia and I could get started on our training session, Tazzy called a meeting and we all gathered in the center of the office.

"Good morning, everybody," Tazzy spoke.

"Good morning," the office girls spoke in unison.

"Is Tina here yet?" Tazzy said, looking around for her.

"Not yet," voices scattered.

"Well, it's going to be a quick meeting. I'll get the small things out of the way. Can everyone please stay away from the thermostat? I've been noticing the temperature is much lower than where I set it. Secondly, when you go into the bathroom, please, please clean up after yourselves. I cannot stress that enough, especially when Mother Nature is calling. No one wants to walk into a bathroom and be greeted with someone else's tampon or what have you. So please, clean up after yourselves, okay? Now, back to business, we really have to stay focused and stay on task. We have to get our volume of claims down. So please, if you must talk, keep it to a minimum and try not to disturb your neighbor. That's it. Any questions?"

"Can you speak up? I can barely hear you," Pam said.

"You need to quit, Pam. You know you can hear that girl," Valerie said, whispering so that Tazzy couldn't hear.

"I said please keep talking to a minimum. Clean up behind yourself. Stay away from the thermostat. And let's try to work on getting our claims down. Did you get it that time, Pam?" Tazzy said, raising her voice.

"Some of it," Pam mumbled, rolling her eyes.

"I'm sure your neighbor will let you in on whatever you missed."

The girls in the office were beginning to disperse when Tazzy stopped them. "Oh, I almost forgot. I'd like to welcome our newest employee, Michael Forrester," Tazzy said, pointing at me. "Please do your best to make Michael feel as comfortable as possible. Have a nice day, people!"

I waved to the girls to acknowledge Tazzy's announcement, then we went back to our desks. Cynthia and I sat down together at my desk to begin my training. As she started to speak, that irrepressible familiar feeling resurfaced.

"Excuse me, Cynthia," I said. "Do I know you from somewhere?"

"I don't think so," Cynthia said with a smile.

"You seem so familiar to me. What's your full name?"

"Cynthia B. Childs."

"What does the 'B' stand for?"

"It stands for 'B' as in B-quiet."

"Are you ashamed of your name?"

"I'm not ashamed. I just don't know want anybody to know what it is." Cynthia laughed. "It is coun-tree."

"You look so familiar to me."

"Everybody tells me I have that kind of face."

"Yeah, maybe that's it!"

Cynthia trained me for that first week and I kept my conversations confined to her ears only. On Wednesday she gave me a list of telephone numbers of the women in the office. Strangely, the list consisted of both work and personal contact numbers. She told me both numbers were listed because during the winter hours they would call each other to make sure each of them made it to their cars safely. Although Upskon was a huge building that employed over five hundred people, the security was a joke. It was common knowledge that security seemed to show up after someone was robbed, stabbed or raped.

The following week, Wanda, Pam, Lisa and I were sitting in the break room for lunch and a conversation sprang up on the radio about men being intimidated by successful women. I sat and listened as they ranted their opinions.

"That's the problem with men nowadays. Every time a woman makes more money than them, they can't take it!" Wanda shouted.

"I know," Pam agreed. "It's hard for me to get a date because I have my own car, my own house, and my own money. Men don't know how to deal with a woman like me."

As I tried to ignore them, I thought to myself, *perhaps men don't want to deal with a woman like you, not because you have a car, a house, or your own money. Maybe, just maybe, it's because you have a rotten-ass attitude that a man can't stand to be around...*